A Startling Discovery

A surprised murmur ran through the crowd as one of the eggs rocked more violently. The dragons on the upper ledges hummed more loudly than ever with encouragement. Then, the moment came. Leaning back, Piemur braced himself as the huge lizard launched skyward. It was only then that the Master came to the startling conclusion that it was not some unknown drudge who had made off with the precious egg.

Dragondrums
by Anne McCaffrey

BANTAM BOOKS
TORONTO · NEW YORK · LONDON · SYDNEY

This low-priced Bantam Book
has been completely reset in a type face
designed for easy reading, and was printed
from new plates. It contains the complete
text of the original hard-cover edition.
NOT ONE WORD HAS BEEN OMITTED.

DRAGONDRUMS

A Bantam Book / published by arrangement with
Atheneum Publishers, Inc.

PRINTING HISTORY

Atheneum edition published March 1979
5 printings through May 1979

Bantam edition / February 1980

2nd printing .. February 1980   4th printing ..... March 1980
3rd printing .. February 1980   5th printing ...... April 1980
6th printing ... September 1981

ISBN 0-553-20722-9

Published simultaneously in the United States and Canada

Bantam Books are published by Bantam Books., Inc. Its trademark, consisting of the words "Bantam Books" and the por-
trayal of a rooster, is Registered in U.S. Patent and Trademark
Office and in other countries. Marca Registrada. Bantam
Books, Inc., 666 Fifth Avenue, New York, New York 10103.

PRINTED IN THE UNITED STATES OF AMERICA

15 14 13 12 11 10 9 8 7

AT THE HARPER CRAFT HALL

Robinton—Masterharper; bronze fire lizard, Zair

Masters: Jerint—Instrument maker
 Domick—Composition
 Shonagar—Voice
 Arnor—Archivist
 Oldive—Healer
 Olodkey—Drummaster

Masterharper Journeymen: Sebell; gold fire lizard, Kimi
 Talmor
 Menolly: nine fire lizards

gold	Beauty
bronze	Rocky
	Diver
brown	Lazybones
	Mimic
	Brownie
blue	Uncle
green	Auntie One
	Auntie Two

Drum Journeymen: Dirzan
 Rokayas

Drum apprentices: Piemur
 Clell

Apprentices: Ranly
 Timiny
 Brolly
 Bonz
 Tilgin

Silvina—headwoman
Abuna—kitchen worker
Camo—half-witted kitchen drudge
Banak—head stockman

AT FORT HOLD

Lord Holder Groghe; gold fire lizard, Merga
N'ton—Weyrleader of Fort Weyr; fire lizard, Tris

AT NABOL HOLD

Lord Holder Meron
Candler—harper
Berdine—journeyman healer
Deckter—grand-nephew of Meron
Hittet—blood relation of Meron
Kaljan—minemaster
Besel—kitchen drudge

AT IGEN HOLD

Lord Holder Laudey
Bantur—harper
Deece—journeyman harper

AT SOUTHERN HOLD

Lord Holder Toric
Saneter—harper
Sharra—Toric's sister

AT BENDEN WEYR

F'lar—Weyrleader
Lessa—Weyrwoman
Felessen—son of F'lar and Lessa
T'gellen—bronze dragonrider
F'nor—brown dragonrider; gold fire lizard, Grall
Brekke—queenrider; bronze fire lizard, Berd
Manora—Headwoman
Merrim—fosterling of Brekke; three fire lizards
Oharan—harper

AT SOUTHERN WEYR

T'kul—weyrleader
Mardra—weyrwoman
T'ron—dragonrider

CRAFTMASTERS

Masterherdsman Briaret
Masterminer Nicat

Benden Weyr

N

W E

S

Bitra Hold

Keroon Hold

Nerat Hold

Southern Current

Cove Hold

Pern

Chapter 1

The rumble-thud-boom of the big drums answering a message from the east roused Piemur. In his five Turns at the Harper Craft Hall, he had never become accustomed to that bone-throbbing noise. Perhaps, he thought, sleepily turning over, if the drums beat every dawn, or in the same sequence, he'd get accustomed enough to sleep through it. But he doubted that. He was naturally a light sleeper, a talent picked up when he'd been a herder's boy and had to keep an ear awake for night alarms among the runner beasts. The facility had often been to his advantage since the other apprentices in his dormitory couldn't sneak up on him with vengeance in mind. And he was often awakened by discreet, dragon-borne visitors coming to see the Masterharper of Pern, or the arrivals and departures of Master Robinton himself, for he was surely one of the most important men on Pern; almost as influential as F'lar and Lessa, the Weyrleaders of Benden. Occasionally, too, on warm summer nights, when the shutters of the main hall were thrown back, the masters and journeymen assuming all the apprentices slept, he'd hear fascinating and uninhibited talk drifting on the night air. A small fellow like himself had to keep ahead of everyone else, and listening often showed him how.

As he tried to get back to sleep for just a little longer in the gray dawn, the drum sequence echoed in his mind. The message had originated from Ista Hold's harper: he had caught the identifying signature. He couldn't be sure of the rest of the message: something about a ship. Maybe he ought to learn message-drum beats. Not that they came in with such frequency now that more and more people owned little fire lizards to take messages round and about Pern.

He wondered when he'd get his hands on a fire lizard

egg. Menolly had promised him one when her queen, Beauty, mated. A nice thought on her part, Piemur reflected, realistically aware that Menolly might not be able to distribute Beauty's eggs as she wished. Master Robinton would want them placed to the Harper Hall's advantage. And Piemur couldn't fault Master Robinton. One day, though, he'd have his fire lizard. A queen, or, at least, a bronze.

Piemur folded his hands behind his head, musing on such a delightful prospect. From having helped Menolly feed her nine, he knew a fair bit about them now. More than some people who had fire lizards, the same people who'd been claiming for Turns that fire lizards were boy's sun-dreams. That is, until F'nor, brown Canth's rider, had Impressed a little queen on a beach in the southern continent. Then Menolly, halfway across Pern, had saved a fire lizard queen's eggs from being drowned in the unusually high tides of that Turn. Now everyone wanted a fire lizard, and admitted that they must be tiny cousins to the great dragons of Pern.

Piemur shivered with delighted terror. Thread had fallen over Fort Hold yesterday. They'd been rehearsing Master Domick's new saga about the search for Lessa and how she'd become Weyrwoman at Benden just before the new Pass of the Red Star, but Piemur had been much more aware of the silvery Threads dropping through the skies above the tightly shuttered and sealed Harper Hall. He'd imagined, as he always did during Threadfall, the graceful passages of the great dragons as their fiery breath charred Thread before it could fall to the ground and devour anything living, before it could burrow into the ground and multiply. Even thinking of that phenomenon made Piemur quiver fearfully again.

Before Master Robinton had discovered Menolly's talent at songmaking, she'd actually lived outside her hold, caring for the nine fire lizards she had Impressed from the rescued clutch. If only, thought Piemur with a sigh, he wasn't immured in the Crafthall; if only he had a chance to search seashores and find his own clutch. . . . Of course, as a mere apprentice, he'd have to give the eggs to his Craft Master, but surely, if he found a whole clutch, Master Robinton would let him keep one.

The sudden raucous call of a fire lizard startled him, and he sat up in alarm. The sun was now streaming across the outer side of the Harper Hall rectangle. He had fallen asleep again. If Rocky was screaming, he was late to help feed. With deft movements, he dressed, except for his boots, and thudded down the steps, emerging into the courtyard just as he heard the second, more urgent summons from a hungry Rocky.

When he saw that Camo was only just trudging up the steps outside the kitchen, clutching his bowl of scraps, Piemur drew a sigh of relief. He wasn't all that late! He thrust his feet into his boots, stuffed the laces inside to save time, and clomped across the court just as Menolly came down the steps from the Main Hall. Rocky, Mimic and Lazy whirled above Piemur's head, chittering hungrily at him to move faster.

Piemur glanced up, looking for Beauty. Menolly had told him that when the little queen was close to mating time she'd seem to be more golden than ever. She was now circling to land on Menolly's shoulder, but she seemed the same color as ever.

"Camo feed pretties?" The kitchen drudge smiled brightly as Menolly and Piemur reached him.

"Camo feed pretties!" Menolly and Piemur spoke the customary reassurance in chorus, grinning at each other as they reached for handfuls of meat scraps. Rocky and Mimic took their accustomed perches on Piemur's shoulders, while Lazy clung with far from indolent strength to his left forearm.

Once the fire lizards settled to the business of eating, Piemur glanced at Menolly, wondering if she'd heard the drum message. She looked more awake than she usually did at this hour, and slightly detached from her immediate task. Of course, she might just be thinking up a new song, but writing tunes was not Menolly's only duty in the Harper Hall.

As they fed the fire lizards, the rest of the Hall began to stir: the drudges in the kitchen were roused to breakfast efforts by Silvina and Abuna; in the junior and senior dormitories, occasional shouts punctuated random noises; and shutters on the journeyman's quarters were being opened to let in the fresh morning air.

Once the fire lizards had wheeled up for their morning stretch of wings, Piemur, Menolly and Camo separated: Camo, with a push from Menolly, was sent back to the kitchen; then she and Piemur went up the main steps of the Harper Hall to the dining room.

Piemur's first class that morning was chorus, for they were, as usual at this time of the Turn, rehearsing the spring music for Lord Groghe's feast. Master Domick had collaborated with Menolly this year and produced an uncommonly singable score for his ballad about Lessa and her golden queen dragon, Ramoth.

Piemur was to sing the part of Lessa. For once, he didn't object to having to sing a female role. In fact, that morning he waited eagerly for the chorus to finish the passage before his first entrance. The moment came, he opened his mouth, and to his amazement no sound emerged.

"Wake up, Piemur," said Master Domick, irritably rapping his stick on the music stand. He alerted the chorus. "We'll repeat the measure before the entrance . . . *if* you're now ready, Piemur?"

Usually Piemur could ignore Master Domick's sarcasm, but since he had been ready to sing, he flushed uncertainly. He took a breath and hummed against his closed teeth as the chorus began again. He had tone, and his throat wasn't sore, so he wasn't coming down with a stuffed head.

The chorus gave him his entrance again, and he opened his mouth. The sound that emerged ranged from one octave to another, neither of which were in the score he held.

A complete and awed silence fell. Master Domick frowned at Piemur, who was now swallowing against a fear that froze his feet to one spot and crept up his bones to his heart.

"Piemur?"

"Sir?"

"Piemur, sing a scale in C."

Piemur attempted to, and on the fourth note, though he had hardened his middle to iron for support, his voice again broke. Master Domick put down his stick and regarded Piemur. If there was any expression in the Composition Master's face, it was compassion, tinged with resigned irritation.

"Piemur, I think you had best see Master Shonagar. Tilgin, you've been understudying the role?"

"Me, sir? I haven't so much as glanced at it. Not with Piemur . . ." The startled apprentice's voice trailed off as Piemur, slowly and with feet he could barely force to move, left the chorus hall and walked across the court toward Master Shonagar's room.

He tried to close his ears to the sound of Tilgin's tentative voice. Scorn gave him momentary relief from his cold fear. His had been a much better voice than Tilgin's would ever be. Had been? Maybe he was just coming down with a cold. Piemur coughed experimentally, but knew even as he did so that no phlegm congested his lungs and throat. He trudged on to Master Shonagar, knowing the verdict and hoping against vain hope that somehow the flaw in his voice was transitory, that he'd manage to keep his soprano range long enough to sing Master Domick's music. Scuffing up the steps, he paused briefly in the threshold to accustom his eyes to the gloom within.

Master Shonagar would only just have arisen and breakfasted. Piemur knew his master's habits intimately. But Shonagar was already in his customary position, one elbow on the wide table, propping up his massive head, the other arm cocked against the columnar thigh.

"Well, it's sooner than we might have expected, young Piemur," the Master said in a quiet tone, which nonetheless seemed to fill the room. "But the change was bound to come sometime." A wealth of sympathy tinged the Master's rich, mellow bass voice. The propping hand came away from the head and brushed aside the tones now issuing from the chorus hall. "Tilgin will never come up to your measure."

"Oh, sir, what do I do now my voice is gone? It's all I had!"

Master Shonagar's surprised contempt startled Piemur. "All you had? Perhaps, my dear Piemur, but by no means all you *have!* Not after five Turns as *my* apprentice. You probably know more about vocal production than any journeyman in the Craft."

"But who would want to learn from me?" Piemur gestured to his slight adolescent frame, his voice cracking dra-

5

matically. "And how could I teach when I've no voice to demonstrate?"

"Ah, but the distressing condition of your singing voice heralds other alterations that will remedy those minor considerations." Master Shonagar waved aside that argument, and then regarded Piemur through narrowed eyelids. "This occasion has not caught *me* . . ." the thick fingers tapped against the bulging chest ". . . unprepared." Now a gusty sigh escaped Master Shonagar's full lips. "You have been without doubt or contradiction the most troublesome and ingenious, the laziest, the most audacious and mendacious of the hundreds of apprentices and voice students it has been my tiresome task to train to some standard. Despite yourself, you have achieved some measure of success. You ought to have achieved even more." Master Shonagar affected a point. "I find it altogether too perverse, if completely in character, for you to decide on puberty *before* singing Domick's latest choral work. Undoubtedly one of his best, and written with your abilities in mind. Do not hang your head in my presence, young man!" The Master's bellow startled Piemur out of his self-pitiful reflections. "Young man! Yes, that's the crux. You are becoming a young man. Young men must have young-manly tasks."

"What?" In the single word, Piemur expressed his disbelief and distress.

"That, my young man, is for the Harper to tell you!" Master Shonagar's thick forefinger pointed first at Piemur and then swung toward the front of the building, indicating Master Robinton's window.

Piemur did not dare permit the hope that began to revive in him to blossom. Yet, Master Shonagar wouldn't lie for any reason, certainly not to give him false hope.

Then they both winced as Tilgin erred in his sight reading. Instinctively glancing at his Master, Piemur saw the pained expression on Master Shonagar's face.

"Were I you, young Piemur, I'd stay out of Domick's sight as much as possible."

Despite his depression, Piemur grinned, wryly aware that the brilliant Composition Master might well decide that Piemur had elected to thwart his musical ambition in this untimely voice change.

Master Shonagar sighed heavily. "I do wish you'd have

waited a trifle longer, Piemur." His groan was wistful as well as resigned. "Tilgin is going to require much coaching to perform creditably. Now, don't you repeat that, young Piemur!" The thick forefinger pointed unwaveringly at Piemur, who affected innocent shock that such an admonition might be needed. "Away with you!"

Obediently, Piemur turned, but he'd gone no more than a few paces to the door when a second shock stopped him. He whirled toward the Voice Master.

"You mean, just now, sir, don't you?"

" 'Just now, sir?' Of course, I mean now, not this afternoon or tomorrow, but now."

"Now . . . and always?" asked Piemur uncertainly. If he could no longer sing, Master Shonagar would take on another special apprentice to perform those personal and private duties for him that Piemur had been undertaking in the past Turns. Not only was Piemur reluctant to lose the privilege of being Master Shonagar's special lad, he honestly didn't wish to end the very rewarding association with the Master. He liked Shonagar, and those services he had performed for his Master had stemmed from that liking rather than a sense of duty. He had enjoyed above all the droll humor and florid speech of his Master, of being teased for his bold behavior and called to task by a man he had never managed to deceive for an instant with any of his strategems or ploys.

"Now, yes," and there was a rumble of regret in Shonagar's expressive voice that eased Piemur's sense of loss, "but assuredly not always," and the Master's tone was brisker with only a hint of resigned irritation that he was not going to be forever rid of this small nuisance. "How can we escape each other, immured as we are in the Harper Hall?"

Though Piemur knew perfectly well that Master Shonagar rarely left his hall, he was obscurely reassured. He made a half turn and then came slowly back.

"This afternoon, you'll need some errands done?"

"You may not be available," said Master Shonagar, his face expressionless, his voice almost as neutral.

"But, sir, who will come to you?" and again, Piemur's voice broke. "You know you're always busy after the midday meal . . ."

"If you mean," and Shonagar spoke with real amusement crinkling his eye folds, "do I plan to appoint Tilgin to the vacancy? Sssssh! I shall, of course, have to devote a great deal of time to improving his voice and musicality, but to have him lurking about on tap . . ." The thick fingers wiggled with distaste. "Away with you. The choice of your successor requires considerable thought. Not, mind you, that there are not hundreds of likely lads who would undoubtedly suit my small requirements to perfection . . ."

Piemur caught his breath in hurt and then saw the twitch of Master Shonagar's expressive brows and realized that this moment was no easier on the older man.

"Undoubtedly . . ." Piemur tried to turn away on that light note but found he could not, wishing that Master Shonagar might just this once . . .

"Go, my son. You will ever know where to find me, should the need arise."

This time the dismissal was final because the Master slanted his head against his fist and closed his eyes, shamming weariness.

Quickly Piemur walked to the entrance, blinking at the bright sunlight after the darker hall. He paused on the bottom step, reluctant to take the final one that severed his association with Master Shonagar. There was a sudden hard lump in his throat that had nothing to do with his voice change. He swallowed, but the sensation of constriction remained. He rubbed at his eyes with knuckles that came away moist and stood, fists clenched at his thighs, trying not to blubber.

Master Robinton had something to tell him about new duties? So his voice change had been discussed by the Masters. To be sure, he wouldn't have been callously thrown out of the Harper Hall and sent in some obscure disgrace back to his herdsman father and the dreary life of a beast farmer simply because he no longer had his soprano voice. No, that wouldn't be his fate, despite the fact that singing was his one undeniable harper skill. As Talmor said of his gitar and harp playing, he could accompany so long as his playing was drowned out by loud singing or other instruments. The drums and pipes he made under Master's Jerint's guidance were only passable and never got stamped for sale at Gathers. He copied scores accurately enough when he put his mind to it, but he always found so many more interesting things to do than spending hours cramping his fingers, to renew Records someone else could do more neatly and in half the time. Yet, when pushed to it, Piemur didn't actually mind scribing, if he were allowed to add his own embellishments. Which he wasn't. Not with Master Arnor looking over his shoulder and muttering about wasted ink and hide.

Piemur sighed deeply. The only thing he was really adept at was singing, and that was no longer possible. Forever? No, not forever! He spread his fingers in rejection of that prospect and then closed them into tighter fists. He'd be able to sing all right: he'd learned too much from Master Shonagar about voice production and phrasing and interpretation, but he might not *have* a voice as an adult. And he wasn't going to sing unless he did! He had his reputation. Better if he never opened his mouth to sing another note. . . .

Tilgin flubbed another phrase. Piemur grinned, listening to Tilgin repeating the phrase correctly. They'd miss Piemur all right! He could sight-read any score, even one of Domick's, without missing a beat or an awkward interval, or those florid embellishments Domick insisted on writing for the treble parts. Yes, they'd miss Piemur in the chorus!

That knowledge fortified him, and he took the final step onto the flagstones of the court. Clipping his thumbs over his belt, he began to saunter toward the main entrance of the Harper Hall. Not, he reminded himself, that a lowly apprentice who has just lost his privileged position, should saunter when sent to the Masterharper of Pern. Piemur squinted into the sunlight at the fire lizards on the roof opposite. He didn't spot Master Robinton's bronze fire lizard, Zair, among those sunning themselves with Menolly's nine. So the Masterharper wasn't with the day as yet. Come to think of it, Piemur reflected, he'd heard the clear baritone voice of the Harper in the Court late last night and the noise of a dragon landing and departing. These days the Harper spent more time away from the Hall than in it.

"Piemur?"

Startled, he glanced up and saw Menolly standing on the top step of the Main Hall. She'd spoken quietly, and when he peered at her, he knew that she knew what had happened to him.

"It *was* rather audible," she said, again in that gentle tone, which both irritated and appeased Piemur. Menolly, of all within the Harper Hall, would sympathize with him most acutely. She knew what it was to be without the ability to make music. "Is that Tilgin singing?"

"Yes, and it's all my fault," Piemur said.

"All your fault?" Menolly stared at him in surprised amusement.

"Why did I have to pick *now* to break my voice?"

"Why indeed? I'm sure you did it only to annoy Domick!" Menolly grinned broadly at him, for they both had experience with Domick's whimsical temper.

Piemur had reached the top step and experienced another shock on this morning of surprises: he could almost look Menolly squarely in the eye, and she was tall for a girl! She reached out and ruffled his hair, laughing as he indignantly swatted her hand away.

"C'mon, Master Robinton wants to see you."

"Why? What'm I going to be doing now? D'you know?"

"Not for me to tell you, scamp," she said, striding on her long legs across the hall and forcing him to a jog pace to keep beside her.

"Menolly, that's not fair!"

"Ha!" She was pleased by his discomfiture. "You've not long to wait. I will tell you this: Domick may not be pleased that your voice changed, but the Master was."

"Aw, Menolly, one little hint? Please? You know you owe me a favor or two!"

"I do?" Menolly savored her advantage.

"You do. And you know it. You could pay me back right now!" Piemur was irritated. Why did she have to pick now to be difficult?

"Why waste a favor when a little patience on your part will bring the answer?" They had reached the second level and were striding down the corridor toward the Harper's quarters. "You'd better learn patience, too, my friend!"

Piemur halted in disgust.

"Oh, c'mon Piemur," she said, with a broad swing of her arm. "You're not a little 'un anymore to wheedle news out of me. And wasn't it you who warned me that you don't keep a Master waiting?"

"I've had enough surprises today," he said sourly, but he closed the distance between them just as she tapped politely on the door.

The Masterharper of Pern, his silvering hair glinting in the sun streaming in his windows, was seated at the worktable, a tray before him, the steam of hot klah rising unnoticed as he offered pieces of meat to the fire lizard clinging to his left forearm.

"Glutton! Greedy maw! Don't claw me, that's bare skin, not padding! I'm feeding you as fast as I can! Zair! Behave yourself! I'm perishing for a taste of my klah, but I'm feeding you first. Good morning, Piemur. You're adept at feeding fire lizards. Pop sustenance into Zair's mouth so I can get some in mine!" The Harper shot a look of desperate entreaty to Piemur.

He whipped around the long worktable and, grabbing up several chunks of meat, attracted Zair's gaze.

"Ah, that's more the thing!" exclaimed Master Robinton after he'd had a long gulp of his klah.

Absorbed in his task, Piemur wasn't at first aware of the Harper's scrutiny, for the man was applying himself to his own food with his free right hand. Then Piemur saw the keen eyes on him, lids narrowed as if weighty from sleep. He could tell nothing from the Harper's expression, for the long face was quiescent, slightly puffy about the eyes from sleep, the grooves from the corners of the mobile mouth pulled down with age and accumulated fatigue rather than displeasure.

"I shall miss your young voice," said the Harper with a gentle emphasis on "young." "But, while we're waiting for you to settle into an adult placement, I've asked Shonagar to release you to me. I've a suspicion that you won't mind too much"—and a smile twitched the Harper's lips—"doing the odd job for me and Menolly and my good Sebell."

"Menolly *and* Sebell?" Piemur gawked.

"I'm not sure I care for that emphasis," said Menolly in a mock growl, subsiding as the Harper threw her a quieting glance.

"I'd be *your* apprentice?" Piemur asked the Harper, holding his breath for the answer.

"Indeed, you'd have to be my apprentice at that," said Master Robinton, his voice and face turning droll.

"Oh, sir!" Piemur was stunned at such good fortune.

Zair squawked petulantly in the little silence, for Piemur had paused in his feeding.

"Sorry, Zair," and Piemur hastily resumed the task.

"However," and the Harper cleared his throat while Piemur wondered what disadvantage to this envious status was about to be disclosed (there had to be one, he knew), "you will have to improve your skill in scribing—"

"We must be able to read what you write," said Menolly, sternly.

"—learn to send and receive message drum accurately and rapidly . . ." He looked at Menolly. "I know that Master Fandarel is very keen to have his new message-sender installed in every hall and craft, but it's going to take far too long to be useful to me. Then, too, there are some messages that should remain privy to the Craft!" He paused, staring long at Piemur. "You were bred on a runner beast hold, weren't you?"

"Yes, sir. And I can ride any runner anywhere!"

Menolly's expression indicated disbelief.

"I can, too."

"You'll have ample chance to prove it, I fear," said the Harper, smiling at his new apprentice's stout claim. "What you will also have to prove, young Piemur, is your discretion." Now the Harper was in solemn earnest, and with equal solemnity, Piemur nodded assurance. "Menolly tells me that despite your incorrigibility on many other counts, you're not given to indiscriminate babbling. Rather," and the Harper held up his hand as Piemur opened his mouth to reassure him, "that you keep close about incidental information until you can use it to your benefit."

"Me, sir?"

Master Robinton smiled at his wide-eyed innocent expression. "You, sir, young Piemur. Although it does strike me that you've exactly the sort of guile—" He broke off, then continued more briskly, leaving unsaid words to tantalize Piemur. "We'll see how you get on. I fear you may find your new role not as exciting as you think, but you will be serving your Craft, and me, very well indeed."

If he couldn't sing for a while, thought Piemur, being the Master's apprentice was the next best thing. Wait'll he told Bonz and Timiny; wouldn't they just choke!

"Ever sailed?" asked Menolly with such a piercing look that Piemur wondered if she'd read his thoughts.

"Sailed? In a boat?"

"That's the general method," she said. "With my luck you'll be a seasicker."

"You mean, I might get to the Southern Continent, too?" asked Piemur, having rapidly added up assorted pieces of information and come to a conclusion; all too hastily spoken, he realized belatedly.

The Harper lost all semblance of lassitude and sat bolt upright in his chair, causing his fire lizard to protest vehemently.

Menolly burst out laughing.

"I told you, Master," she said, throwing up her hands.

"And what makes you mention the Southern Continent?" asked the Harper.

Piemur was rather sorry now that he had.

"Well, sir, nothing special," he said, wondering himself. "Just things like Sebell being gone for a couple of sevendays midwinter and coming back with a tanned face. Only I'd known he'd not been in Nerat or Southern Boll or Ista. There's been talk, too, at the Gathers that even if dragonriders from the north aren't supposed to go south, some of the Oldtimers have been seen here in the north. Now, if I was F'lar, I'd sort of wonder what those Oldtimers were doing north. And I'd try to keep them south, where they're supposed to be. And there're all these holdless men, looking for someplace to live, and no one seems to know how big the Southern Continent is and if . . ." Piemur trailed off, daunted by the keen scrutiny of the Master Harper.

"And if . . . ?" Master Robinton urged him to continue.

"Well, I've had to copy that map F'nor made of the Southern Hold and Weyr, and it's small. No bigger'n Crom or Nobol, but I've heard from weyrfolk at High

Reaches who were *in* the south before F'lar exiled the worst of the Oldtimers, and they said they were sure the Southern Continent must be pretty big." Piemur gestured broadly.

"And . . . ?" The Harper's encouragement was firm.

"Well, sir, if it were me, I'd want to know, 'cause sure as eggs hatch, there's going to be trouble with those Oldtimers south"—he jerked his thumb in that direction— "and trouble with the holdless men in the north," he turned his thumb back. "So when Menolly talks about sailing, I know how Sebell got south without being taken by a dragon. Which Benden Weyr wouldn't permit 'cause they promised that northern dragons wouldn't go south, and I don't think Sebell could swim that far. If he can swim."

Master Robinton began to laugh, a soft chuckle, and he slowly swung his head from side to side.

"I wonder how many more people have put the same pieces together, Menolly?" he asked, frowning. When his journeywoman shrugged, he added to Piemur. "You've kept such notions to yourself, young man?"

Piemur gave a snort, realized he must be more circumspect with the Master of his Craft and said quickly, "Who pays any attention to what apprentices think or say?"

"Have you mentioned these notions to anyone?" The Harper was insistent.

"Of course not, sir." Piemur tried to keep indignation from his tone. "It's Benden's business, or Hold business, or Harper business. Not mine."

"A chance spoken word, even by an apprentice, can sift through a man's thoughts till he forgets the source and remembers the intent. And repeats it inadvisedly."

"I know my loyalty to my Crafthall, Master Robinton," said Piemur.

"I'm sure of your loyalty," the Harper said, nodding his head slowly, his eyes still holding Piemur's. "I want to be certain of your discretion."

"Menolly'll tell you; I'm not a babblemouth." He looked at Menolly for her support.

"Not normally, I'm sure. But you might be tempted to speak when taunted by others."

"Me, sir?" Piemur's imagination was genuine. "Not me, sir! I may be small, but I'm not stupid."

"No, one could not accuse you of that, my young friend, but as you've already pointed out, we are living in an uncertain Turn. I think . . ."

The Harper broke off, staring out the window, frowning absently. Abruptly he made a decision and regarded Piemur for a long moment. "Menolly told me you were quick-witted. Let's see if you comprehend the reason behind this: you will not be known as *my* apprentice . . ." and Master Robinton smiled understandingly at Piemur's sharp intake of breath. Then he nodded with approval as Piemur promptly schooled his expression to polite acceptance. "You will be told off as apprentice to the Drummaster, Olodkey, who will know that you are under my orders as well. Yes"—and the crispness of Master Robinton's tone told Piemur that he was pleased by this solution, and Piemur had better be—"that will serve. The drummers must, of course, keep irregular hours. No one would note your absences or think anything of your taking messages."

Master Robinton put his hand on Piemur's shoulder and gave him a little shake, smiling kindly.

"No one will miss your boyish treble more than I, lad, except possibly Domick, but here in the Harper Hall, some of us listen to other tunes and drum a different beat." He gave Piemur another shake, then cuffed him on the shoulder encouragingly. "I don't want you to stop listening, Piemur, not if you can take isolated facts and put them together as well as you just did. But I also want you to notice the way things are said, the tone and inflection, the emphasis."

Piemur mustered a grin. "What a harper hears is for the Harper's ears, sir?"

Master Robinton laughed. "Good lad! Now, take this tray back to Silvina and ask her to fit you out with wherhide. A drummer has to be at his post in all weathers!"

"You don't need wherhide on the drumheight!" exclaimed Piemur. Then he grinned as he cocked his head at his master. "You do need it if you're riding a dragonback, though."

"I told you he was quick," said Menolly, grinning at the Harper's consternation.

"Scamp! Rascal! Impertinent snip!" cried the Harper, dismissing him with a vigorous wave of his hand that set

Zair squawking. "Do as you're told and keep your notions to yourself!"

"Then I will be riding dragons!" said Piemur, and when he saw Master Robinton rise half out of his chair, he quickly slipped out of the room.

"What did I tell you, Master," said Menolly, laughing. "He's quick enough to be very useful."

Though the glint of amusement remained in his eyes, the Harper stared thoughtfully at the closed door, his fingers tapping idly on his chair arm.

"Quick yes, but a shade young . . ."

"Young? Piemur? He was never young, that one. Don't let that innocent, wide-eyed stare of his fool you. Besides, he'd got fourteen Turns, almost as old as I was when I left Half-Circle Sea Hold to live in the Dragon Stones' cave with my fire lizards. And what else can be done with all his energy and mischief? He's simply not suited for any other section of this Craft. Master Shonagar was the only person who had half a chance of keeping him out of trouble. Old Arnor couldn't, nor Jerint. It's got to be Olodkey and the drums."

"I could almost see the merit of the Oldtimers' attitudes," said the Harper on the end of a heavy sigh.

"Sir?" Menolly stared at him, startled as much by the abrupt change of subject as the sense of what he said.

"I wish we hadn't changed so in this last long Interval."

"But, sir, you've been supporting all the changes F'lar and Lessa have advocated. And Benden's been right to make those changes. They're united Hall and Hold behind the Weyrs. Furthermore," and Menolly took a deep breath, "Sebell told me not so long ago that before this Pass of the Red Star began, harpers were nearly as discredited as dragon riders. You've made this Hall into the most prestigious craft on Pern. Everyone respects Masterharper Robinton. Even Piemur," she added with a laugh trembling in her voice as she struggled to relieve her master's melancholy.

"Ah, now, there's the real accomplishment!"

"Indeed it is," she said, ignoring his facetiousness. "For he's very hard to impress, I assure you. Believe me, too, that he won't be in the least distressed to do for you what he does naturally for himself. He's always heard the gossip at Gathers and told me, knowing I'd tell you. 'What a harper hears is for the Harper's ears.'" She laughed to find Piemur's saucy quip so applicable.

"It was easier during the Interval. . . ." Robinton said, with another long sigh. Zair, who'd been cleaning himself, chirped in a querying way, tilting his head and peering with earnestly whirling eyes at his friend. The Harper smiled as he stroked the little creature. "Boring, too, to be completely candid. Still, it won't be that long an assignment for Piemur, will it? His voice ought to settle within the Turn, and he can resume his place as a soloist. If his adult voice is half as good as his treble, he'll be a better singer than Tagetarl."

Seeing that that prospect cheered her Master, Menolly smiled.

"The dream message was from Ista Hold. Sebell's on his way back with those herbal medicines Master Oldive wanted. He'll be at Fort Sea Hold by late afternoon tomorrow if the wind holds."

"Indeed? I'll be very interested to hear what our good Sebell has for his Harper's ears."

Chapter 2

The tray Piemur was carrying was all that restrained him from jumping into the air and kicking his heels together in his jubilation. Working for Master Robinton, no matter how indirectly, and being apprenticed to Master Olodkey, was no loss of prestige and much more than he had dared contemplate. Not, Piemur admitted to himself, that he'd given much thought to his future.

Of course, one never saw much of Master Olodkey about the Hall. He kept to the drum height, a lean, slightly stooped figure of a man with a big head and coarse bristling brown hair that seemed to stand out from his skull to give him the appearance, the irreverent said, of one of his own bass drumsticks. Others insisted that he was deaf from years of pounding the great message-drums for the Harper Hall. Except for drumbeats, they hastily amended, which he didn't need to hear: he felt the vibrations in the air.

Piemur considered his new apprenticeship and found it good: there were only four other apprentices, seniors all, and five journeymen serving Master Olodkey. Granted that Piemur had been Master Shonagar's special, but Master Shonagar was responsible for every singer in the Hall, whereas Master Olodkey rarely had more than ten harpers looking to him. Piemur again was in a select group. Even more select if he'd been permitted to announce the full truth.

He skittered down the steps, balancing the tray deftly. Maybe, once he'd proved to the Masterharper that he could keep his mouth sealed . . . And Master Robinton was wrong to think that any could extract information from Piemur that Piemur didn't care to divulge. Nothing pleased Piemur more than "knowing." He didn't necessarily have to show off to other people how much he "knew."

The fact that he, Piemur, an insignificant herdsman's son from Crom, knew, was sufficient.

He wished he hadn't been so brash, mentioning the Southern Continent, but the reactions had proved that his guess was accurate. They had been down to the south: at least Sebell had, and probably Menolly. If they'd gone, then the Harper needn't risk the trip with such eyes and ears to do the hard work.

Piemur hadn't had much to do with the Oldtimers before F'lar had ordered them exiled to the Southern Continent. For this he was fervently grateful as he'd heard enough about their arrogance and greed. But if he, Piemur, had been exiled, he wouldn't have just stayed put. He couldn't understand why the Oldtimers had quietly accepted their humiliating dismissal. Piemur calculated that some two hundred and forty-eight Oldtimers and their women had gone to the Southern Continent, including the two dissatisfied Weyrleaders, T'ron of Fort and T'kul of the High Reaches. Seventeen Oldtimers had returned north, accepting Benden as their leader or so Piemur had heard. Most of the exiled men and dragons had been well on in Turns, so they were no real loss to the dragon strength of Pern. Old age and sickness had claimed almost forty dragons in the first Turn, and almost as many had gone *between* this Turn. Somehow that struck Piemur as being rather careless of dragons, even Oldtimer ones.

He stopped abruptly, aware of a tantalizing aroma wafting from the kitchens. Bubbly berry pies? And just when he needed a real treat! His mouth began to water in anticipation. The pies must be just out of the bake oven or surely he would have discerned that fragrance before.

He heard Silvina's voice rising above the working noises and grimaced. He could've gotten a few pies out of Abuna with no trouble. But Silvina wasn't often taken in by his starts and schemes. Still . . .

He let his shoulders sag, dropped his head and began to shuffle down the last few steps into the kitchen level.

"Piemur? What are you doing here at this hour? Why do you have the Harper's tray? You should be rehearsing . . ." Silvina took the tray from his hands and stared at him accusingly.

"You didn't hear?" Piemur asked in a low, dejected voice.

"Hear? Hear what? How could anyone hear anything in this babble? I'll . . ." She slipped the tray onto the nearest work surface and, putting her finger under his chin, forced his head up.

Piemur was rather pleased to be able to squeeze moisture from the corners of his eyes. He narrowed them quickly for Silvina wasn't easily fooled. Though, he told himself hastily, he *was* very sorry he wouldn't be singing Domick's music. And he was sorrier that Tilgin was!

"Your voice? Your voice is changing?"

Piemur heard the regret and dismay in Silvina's hushed tone. It occurred to him that women's voices never did change, and that she couldn't possibly imagine his feelings of total loss and crushing disappointment. More tears followed the first.

"There, lad. The world's not lost. In a half-Turn or less your range'll settle again."

"Master Domick's music was just right for me . . ." Piemur did not need to fake the ragged tones.

"To be sure, since he wrote it with you in mind, scamp. Well, wouldn't you know? Though I can't for the life of me believe you could contrive to change your voice to spite Domick—"

"Spite Master Domick?" Piemur widened his eyes with indignation. "I wouldn't do such a thing, Silvina."

"Only because you couldn't, rascal. I know how you hate singing female parts." Her voice was acerbic, but her hand under his chin was gentle. She took a clean corner of her apron and blotted the tears on his cheeks. "As luck would have it, I seem to be prepared with an easement for your tragedy." She propelled him before her, motioning toward the trays of cooling pies. Piemur rapidly wondered if he ought to dissemble. "You can have two, one for each hand, and then away with you! Have you seen Master Shonagar yet? Watch those pies! They're just out of the oven."

"Hmmmm," he replied, biting into the first pie despite her admonition. "It's the only way to eat 'em," he mumbled through a mouthful so hot that he had to suck in cool air to ease the burning of his gums. "But . . . I'm to get wherhide clothes."

"You? In wherhide? Why would you need wherhide?" She frowned suspiciously at him now.

"I'm to study drum with Master Olodkey, and Menolly asked me could I ride runners, and Master Robinton said I was to ask you for wherhide."

"All three of them in it? Hmmm. And you'd be apprenticed to Master Olodkey?" Silvina considered the matter and then eyed him shrewdly. He wondered should he tell Menolly that Silvina hadn't been taken in by their stratagem of making him a drummer. "Well, I suppose you'll be kept out of mischief. Though I, for one, doubt it's possible. Come on then. I do have a wherhide jacket that might fit." She cast him a calculating look as they moved toward the storage section of the kitchen level. "Let's hope it'll fit for a while because sure as eggs hatch, I shan't be able to pass it on to anyone else the way you mangle your clothes."

Piemur loved the storerooms, redolent with the smell of well-cured hides and the eye-smarting acridity of newly dyed fabrics. He liked the glowing colors of the cloth bales, the jumble of boots, belts, packs hanging from hooks about the walls, the boxes with their odd treasures. Silvina rapped his knuckles with her keys several times for opening lids to investigate.

The jacket fit, the stiff new leather bucking against his thighs as he pranced about, swinging his arms to make the shoulders settle. It was long in the body, but Silvina was pleased: he'd need the length. Fitting him with new boots showed her how ragged his trousers were, so she found him two new pairs, one in harper blue and the other in a deep gray leather. Two shirts with sleeves too long, but which no doubt would fit him perfectly by midwinter, a hat to keep his ears warm and his eyes shaded, and heavy riding gloves with down-lined fingers.

He left the stores, his arms piled high with new clothes, boots dangling from their laces over his shoulder and bumping him front and back, his ears ringing with Silvina's promise of dire things happening to him if he snagged, tore, or scuffed his new finery before he'd had it on his back a sevenday.

He happily employed the rest of the morning by dressing in his new gear, examining himself from all angles in the one mirrored surface of the apprentice dormitory.

He heard the burst of shouts as the chorus was released and peered cautiously over the sill. Most of the boys and young men swarmed across the Court to the Hall. But Master Domick, music rolled in one fist, strode purposefully toward Master Shonagar's hall. The last to exit was Tilgin, head bowed, shoulders slumped, weary from what must have been an exhausing rehearsal. Piemur grinned; he had warned Tilgin to study the part. One never knew when Master Domick might call on the understudy. There was always the chance of a bad throat or a hacking cough for a soloist. Not that Piemur had ever been sick for performance . . . until this one. Piemur gave a sour note. He really had wanted to sing Lessa in Domick's ballad. He'd sort of counted on coming to the Benden Weyrwoman's notice that way. It was always wise to be known to the two Benden Weyrleaders, and this would have been the perfect opportunity.

Ah well, there were more ways of skinning a herdbeast than shaving him with a table-knife.

He folded his new clothing carefully in his bedpress, giving the fur a smoothing twitch. Then quickly glanced out the window again. Now, while Master Domick was busy with Master Shonagar, would be the time for him to slip into the dining hall. Keep out of sight, and soon enough he'd be out of Domick's mind. Not that Piemur was at fault. This time.

A shame really. Lessa's melody was the loveliest Domick had ever written. It had so suited his range. Once again a lump pushed up in his throat at the sadness of the lost opportunity. And probably a Turn before he could try to sing again. Nor was there a guarantee that he'd have anywhere near as good a singing voice as an adult as he'd had as a boy. None at all. He'd miss being able to astonish people with the pure tone he could produce, the marvelous flexibility, the perfect sense of pitch and timing, not to mention his particularly acute skill at note-reading.

His reflections caused him sufficient pangs of regrets so that, when he drifted past the first group of apprentices in the court, they paused in their play and watched his slow progress with awed silence.

He trudged up the steps, past apprentices and journeymen, eyes down, hands flopping at his sides, the picture of dejection. Scorch it, would he have to pretend to have lost his appetite? He could smell roast wherry, succulent, and dripping with juices. And then, berry pies.

However, if he managed his tablemates adroitly . . . Hunger warred with greed, and there was nothing feigned about his expression of sad reflection when the dining room began to fill.

Piemur, deep in his plans, was aware of being flanked by silent boys. But the chubby fist visible on the left was Brolly's. The stained, dirty, calloused, nail-bitten hand on the right was Timiny's. His good friends were standing by him in this moment of loss. He let out a long, draggling sigh, heard Brolly shift his feet uncomfortably, saw Timiny extend his hand tentatively to draw it back slowly, uncertain how a gesture of sympathy would be received. Well, Timiny might just give him both pies, Piemur thought.

Suddenly everyone moved, and a quick glance at the round table told Piemur that Master Robinton had taken his place. A flash of blue and gray past his lowered eyes was probably Menolly moving to take her place at a journeyman's table.

Ranly and Bon sat directly opposite Piemur, regarding him with wide and worried eyes. He gave them a sad half-smile. When the platter of roast wherry slices came to him, he heaved another sigh and fumbled for a slice. He stared at it on his plate instead of attacking it immediately. But then, generally, he'd have taken as many slices as he could knife onto his plate without raising uproars from his mates. He did like roast tubers, but restrainedly took only a small one. He ate slowly so that his stomach would think it was getting more. A rumbling belly would ruin his ploy for bubbly pies.

None of his friends spoke, either to him or to each other. At their end of the table, gloomy silence prevailed. Until the bubbly pies were served. Piemur maintained his air of tragic indifference as the first ripple of delighted surprise sighed down from the kitchen end of the table. He could hear the rise of happy voices, the quick interest of his friends as they saw the burden of the sweet tray.

"Piemur, it's bubbly pies," said Timiny, pulling at his sleeve.

"Bubbly pies?" Piemur kept a querulous note in his voice, as if even bubbly pies had no magic to revive him.

"Yes, bubbly pies," said Brolly, determined to rouse him.

"Your very first favorite, Piemur," said Bonz. "Here, have one of mine," he added and, with only an infinitesimal show of reluctance, pushed the coveted pie across to Piemur.

"Oh, bubbly pies," repeated Piemur on the end of a quavering semi-interested sigh and picked up one of the offerings as though he was forcing himself to exhibit interest.

"It's an awfully good bake, Piemur." Ranly bit into his with exaggerated relish. "Just take a bite, Piemur. You'll see. Get a bubbly or two inside you, and you'll feel more like yourself. Imagine! Piemur not wanting all the bubblies he can eat!" Ranly glanced at the others, urging them to second him.

Bravely Piemur ate slowly of the first bubbly pie, wishing they were still hot.

"That did taste good," he said with a trifle brighter tone and was promptly encouraged to eat another.

By the time he had consumed eight because three more were donated from the other end of the table, Piemur affected to lose the edge of his gloom. After all, ten bubbly pies when he might only have had two was a good day's scrounge.

The journeyman rose to deliver announcements and assignments. Piemur toyed with the notion of several different reactions to the news of his change in status. Shock, yes! Delight? Well, some because it was an honor, but not too much, otherwise they might doubt the performance that had won so many pies.

"Sherris, report to Master Shonagar . . ."

"Sherris?" Surprise, shock, and consternation, totally unrehearsed or anticipated brought Piemur straight up off the bench and prompted his neighbors to seize him by the shoulders and push him down. "Sherris? That little snip, that wet-eared, wet-bottomed, wet-bedded—"

Timiny clamped his hand firmly over Piemur's mouth,

and the next few announcements were lost to that section of the apprentice tables. Indignation revitalized Piemur, but he was no match for the concerted efforts of Timiny and Brolly, determined that their friend should not suffer the extra humiliation of a public reprimand for interrupting the journeyman.

"Did you hear, Piemur?" Bonz was saying, leaning across the table. "Did you not hear?"

"I heard that Sherris is to be Master . . ." Piemur was sputtering with rage. There were a few truths Master Shonagar ought to know about Sherris.

"No, no, about you!"

"Me?" Piemur ceased his struggles, abruptly horrified by the sudden thought that maybe Master Robinton had changed his mind, that some further investigation had led him to believe Piemur was unsuitable, that all the morning's bright prospect would be wrenched from his grasp.

"You! You're to report to . . ." and Bonz paused to give additional weight to his final words, "Master Olodkey!"

"To Master Olodkey?" Relief gave Piemur's reaction genuine force. Then he looked wildly around for the Drummaster.

Bonz's elbow suddenly digging into his ribs alerted him, and there was Dirzan, Master Olodkey's senior journeyman, staring down at them, fists against his belt, a wary and disapproving expression on his weathered face.

"So we get saddled with you, eh, Piemur? I'll tell you this, you watch your step with our Master. Quickest man in the world with a drumstick, and he doesn't always use it on the drums!" He eyed Piemur significantly and then, with a sharp gesture, indicated that Piemur should follow him.

Chapter 3

The rest of that day was not quite as joyful for Piemur. At Dirzan's order, he moved his gear from the senior apprentice dormitory to the Drummers' quarters, four rooms adjacent to the height, separate from the rest of the Hall. The apprentices' room was cramped and would be more so when the spare cot for Piemur was added. The journeymen's quarters were hardly more spacious, nor Master Olodkey's, though he had his small room to himself. The largest room was both for the instruction and living. Beyond, separated by a small hallway, was the drum room, with the great metal message-drums shining in the afternoon sun. There were several stools for the watchdrummer, a small workable to write down the messages, and a press, which became the bane of Piemur's mornings. It contained the polish and cloths required to keep that eye-blinding shine on the drums. Dirzan took evident relish in telling Piemur that, by custom, the newest apprentice was required to maintain their brilliance.

The drumheights were always manned save for the "dead" time, four hours in the depth of night, when the eastern half of the continent was still sleeping and the western half just retiring. Piemur wanted to know what happened if an emergency occurred in the dead time and was crisply informed that most drummers were so attuned to an incoming message that even in the shielded quarters the vibrations had been known to alert them.

As part of his apprentice training, Piemur had dutifully learned the identifying beats of each of the major holds and crafthalls, and the emergency signals, like "threadfall," "fire," "death," "answer," "question," "help," "affirmative," "negative," and a few useful phrases. When Dirzan first showed him the mass of drum messages that he would be expected to memorize and perform, he began to wish fervently that his voice would settle before winter came. Dirzan ruthlessly loaded him down with a column of frequently used beat measures to learn by the next day, telling him to practice quietly, using sticks on the practice block, and left him.

In the morning, writing under Dirzan's full attention Piemur struggled through the lesson. He almost cried out with relief when Menolly appeared. She ignored him.

"I need a messenger. Can I steal Piemur?"

"Certainly," Dirzan said without surprise, since that task was also a function of drum apprentices. "He can practice his lesson on his way, I expect. I expect he'd better."

Piemur groaned to himself at this partial reprieve, but kept a carefully contrite expression on his face for Dirzan's benefit.

"Did you get riding gear yesterday from Silvina?" Menolly asked him, her face unrevealing. "Get it on," she said when he nodded, gesturing him to be quick about changing.

She was laughing with Dirzan when he reappeared, but broke off her conversation, motioning Piemur to follow her. She took the steps from the drumheights at a clip.

"You said you'd ridden runners?" she asked.

"Sure. I'm herder bred, you know." He was a bit miffed.

"That doesn't necessarily mean that you've ridden runners."

"Well, I have."

"You'll have a chance to prove it," she said, awarding him a curious smile.

Piemur stared hard at her profile as they made their way out of the arch entrance and across the broad Gather meadow in front of the Harper Hall. To their left towered the cliff that housed Fort Hold, and the rows of cots that huddled in the bosom of the sturdy precipice. On the fire heights of the Hold, the brown dragon stood, looking more massive silhouetted against the bright sky, one wing extended, which his rider was grooming.

Piemur felt a surge of reverence for dragons and their riders, reinforced by the sight of Beauty, Menolly's queen fire lizard, alighting on her friend's padded shoulder, while the rest of Menolly's fair cavorted in the air above them.

Her head raised, Menolly smiled at her playful friends and told them they were going for a ride. Did they care to come along? Chirruping and excited aerial displays greeted her question, and Piemur watched, as ever envious, while Beauty stroked Menolly's cheek with her wedge-shaped head and crooned into her ear, the jewel-faceted eyes bright blue with pleasure. Grimly, Piemur forebode to ask the questions that seethed in his mind as they walked in silence toward the great caverns carved into the Fort cliff to house the herdbeasts, wherry flocks and runners. Inside the cavern, the head stockman approached with a smile for Menolly. Her fire lizards whirled into the cavern and sought perches on the curious beams that supported the ceiling, beams that had been fashioned by long-lost skill of the ancients. No one even knew from what substance they had been contrived.

"Off again, Menolly?"

"Again," she said with a slight grimace. "Banak, have you gear for a beast for Piemur, too? As easy for me to have the second runner ridden as led."

"A' course," and the man led the way to the enclosure where the backpads and headgear were hung on racks. After a close look at Piemur, he selected pad and gear, handed Menolly hers. They followed him down the aisle of open-ended stalls. "Your usual is third down, Menolly."

"See if Piemur remembers how to go on," she said to Banak.

The man smiled and handed Piemur the gear. With a degree of assurance he didn't feel, Piemur made the clucking sound it was wise to use to announce human presence to a runner beast. They weren't intelligent creatures, responding to a narrow set of noises and nudges, but, within that limited scope, quite useful. They weren't even pretty, being thin necked, heavy headed, long backed, lean bodied, with spindly legs. Their hide was covered in a coarse fur and ranged in color from a dirty white to a dark brown. They were more graceful than herdbeasts but by no stretch of the imagination as beautiful as dragons or fire lizards.

The creature Piemur was to ride was a dirty brown. He threw the mouth rope over its neck, and by pinching its nose holes, forced it to open its mouth to receive the metal mouthpiece. Quickly grabbing its ear, Piemur managed to get the headstall in place. It snorted as if mildly surprised. Not half as surprised as Piemur that he'd remembered that little trick. He heard Banak grunt. He slapped the pad in place and tightened the midstrap, wondering if this thing would give him any trouble once he was astride it.

Untying its halter, he backed it out and found Menolly as the aisle, holding her larger beast. She examined the gear on his.

"Oh, he did it right," said Banak, nodding approval and waving them to go on as he turned to the rear of the cavern on his own affairs.

It had been a long time since Piemur had been bestride a runner. Fortunately, this creature was docile, and its pacing stride smooth as Menolly set off briskly down the eastern roadway.

There was a knack of easing yourself on a runner's pad. Piemur found himself almost unconsciously assuming the position; sitting on one buttock, extending his left leg as far as the toe-hold strap would go, while cocking the knee of his right leg firmly against the runner's side. A rider would change sides often in trip. For a girl seahold bred, Menolly rode with the ease of much practice, Piemur noted.

All the way down to the sea hold, Piemur kept his mouth shut. He'd be scorched if he'd ask her why they were going there. He doubted that the sole purpose of this excursion was to see if he could ride runners or keep his mouth shut. And what had she meant by easier to have a second runner ridden than led? This reticent, assured Menolly on Harper business was quite different from the girl who let him feed her fire lizards, and a long stride from his recollections of the shy and self-effacing newcomer to the Harper Hall three Turns back.

Once they reached Fort Sea Hold, Menolly tossed him her beast's mouth rope, told him to take them to the hold's beastmaster, ease the backpads, water them and see if they could have some feed. As Piemur led the creatures away, he noticed that she went to the harbor wall, shading one hand as she peered at the eastern horizon. Why was she waiting for a ship? Or had that something to do with the drum message from Ista Hold the other morning?

The beastmaster greeted him cheerfully enough and helped him attend the runners.

"You'll be likely heading back to the Hall as soon as the ship docks," said the man. "I'll pad up Sebell's beast, so he's ready. Soon's we got these comfortable, you just pop into my hold there, and my woman'll fix you a bite to eat. Boy your age could always do with a bit, I'm sure. One thing about seaholding, you've always the extra to feed, even in Threadfall."

His hospitality included Menolly when she came in; after Piemur too had seen the speck far out on the sea. He knew that he'd have a chance to rest his weary bones as well as exercise his jaw.

Sebell had a runner stabled here, huh? Sebell borne by a westbound ship. Which suggested that Sebell had also sailed from this seahold. Piemur tried to remember how long it had been since he'd seen Sebell about the Hall, and couldn't.

Fort Sea Hold possessed a natural deep harbor so that the incoming ship sailed right up to the stone-lined side. Seamen on shore as well as on the ship neatly tied her thick lines to the bollards on the wall. Sebell was not immediately visible, though as Menolly's fire lizards did a welcoming display above the ship's rigging, the westering sun glinted off two golden bodies, Sebell's queen, Kimi, as well as Menolly's Beauty. Piemur didn't spot Sebell in the bustle of people unloading the ship until suddenly he appeared right in front of them, heavy bags draped across his shoulders and arms. A seaman carefully laid two more filled sacks at his feet. Enough to load down a runner beast, all right.

"Good trip, Sebell?" asked Menolly, picking up one of the sacks and slinging it with a deft twist of her wrist to her back. "Give Piemur at least one yoke of those," she added, and Piemur sprang quickly to relieve Sebell of some of his burden, fingering the bulges to see if he could identify the contents. "And don't maul it, Piemur. The herbs will be crushed soon enough!"

Herbs?

"Piemur? What're you doing here? Shouldn't you be rehearsing?" began Sebell. His smile was pleasant and the whiteness of his teeth stood out against dark tanned skin.

Herbs and a tan? Piemur would bet every mark he had that Sebell had just returned from the Southern Continent.

"Piemur's voice has broken."

"It has?" There was no doubting Sebell's pleasure at the news. "And Master Robinton's agreeable?"

Menolly grinned. "With a slight variation, according to the wisdom of our good Master!"

"Oh?" Sebell glanced first at Piemur and then back to Menolly for explanation.

"He's been told off as apprentice to Master Olodkey."

Sebell began to chuckle then. "Shrewd of Master Robinton, very shrewd! Right, Piemur?"

"I guess so."

At such a sour rejoinder, Sebell threw his head back and laughed, startling his queen who'd been about to land on his shoulder. She flew about his head, scolding, joined by Beauty and the two bronzes. Sebell threw an arm across Piemur's shoulders, telling him to cheer up, and draped his other arm about Menolly. Then he guided them toward the holdstables.

There was a look on Sebell's face that suggested to Piemur that the companionable arm about his shoulders had been an excuse for the one about Menolly's. The observation cheered Piemur for he knew something no other apprentice did. Maybe not even Master Robinton. Or did he?

Variations on that notion contented Piemur on the initial leg of their hallward trip. The last three hours were spent in increasing physical discomfort. For one thing, he had sacks strapped front and back of his pad and another slung over his shoulder. It was difficult to adjust his rear end and find a spot not already beaten to a pulp by the runner beast's action. Rather unfair of Menolly, Piemur thought with some rancor, to include him on an eight-hour ride his first time on a runner in Turns.

He was immensely relieved that he wasn't expected to tend the mounts, too, as they handed mouth ropes to Banak. Then, Piemur wished he'd been able to dismount in the Harper Hall courtyard, for his stiff and seemingly reshaped legs made the short walk from beasthold to Hall an unexpected torture. Sourly he listened to Menolly and Se-

bell chatting as they preceded him. They talked of inconse-
quentialities so that Piemur couldn't even ignore his aches by
concentrating on their comments.

"Well, Piemur," said Menolly as they climbed the steps
to the Hall, "you haven't forgotten how to pace a beast.
Shells, what's the matter with you?"

"It's been five bloody Turns since I've ridden one," he
said, trying to straighten his sorely afflicted back.

"Menolly! That's plain cruel," cried Sebell, trying to
keep a straight face. "Into the hot baths with you, lad,
before you harden in that posture."

Menolly was instantly contrite, with protests of dismay
and apology. Sebell guided him to the bathing room, and
when Menolly brought a tray of hot food for them all, she
served Piemur as he floated in the soothing water. To Piemur's utter embarrassment, Silvina appeared as he was patting his sore spots dry. She proceeded to slather him with
numbweed salve and, making him lie down, massaged his
back and legs. Just when he thought he'd never move
again, Silvina made him get to his feet. Strangely enough,
he could walk more normally. At least the numbweed
deadened the muscular aches enough for him to make his
own way across the court and up to three flights to the
drumheights.

He slept through three drum messages the next morning,
the fire lizards' feeding and half the chorus rehearsal with
instruments. When he woke, Dirzan gave him time for a
cup of klah and a meatroll, then quizzed him on the drum
measures assigned him the day before.

To Dirzan's amazement, Piemur beat them out time-
perfect. He'd had plenty of hours in which to memorize
them on that runner ride. As a reward, Dirzan gave him
another column of measures to learn.

The numbweed salve had worn off, and Piemur found
sitting on the stool during his lesson agonizing. He had
rubbed his seat bones raw, a combination of the stiffness
of his new trousers and the riding. This affliction pro-
vided him with an opportunity to visit Master Oldive after
lunch. Although Sebell's sacks were in evidence in Master
Oldive's quarters, even to some herbs piled on the worktable, Piemur pried no new snippets of information from the

Master Healer. Not even if this had been the first shipment of such medicines. He did learn that galls hurt more when treated than when sat on. Then the numbweed took over. Master Oldive said he was to use a cushion for sitting for a few days, wear older, softened pants, and ask Silvina for a conditioner to soften his wherhide.

No sooner had he returned to the drumheights, than he was sent with a message for Lord Groghe to Fort Hold, and when he came back, set to stand a listening watch.

He saw Menolly and Sebell the next morning when he fed his trio of fire lizards but, apart from solicitous inquiry about his stiffness, the two harpers were not talkative. The next day Sebell was gone, and Piemur didn't know when or how. He was able, however, to observe, from the drumheights, the comings and goings, in and out of Fort Hold, of riders on runners, of two dragons and an incredible number of fire lizards. It occurred to him that while he had been congratulating himself on knowing most of what went on in the Harper Hall, the drumheights let him observe the larger world which, up till that day, had been unremarked by himself.

Several messages came in that afternoon, two from the north and one from the south. Three went out; one in answer to Tillek's question from the north; an originating message to Igen Tanner Hall; and the third to Master Briaret, the Masterherdsman. To tantalize him, all the messages were too quickly delivered for him to recognize more than a few phrases. Infuriated to be in a position to know more and unable to exercise the advantage to the full, Piemur memorized two columns of drum measures. If his zeal surprised Dirzan, it irritated his fellow apprentices. They presented him with several all too forceful arguments against too much application on his part. Piemur had always relied on being able to outrun any would-be adversaries, but he discovered that there was no place to run to in the drumheights. While nursing his bruises, he stubbornly learned off three more columns, though he kept this private, tempering his recitations to Dirzan. Discretion, he was learning, is required on many different levels.

He was not sorry six days later to be told to take a message to a minehold situated on an awkward ridge in the

Fort Hold Range. With a signed, Harper-sealed tube of record hide, he mounted the same stolid runner beast Banak had given him for the previous trip.

Gingerly settling the seat of his now well-softened wher-hide pants onto the pad, Piemur was relieved to feel no discomfort from his tail bones as the creature moved off. The journey should take him two to three hours, Banak said, as he'd pointed out to him the correct southwestern track. Three hours was probably correct, Piemur thought as his efforts to increase the pace of his runner failed. By the time the wide track had narrowed to a thinner trace, winding against a stony hillside, with deep gorges on the outside, Piemur was quite willing to let his runner go at that steady, careful pace. As he figured it would have taken the Fort Hold watchdragon only a few moments to make the trip, and the watchdragon's rider was quite willing to oblige the Masterharper of Pern, he wondered why he'd been sent. Until he delivered his message tube to the taciturn mineholder.

"You're from the Harper Hall?" The man scowled at him dubiously.

"Apprentice to Master Olodkey, the Drummaster!" This could be some sort of test of his prudence.

"Wouldn't have thought they'd send a boy on this errand," he said with a skeptical grunt.

"I've fourteen Turns, sir," Piemur replied, trying to deepen his tone without notable success.

"No offense meant, lad."

"None taken." Piemur was pleased that his voice remained steady.

The Miner paused, his gaze drawn upward. Not, Piemur noticed, in the direction of the sun. When the Miner began to scowl, Piemur also looked up. Though why the Miner should register displeasure at the sight of three dragons in the sky, Piemur couldn't guess. True, Thread had fallen only three days before, but you'd think dragons would be a reassuring sight at any time.

"There's feed and water in the shed," said the Miner, still watching the dragons. He gestured absently over his left shoulder.

Obediently Piemur started to lead the runner around, hoping that there would be something for himself as well when he'd tended the beast. Suddenly, the Miner let out a startled oath and retreated into his holdcot. Piemur had only reached the shed when the Miner came striding after him, thrust a small bulging sack at him.

"This is what you were sent for. Tend your beast while I tend these unexpected arrivals."

Piemur's trained ear did not miss the apprehension in the Miner's tone nor the implicit command that Piemur was to remain out of sight. He made no comment, stuffing the small sack in his belt pouch while the Miner watched. The man left as Piemur vigorously pumped water into the trough for his thirsty beast. As soon as the Miner reached his cot, Piemur changed his position so that he had a clear view of the one reasonably level area of the minehold where dragons could land.

Only the bronze did. The two blues settled on the ridge above the mine opening. Sight of the great beast that backwinged to the ground told Piemur all he needed to know to understand the Miner's grimness. Before their exile south, the Oldtimers from Fort Weyr had made few appearances, but Piemur recognized Fidranth by the long sear scar on his rump and T'ron by the arrogant swagger as he strode up to the minecot. Piemur didn't need to hear the conversation to know that T'ron's manner had not altered in his Turns south. With a very stiff bow, the Miner stepped aside as T'ron, slapping his flying gloves against his thigh, strode disdainfully into the cothold. As the Miner followed, he glanced toward the shed. Piemur ducked behind the runner.

It needed little wit now to realize why the Miner had thrust the sack at him. Piemur investigated the contents: only four of the blue stones that spilled into his hand had been cut and polished. The others, ranging from one the size of his thumbnail to small uneven crystals, were rough. The blue sapphires were much prized by the Harper Hall, and stones as large as the four cut ones were mounted as badges for Masters of the Craft. Four cut stones? Four new masters walking the tables? Would Sebell be one of them, Piemur wondered.

Piemur thought a moment and then slipped the cut stones carefully, two and two, into his boots. He wiggled his feet until the stones settled, sharp lumps against his ankles but they'd not slip out. He hesitated as he was about to stow the sack in his pouch. He doubted T'ron would stoop to searching a lowly apprentice, but the stones made a suspicious bulge. Checking the leather to make sure it bore no miner's mark, he wrapped the thong on the back-pad ring beside his drinking flask. Then he took off his jacket, folding the harper badge inside before he slung it over the pump handle. Trail dust had turned his blue pants to a nondescript gray.

A clink of boot nails on the ridge stone warned him and, whistling tunelessly, he picked up the beast's feet in turn, checking for stones in the cleft hooves.

"You there!"

The peremptory tone irritated Piemur. N'ton never spoke like that, even to a kitchen drudge.

"Sor?" Piemur unbent and stared around at the Old-timer, hoping his anxious expression masked the anger he really felt. Then he glanced apprehensively at the Miner, saw a harsh wariness in the man's eyes and added in his best hillhold mumble, "Sor, he was that sweated, I've had a time cleaning him up."

"You've other work to do," said the Miner in a cold voice, jerking his head toward the cothold.

"A day too late, am I, Miner? Well, there's been yester-day's work and this morning's." The Oldtimer supercil-iously gestured the Miner to precede him toward the open shaft.

Piemur watched, keeping a dull expression on his face as the two men disappeared from sight. Inwardly he was right pleased with his dissembling and was positive he'd seen an approving glint in the Miner's eyes.

By the time he had finished grooming the runner from nose to dock, T'ron and the Miner had not yet reappeared. What other work would he have to do if he were a genuine miner's apprentice? It would be logical for him to stay far away from the shaft at the moment, for he'd be scared of the dragonrider if not of his master. Ah, but the Miner had indicated the cothold.

Piemur pumped water into a spare pail and lugged it back to the cothold, ogling with what he hoped was appro-priate fear the blue dragons ensconced on the ridge, the riders hunkered between them.

The minecot was divided into two large rooms, one for sleeping, the other for relaxing and eating, with a small portion curtained off for the Miner's privacy. The curtain was open, and plainly the disgruntled dragonrider had searched the press, locker and bedding. In the kitchen area, every drawer was open and every door was ajar. A large cooking pot on the hearth was boiling so hard its contents frothed from under its cover. Not wishing what might be his meal in the ashes, Piemur quickly swung the pot away from the full heat of the fire. Then he began to tidy the kitchen area. No lowly apprentice would enter the Master's quarters, however humble, without direct permission. He heard voices again, the Miner's low comments and T'ron's angry reproaches. Then he heard the sounds of hammers against stone and ventured to look cautiously through the open window.

Six miners were squatting or kneeling, carefully chipping rough dark stone and dirt from the blue crystals possibly within. As Piemur watched, one of the miners rose, extending the palm of his hand toward the Miner. T'ron intercepted the gesture and held the small object up to the sun. Then he gave an oath, clenching his fist. For a moment, Piemur thought that the Oldtimer was going to throw the stone away.

"Is this all you're finding here now? This mine produced sapphires the size of a man's eye—"

"Four hundred Turns ago it did indeed, Dragonrider," said the Miner in an expressionless voice that could not be construed either as insolent or courteous. "We find fewer stones nowadays. The coarse dust is still good for grinding and polishing other gems," he added as the Oldtimer stared at the man carefully brushing what seemed like glistening sand into a small scoop, which he then emptied in a small lidded tub.

"I'm not interested in dust, Miner, or flawed crystals." He held up his clenched fist. "I want good, sizable sapphires."

He continued to stand there, glaring at each of the miners in turn as they tapped cautiously away. Piemur, hoping that no larger sapphires would be discovered, made himself busy in the kitchen.

By the time the sun was westering behind the highest of

the ridges, only six medium to small sapphires had rewarded T'ron's afternoon vigil. Piemur was not the only one to watch, half-holding his breath, as the Oldtimer stalked to Fidranth and mounted. The old bronze showed no faltering as he neatly lifted in the air, joined by the two blues. Only when the three had winked out *between* did the miners break into angry talk, crowding up to the Miner, who brushed them aside in his urgency, to get to the minecot.

"I see why you're a messenger, young Piemur," said the Miner. "You've all your wits about you." Grinning, he extended his hand.

Piemur grinned back and pointed toward his backpad and the sack with its precious contents, looped in plain sight to the ring. He heard the Miner's astonished oath, which turned into a roar of laughter.

"You mean, he spent all afternoon facing what he wanted?" cried the Miner.

"I did put the cut gems in my boots," Piemur said with a grimace for one of the stones had rubbed his ankle raw.

As the Miner retrieved the sack, the others began to cheer, for they'd had no chance to learn that the Miner had managed to save the product of several sevendays' labor. Piemur found himself much admired for his quick thinking as well as his timely arrival.

"Did you read my mind, lad," asked the Miner, "to know that I'd told the old grasper I'd sent the gems off yesterday?"

"It seemed only logical," Piemur replied. He'd taken his boots off just then, examining the scratches the sapphires had made. "It would've been a crying shame to let old T'ron get away with these beauties!"

"And what are we going to do, Master," asked the oldest journeyman, "when those Oldtimers come back again in a few sevendays' and take what we've mined? That placer's not played out yet."

"We're closing up here tomorrow," said the Miner.

"Why? We've just found more—"

The Miner signaled silence abruptly.

"Each craft has its privacies," said Piemur, grinning broadly. If the Miner felt an apprentice required no apology for such curtness, he would not be admonished for impertinence for repeating a well-known rule. "But I shall have to mention this to Master Robinton, if only to explain why I'm so late returning."

"You must tell the Masterharper, lad. He's got to know if no one else. I'll tell Masterminer Nicat." Then he swung about the room with a warning look at each of his own craftmen. "You all understand that this matter goes no further? Well and good. T'ron got only a few flawed stones—you were all very clever with your hammers today, though I deplore cracking good sapphires." The Miner sighed heavily for that necessity. "Master Nicat will know which other miners to warn. Let the Oldtimers seek if it amuses them." When the older journeyman laughed derisively, the Miner went on, raising an admonishing finger at him. "Enough! They are dragonmen, and they did help Benden Weyr and Pern when aid was badly needed!" Then he turned to Piemur. "Did you save any of our stew, lad? I've the appetite of a queen dragon after clutching."

Chapter 4

That day held one more event! At sunset, as Piemur was helping the apprentice bring in the miners' runners from the pasture, he heard the shrill cry of a fire lizard. Glancing up, he saw a slender body, wings back, drop with unnerving speed in his direction. The apprentice dropped to the ground, covering his head with his arms. Piemur braced his legs, but the bronze fire lizard did not come to his shoulder. Instead, Rocky spun round his head, berating him, his jewel-faceted eyes spinning violently red and orange in anger.

It took Piemur a few minutes to talk Rocky into landing on his shoulder and even more time to soothe the little creature until his eyes calmed into tones of greeny blue. All the time the miner apprentice watched, eyes bugged out.

"There now, Rocky. I'm all right, but I have to stay the night here. I'm all right. You can tell Menolly that you've found me, can't you? That I'm all right?"

Rocky gave a half-chirp that sounded so skeptical Piemur had to laugh.

"Is that fire lizard yours?" asked the Miner curiously as he approached Piemur, eyeing Rocky all the time.

"No, sir," said Piemur with such chagrin the Miner smiled. "This is one of Menolly's, Master Robinton's journeywoman. His name is Rocky. I help Menolly feed him mornings, because she's got the nine and they're a right handful, so he knows me pretty well."

"I didn't think the creatures had enough sense to find people!"

"Well, sir, I have to say it's the first time it's happened to me," and Piemur couldn't suppress the smug satisfaction he was feeling that Rocky had been able to find him.

"Now that he's found you, what good will that do?" asked the Miner with a revival of his skepticism.

"Well, sir, he could go back to Menolly and make her understand that he's seen me. But it would be much more useful if you'd let me have a bit of hide for a message. Tied on his leg, he'll take it back, and they'll know exactly. . . ."

The Miner held up his hand admonishingly. "I'd rather nothing in script about the Oldtimers' visit."

"Of course not, sir," replied Piemur, offended that he needed to be cautioned.

A terse message was all he could scribe on the scrap of hide the Miner grudgingly produced for him. The hide was so old, had been scraped so often for messages, that the ink blurred as he wrote. "Safe! Delayed!" Then it occurred to him to add in drum measures, "Errand completed. Emergency. Old Dragon."

"You've a way with the little things, haven't you?" said the Miner with reluctant respect as he watched Piemur tying the message on Rocky's leg, an operation the fire lizard oversaw as carefully as the Miner.

"He knows he can trust me," said Piemur.

"I'd say there were not many," replied the Miner in such a dry tone that Piemur stared at him in surprise. "No offense meant!"

Piemur had to concentrate just then on imagining Menolly as strongly as he could in his mind. Then, lifting his hand high, he gave a practiced flick to send Rocky into flight.

"Go to Menolly, Rocky! Go to Menolly!"

He and the Miner watched until the little fire lizard seemed to disappear in the dimming light to the east. Then the apprentice called them to their meal.

As he ate, Piemur wondered what the Miner had meant by that remark. "Not many that fire lizards could trust?" "Not many people that trusted Piemur?" Why would the Miner say a thing like that? Hadn't he saved the miners' sapphires for them? It wasn't as if he'd told any lies to do so. Further he'd never taken any real advantage of his friends in bargaining at a Gather or failing to keep a promise. All of his friends came to him for help. And, Shells, wasn't the Masterharper entrusting him with this errand? And knowing about Harper Hall secrets? What had the Miner meant?

"Piemur!" Someone shook him by the shoulder.

Abruptly the young harper realized that he'd been addressed several times.

"You're a harper! Can you not give us a song?"

The eagerness of the request from men isolated for long periods of time in a lonely hold gave Piemur a genuine pang of regret.

"Sirs, the reason I'm messenger is that my voice is changing and I'm not allowed to sing just now. But," he added seeing the intense disappointment on every face, "that doesn't mean I can't talk them to you. If you've something I can drum to give the rhythm."

After several attempts, he found a saucepan that did not sound too flat, and while the men stomped their heavy boots in time, he talked the newest songs from the Harper Hall, even giving them Domick's new song about Lessa. The Shell knew when they'd hear it sung, though no one was supposed to hear it until Lord Groghe's feast. If the performance of the spoken song lacked much in Piemur's estimation, Master Shonagar couldn't hear, Domick would never know, and the men were so grateful that he felt completely justified.

He left the minehold with the first rays of the sun and made the trip back to the Harper Hall at a downhill pace that all but forced his voice back up to the treble range. At times his runner slithered unnervingly down tracks that they had laboriously climbed the day before. Piemur closed his eyes, held tightly to the saddle pad, and fervently hoped not to go sailing off the track into the deep gorges. When he returned the stolid runner to Banak, it was barely sweated under the midstrap while Piemur knew that his armpits and back were damp with perspiration.

"Safe back, I see," was Banak's only remark.

"He may be slow, but he's sure-footed," said Piemur with such exaggerated relief that Banak laughed.

As Piemur jogged into the Harper Hall court, he heard Tilgin bravely singing his first solo as Lessa. Piemur grinned to himself, for Tilgin's voice sounded tired even if he was note-wise. None of Menolly's fair was sunning on the ridge, but Zair was sprawled on the ledge of the Harper's window so Piemur took the steps two at a time. While he sort of wished someone would encounter him on his triumphant return, he was also relieved that he'd have no temptation to blurt out his adventures.

Master Robinton's greeting, however, was warm enough to make Piemur puff his chest out in pride.

"You make the most of your opportunities, young Piemur—but kindly explain your cryptic measures before I burst with curiosity! 'Old dragon' does mean oldtimers, I take it?"

"Yes, sir," and Piemur took the seat the Harper indicated and began. "T'ron and Fidranth with two blue dragons came to relieve the Miner of his sapphires!"

"You're positive beyond doubt that it was T'ron and Fidranth?"

"Positive! I did see them once or twice before they were exiled. Besides, the Miner knew them all too well."

The Harper gestured for him to continue, and the day's events made good telling with the best of all audiences in the Masterharper, who listened intently without a single interruption. He then asked Piemur to repeat, this time questioning a detail here, a response there, and extracting from Piemur every nuance of the confrontation of Miner and Oldtimer. He laughed appreciatively at Piemur's strategy and lauded his caution of putting the four cut gems in his boots. It was only then that Piemur remembered to hand the precious stones to the Harper. The sun sparkled off the facets as the sapphires lay on the table.

"I'll have a word with Master Nicat myself. And I think I'll see him today," said Robinton, holding up one of the gems between thumb and forefinger and squinting at it in the sunlight. "Beautiful workmanship! Not a flaw!"

"That's what the Miner said," and then Piemur daringly added. "I gather it's not easy to find the right blues for masterharpers."

Master Robinton regarded Piemur, a startled expression on his face, which changed to amusement. "You will keep that to yourself as well, young man!"

Piemur nodded solemnly. "Of course, if I'd had a fire lizard of my own, you wouldn't have had to worry about me and the stones, and perhaps something could have been done about T'ron."

The Harper's face altered and the flash in his eyes had

nothing to do with amusement. Now Piemur couldn't imagine what had prompted him to say such a thing. He didn't even dare look away from the Harper's severe gaze, although he wanted more than anything else to creep away and hide from his Master's disapproval. He did stiffen, fully expecting a blow for such impertinence.

"When you can keep your wits about you as you did yesterday, Piemur," said Master Robinton after an interminable interval, "you prove Menolly's good opinion of your potential. You have also just proved the main criticism that Hall masters have expressed. I do not disapprove of ambition, nor the ability to think independently, but," and suddenly his voice lost the cold displeasure, "presumption is unforgiveable. Presuming to criticize a dragonrider is the most dangerous offense against discretion. Further," and the Harper's finger was raised in warning, "you are rushing toward a privilege you have by no means earned. Now, off with you to Master Olodkey and learn the proper drum measure for 'Oldtimer.'"

The kindly note in his tone was almost too much for Piemur, who could more easily have borne blows and a tirade for his transgressions. He made his way to the door as fast as his leaden legs could bear him.

"Piemur!" Robinton's voice checked him as he fumbled for the latch. "You did handle yourself very well at the Minehold. Only do," and the Harper sounded as resigned as Master Shonagar often had, "do please try to guard your quick tongue!"

"Oh, sir, I'll try as hard as I can, really I will!" His voice cracked ignominiously, and he spun around the door so that the Harper wouldn't see the tears of shame and relief in his eyes.

He stood for a moment in the quiet hall, intensely grateful that it was empty at this time of day as he conquered dismay at his untimely insolence. The Harper was so right: he had to learn to think before he spoke; he never should have blurted out that unfortunate criticism of dragonriders. He'd've rated a right sound beating from any other Master. Domick wouldn't have hesitated a moment, nor even languid Master Shonagar, whose hand he'd felt many a time for his brashness. But how had he dared criticize dragonriders, even Oldtimers, to Master Robinton? Certainly that took the prize for impudence, even from him.

Piemur shivered and vowed fervently to mind his thoughts and, even more carefully, his tongue. Particularly now, when he did know something of real significance. For he had been aware, previous to his imprudent comment, that the appearance of the Oldtimers at the mine, not to mention their errand, was unwelcome news to the Harper.

Besides, what *could* have been done about the Oldtimers' illegal return to the North?

Piemur gave his own ear a clout that made his eyes swim and then started down the corridor. Now, how was he to find out the drum code for Oldtimers? Under the circumstances he couldn't just ask Dirzan outright without having to explain why he needed to know. Nor could he ask one of the other apprentices. They were annoyed enough with him and his quick studying. There'd be a way, he was sure.

Then he wondered why Master Robinton had asked him to find out. Was it a code he'd need? Did that mean the Harper expected this wouldn't be the first such visit by the Oldtimers? Or what?

The speculations on this subject occupied Piemur's mind off and on for the next few days until he did have the chance to check the code.

Somewhat to Piemur's disgust, Dirzan treated him as if he had deliberately protracted his errand to avoid polishing the drums. This was his first task, and because Piemur couldn't polish when the drums were in use, it dragged on until the midday meal.

That afternoon Piemur began to participate in another activity of the drumheights, since he had unfortunately learned the drum measures so well. All apprentices were supposed to stop and listen when messages came in and write down what they heard, if they could. Then Dirzan checked their interpretations of the message. It seemed harmless enough, but Piemur soon learned that it was one more road to trouble for him. All drum messages were considered private information. A bit silly to Piemur's way of thinking, since most journeymen and all masters had to be adept in drum messages. A full third of the Harper Hall would understand most of a drum message booming across the valley. Nonetheless, if word of something especially sensitive became common knowledge about the Hall, it was deemed the fault of a gossipy drum apprentice. Piemur was twigged for that role now!

When Dirzan first accused him of loose talk, a day or two after he started writing messages, he stared in utter astonishment at the journeyman. And got a hard clout across the head for it.

"Don't try your ways on me, Piemur. I'm well aware of your tricks."

"But, sir, I'm only in the Hall at mealtimes, and sometimes not even then."

"Don't answer back!"

"But, sir . . ."

Dirzan fetched him another clout, and Piemur nursed his grievance in silence, rapidly trying to figure out which of the other apprentices was making mischief for him. Probably Clell! And how was he going to stop it? He certainly didn't want Master Robinton to hear such a wretched lie.

Two days later a rather urgent message for Master Oldive was drummed through from Nabol. As Piemur was on duty, he was dispatched with it to the Healer. Mindful of a possible repeat accusation, Piemur noted that no one was about in court or hall as he delivered his message. Master Oldive bade him wait for a reply which he wrote on a then carefully folded sheet. Piemur raced across the empty court, up the stairs to the drumheights and arrived out of breath, shoving the note into Dirzan's hand.

"There! Still in its original folds. I met no one coming or going."

Dirzan stared at Piemur, his scowl deepening. "You're being insolent again." He raised his hand.

Piemur stepped back deliberately, catching sight of the other apprentices watching the scene with great interest. The especially eager glint in Clell's eyes confirmed Piemur's suspicion.

"No, I'm trying to prove to you that I'm no babblemouth, even if I did understand that message. Lord Meron of Nabol is ill and requires Master Oldive urgently. But who'd care if *he* died after what he's done to Pern?"

Piemur knew he'd merited Dirzan's blow then and didn't duck.

"You'll learn to keep a civil tongue in your head, Piemur, or it's back to the runner hold for you."

"I've a right to defend my honor! And I can!" Piemur caught himself just in time before he blurted out that Master Robinton could attest to his discretion. As rife with rumor as the Harper Hall generally was, there hadn't been a whisper about the Oldtimers' raid on the mine.

"How?" Dirzan's single derisive word told Piemur forcibly how very difficult that would be without being rightfully accused of indiscretion.

"I'll figure a way. You'll see!" Piemur glared impotently at the delighted grins of the other apprentices.

That night, when everyone else slept through the dead hours, Piemur lay awake, restless with agitation. The more he examined his problem, the harder it was to solve it without being indiscreet on some count or another. When he'd still been free to chatter with his friends, he could have asked the help of Brolly, Bonz, Timiny or Ranly. Among them, they'd surely have been able to discover a solution. If he approached Menolly or Sebell about such a piffling problem, they might decide he wasn't the right lad for their needs. They might even consider his complaint a lack of discretion in itself.

How right Master Robinton had been when he said that Piemur might possibly be plagued into disclosing matters best left unmentioned! Only how could the Harper have known that Piemur was stuck in the one discipline, as a drum apprentice, where he was most likely to be accused of indiscretions?

One possibility presented itself to his questioning mind: the apprentices, even Clell as the oldest, were still plodding through the medium hard drum measures. Therefore some parts of every long message reaching the Harper Hall were incomprehensible to them. Now, if Piemur learned drum language beat perfect, he'd understand the messages in full. Not that he'd let Dirzan know that when he wrote the message down for him. But he'd keep a private record of everything he translated. Then, the next time there was a rumor of a half-understood message, Piemur would prove to Dirzan that he had known *all* the message, not just the parts the other apprentices had understood.

To further achieve his end, Piemur kept to the drumheights even at mealtimes. Preferably within the sight of Dirzan, the Master, or one of the other duty journeymen. If he wasn't near others, he couldn't be accused of gossiping to them. Even when he was sent on message-runs, he made the return trip so fast no one could possibly accuse him of dawdling and gossiping on the way. The only other time he was in the court was to help Menolly feed the fire lizards. Messages came through, some of them urgent, some tempting enough, Piemur would have thought, for one of the apprentices to repeat, but no whisper of rumor repaid his immolation. In despair he gave up his plan and tore up the messages he had written. But he still held himself away from others.

He wasn't certain how much more of this he could endure when Menolly appeared in the drumheights just after breakfast one morning.

"I need a messenger today," she said to Dirzan.

"Clell would—"

"No. I want Piemur."

"Now, Menolly, I wouldn't mind letting him go for a minor errand but—"

"Piemur is Master Robinton's choice," she said with a shrug, "and he's cleared this with Master Olodkey. Piemur, get your gear together."

Piemur blandly ignored the black looks Clell directed his way as he crossed the living room.

"Menolly, I think you ought to mention to Master Robinton that we haven't found Piemur too reliable—"

"Piemur? Unreliable?"

Piemur had been about to whip around and defy Dirzan, but the amused condescension in Menolly's tone was a far better defense than any he could muster under his circumstances. In one mild question, Menolly had given Dirzan, not to mention Clell and the others, a lot to think about.

"Oh, he's been bleating to you, has he?"

Piemur could hear the sneer in the journeyman's voice. He took a deep breath and continued to gather his things.

"In point of fact," and now Menolly sounded puzzled, "he's not been talkative at all, apart from commenting on the weather and the condition of my fire lizards. Should he have reason to bleat, Dirzan?"

Piemur half-ran back into the room, to forestall any explanation by the journeyman. This opportunity was playing beautifully into his hands.

"I'm ready to go, Menolly."

"Yes, and we have to move fast." It was obvious to Piemur that Menolly had wanted to hear Dirzan's reply. "I'll be back to you on this, Dirzan. C'mon, Piemur!"

She led the way down the steps at a clatter, and only when they had passed the first landing did she turn to him.

"What have you been up to, Piemur?"

"I haven't been up to anything," he replied with such vehemence that Menolly grinned at him. "That's the trouble."

"Your reputation's caught up with you?"

"More than that. It's being used against me." As much as Piemur wanted to expand, the less he said, he decided, even to Menolly, the stronger his position.

"The other apprentices against you? Yes, I saw their expressions. What did you do to set them so?"

"Learned drum measures too fast is all I can think of."

"You sure?"

"I'm bloody sure, Menolly. D'you think I'd do anything to get in the Masterharper's bad record?"

"No,' she said thoughtfully as they skipped down the last flight. "No, you wouldn't. Look, we'll sort it out when we come back. There's a Gather today at Igen Hold. Sebell and I are to be there as harpers, but Master Robinton wants you to play scruffy boy apprentice."

"Can I ask why?" Piemur delivered the question on the end of a long suffering sigh.

Menolly laughed and reached out to ruffle his hair.

"You can, but I've no answer. We weren't told either. He just wants you to wander about the Gather and listen."

"Has he got Oldtimers on his mind?" Piemur asked as casually as he could.

"I'd say he probably does," Menolly answered after a thoughtful moment. "He's been worried. I may be his journeywoman, but I don't always know what's on his mind. Neither does Sebell!"

They had reached the archway now and turned toward the Gather meadow.

"I'm to ride a dragon?" asked Piemur. He lurched to a

stop, his eyes bulging out at the scene before him. Bronze Loith was shaking his wings out in the sun, his great jeweled eyes gleaming blue-green as he turned his head to watch the antics of the fire lizards. Dwarfed by his bulk, the tall figures of N'ton, Fort Weyrleader, and Sebell stood by his shoulder.

"C'mon, Piemur. We mustn't keep them waiting. The Gather at Igen is already well started."

Piemur struggled into his wherhide jacket, making that an excuse for falling behind Menolly. Actually he was both terrified and overjoyed at the prospect of riding a dragon! All those cloddies up there in the drumheights! He hoped that they were watching, that they'd see him riding off on a dragon! That'd teach them to smear his reputation. He pushed from his mind the corollary that the privilege of flying a dragonback would make his lot with his fellow apprentices that much harder. What mattered was the now! Piemur was going to ride a dragon.

N'ton had always been Piemur's ideal of a dragonrider: tall, with a really broad set of shoulders, dark brown hair slightly curled from being confined under a riding helmet, an easy, confident air reflected by a direct gaze and a ready smile. The contrast between this present Fort Weyrleader and his disgruntled predecessor, T'ron, was more vividly apparent as N'ton smilingly greeted the harpers' apprentice.

"Sorry your voice changed, Piemur. I'd been looking forward to Lord Groghe's Gather and that new Saga I've heard so much about from Menolly. Have you ridden dragonback before, Piemur? No? Well, up with you, Menolly. Show Piemur the knack."

As Piemur attentively watched Menolly grab the riding strap and half-walk up Lioth's shoulder, swing her leg agilely over the last neck ridge, he still couldn't believe his good fortune. He could just imagine T'ron permitting a journeyman, much less an apprentice lad, to ride his bronze.

"See how it was done? Good. Up with you then, Piemur!" Sebell gave him an initial boost, and Menolly leaned over with a helping hand and a guide rope. It seemed a long way up a dragon's shoulder.

Piemur grabbed the rope and just as he planted his

booted foot on Lioth's shoulder, he wondered if he'd hurt the dragon's smooth hide.

N'ton laughed. "No, you won't hurt Lioth with your boots! But he thanks you for worrying."

Piemur was so startled that he almost lost his grip.

"Reach up, Piemur," Menolly ordered.

"I didn't know he'd hear me," he said in a gasp as he settled astride Lioth's neck.

"Dragons hear what they choose to," she said, grinning. "Sit back against me. Sebell's got to fit in front of you!"

The words were barely out of her mouth before Sebell had swung up with the ease of considerable practice and settled himself before Piemur. N'ton followed, passing back the riding straps. Piemur thought that a needless caution. His legs were wedged so tightly between Menolly's and Sebell's, he couldn't have moved if he had to. Then Sebell peered over his shoulder at him.

"You'll have heard a lot about *between*, I expect, but I'll warn you now: it's scary even when you know what to expect."

"Right, Piemur," Menolly added, circling his waist with her arms. "I've got you tight, and you hang on to Sebell's belt."

"You won't feel once we're *between*," Sebell continued. "There's nothing *between* except cold. You won't be able to feel Lioth beneath your legs nor our legs against yours, nor your hands about my belt. But the sensation lasts only a few heartbeats. They'll sound very loud to you. Just count 'em. We'll be doing the same thing, I assure you!" Sebell's grin absolved Piemur from any expression of fear or doubt.

Piemur nodded, not trusting himself to speak. He didn't care what happened *between*. At least, he would have experienced it, which very few apprentice harpers could say.

Suddenly there was a great heave, and he cracked his chin against Sebell's shoulderblade. Inadvertently looking down, he saw the ground moving away from him as Lioth sprang skyward. He could feel the great muscles along Lioth's neck as the fragile-seeming wings took their first all-important downsweep. Then the Gather meadow and the Harper Hall seemed to rush away, and they were on a level with the Hold fire-heights.

Sebell gave Piemur's hands, clutching his belt, a warning squeeze. The next heartbeat and there was nothing but a cold so intense that it was painful. Except that Piemur couldn't feel pain with his body, only sense that his lack of tactile contact with reality included everything except the wild beating of his heart against his ribcage. Ruthlessly he clamped down on the instinct to scream. Then they were back in the world again, Lioth gliding effortlessly down to the right, a tremendous expanse of golden ground beneath his wings. Piemur shuddered again and kept his eyes fixed on Sebell's shoulders. Hard as Piemur wished he wouldn't, Lioth continued to glide downward, dipping sideways at unnerving angles. Suddenly Piemur could hear fire lizards chittering, and despite his resolve not to look around, found himself watching them zip about the dragon.

"It is scarey to look down," Menolly's voice said in his ear. "It's worse when they . . . ahhhhh. . . ."

Piemur felt his stomach drop and, to his horror, his seat seemed to leave the dragon's neck. He gasped and clutched more tightly at Sebell, feeling the man's diaphragm muscles move as he chuckled.

"That's what I mean!" said Menolly. "N'ton says it's only air currents, pushing the dragons up or letting them down."

"Oh, is that all?" Piemur managed to get the words out in a rush, but his voice betrayed him. "All" came out in a two-octave crack.

Menolly didn't laugh, and he felt more kindly toward her than at any other time in their association.

"It always scares me," she said in a comforting shout by his left ear.

He was just getting accustomed to this additional hazard of flying dragonback when Lioth seemed to be diving straight for the Igen River bed. He was pressed back against Menolly and didn't know whether to clutch more fiercely at Sebell's belt or relax into the pressure.

"Don't forget to breathe!" Menolly was shouting and, at that, he barely heard her words as the wind ripped sound away.

Then Lioth leveled and began to circle at a gentler rate of descent toward the now-visible rectangle of a Gather.

To the left was the river, a broad, muddy stream between red sandstone banks. Small sailing craft skimmed the surface on a current that must be swifter than the turgid surface suggested. To the right was the broad, clean-swept rock shelf that led up to Igen Hold, a safe distance above the highest flood marks left by the river on the sandstone banks. Behind Igen Hold rose curious, wind-fashioned cliffs, some of which made additional holds for Igen's people, for there were no rows of cotholds adjoining the main Hold here. Igen Hold also had no fire-heights, not needing any since there was nothing but sand and stone around the Hold proper, to which Thread could do no harm. The lands that supplied Igen Hold were around the next bend of the river, where the waters had been led inland by canals to supply watergrain fields.

Piemur wasn't sure that he would like living in such a barren-looking Hold, even if no Thread could ever attack it. And it was hot!

Red dust puffed up as Lioth landed, and suddenly Piemur was unbearably warm. He began to unbelt his wherhide jacket before he released the riding strap and noticed that Menolly was as quick to strip helmet, gloves and jacket.

"I always forget how hot it is at Igen," she said, fluffing out her hair.

"The dragons love it," said N'ton, pointing beyond the Hold to where the rough shapes that Piemur had assumed were rock now became recognizable as dragons, stretched out to bake in the sun.

It was as he was sliding down Lioth's shoulder that Piemur noticed the curious construction of the Gather rectangle. There didn't seem to be any walkway. The only open space was the customary central square for dancing. Though who'd have the energy to dance in this heat he didn't know.

Then Piemur ducked while Lioth showered them all with sand as he vaulted into the air and winged to join the other sunbathing dragons. The fire lizards—N'ton's Tris, Sebell's Kimi and Menolly's nine—swirled up and away and were met, midair, by other fire lizards, the augmented fair swirling higher and higher in the joy of meeting.

"That'll occupy them for a while," said Menolly, then

she turned to Piemur. "Give me your flying gear and I'll leave it at the Hold till you need it again."

"We must pay our respects to Lord Laudey and the others," said Sebell, bringing out a handful of marks from his pocket. He presented Piemur with an eighth piece and two thirty-seconds. "I'm not being stingy, Piemur, but you'd be questioned if you had too many marks about you. And I don't think Igen Hold runs to bubbly pies."

"Too hot to eat 'em anyway." Piemur mopped his sweaty forehead with one hand as he gratefully slid the marks into his pouch.

"But they do make a confection of fruits that you might like," said Sebell. "Anyway, move around and listen. Don't get caught being nosy and come up to the Hold for the evening meal. Ask for Harper Bantur if you have any trouble. Or Deece. He remembers you."

They had reached the edge of the Gather tents, and now Piemur realized that walking space existed but was considerately covered with tenting to deflect the worst of the sun's baking heat. It was simple now for Piemur to move away from the journeymen harpers and the Weyrleader in the steady flow of people sauntering past the Gather stalls. He saw Menolly turn about, trying to see where he had got to, then Sebell spoke to her, and she shrugged and moved on with him.

Almost immediately Piemur noticed one great difference between this and the Gathers he had attended in the west: people took their time. In order to separate himself from his craftmates, Piemur had deliberately lagged behind, but when he would have stepped out again at his customary pace, he hesitated. No one was moving briskly at all. Gestures and voices were languid, smiles slow, and even laughter had a lazy fall. A great many people carried long tubes from which they sipped. Stalls dispensing drinks, chilled water, as well as sliced fruits, were frequently placed and well-patronized. About every ten stalls or so, there were areas where people lounged, either on the sand or on benches placed about the edges. The tenting was raised in corners to catch breezes sweeping up from the river, cooling the lounge areas and the walkway.

Piemur did one complete walkabout of the Gather rectangle. He could appreciate that, despite breezeways and the expenditure of the minimum of physical effort, people did not do much talking as they strolled from stall to stall. The talking, either conversation or bartering, was done while both parties sat comfortably. So he used one thirty-second piece on a long tube of fruit juice and some succulent slices of a rind-melon, found himself an inconspicuous spot in one lounge area, and settled to listen as he sipped his drink and ate.

At first he didn't quite catch the softer drawl of these south-easterners. The low-pitched conversation between two men on his left turned out to be the innocuous boasting of one about the breeding lines of the splay-footed runners he was hoping to barter profitably while the other man kept extolling the virtues of the currently favored strain. Disgusted at such a waste of his time, Piemur focused his ears on the group of five men on his right. They were blaming the weather on Thread, the bad crops on the weather and everything else except their lack of industry, which Piemur thought would be the real problem. A group of women were also murmuring against the weather, their mates, their children and the nuisancy children of other holds, but all in a fairly comfortable, tolerantly amused fashion. Three men, with their heads so close together no sound passed their shoulders, finally parted, but not before Piemur saw a small sack pass from one to another and decided that they must only have been bargaining hard. The runnermen left and a new pair took their places, composed their loose robes about them, leaned back and promptly went to sleep. Piemur found himself growing more heavy-eyed and sipped the last of his juice to keep him awake, wondering if he would find another lounge area as dull.

A combination of excited voices and a chill breeze woke him. He stared about him, wondering if he had missed a drum message, and then oriented himself. Night had fallen and, with the set of the sun, the cooler winds of evening blew cheerfully through the raised flaps. There was no one else in the tent with him, but he could smell the aroma of roasting meats and scrambled to his feet. He'd be late at the Hold for his supper, and he was hungry.

Cool evening had enlivened everyone, for the walkway was now full of quickly stepping, chattering people, and Piemur had to duck and dart his way out of the Gather tents. The dragon lumps on the Hold cliff turned their brilliant lanterns of eyes on the doings below them, rivaling the blazing glow baskets set on high standards about the Gather grounds.

No one challenged Piemur at the Hold courtyard gates, and he found the main Hall by simply following the general drift of the well-dressed people.

Lord Laudey, according to Harper Hall gossip, was not a very outgoing man, but at a Gather, every Holder did make an effort. The principal men and craftmasters of his Hold were invited with their immediate families to dine in the Hold Hall, as well as such dragonriders and visiting Lord Holders, Craftmasters and Masters who might be attending the Gather.

By custom, the harpers ate at the first table below the main one. Piemur had never seen the resident Harper, Bantur, and hoped that Menolly and Sebell were already at the table. They were, and chatting in high spirits with Deece, who'd been seconded to Bantur the night Menolly had walked the tables to become a journeywoman, and with Strud, who'd been posted to a sea hold on Igen River that same night. Gray of hair but with bright and unusually blue eyes, Bantur welcomed Piemur with such friendliness for a mere apprentice that Piemur was made more uncomfortable by kindness than he would have been by taciturnity. Bantur insisted on getting him fresh meats and tubers from one of the drudges and heaped his plate so high with choice cuts that Piemur's eyes boggled.

The other harpers talked while he ate, and when he had finally swallowed the last morsel, Bantur suggested they all leave to make room for more of Lord Laudey's guests. Then Bantur asked if Piemur would take a harper's turn on drum or gitar and, when Piemur saw Sebell's discreet nod, he agreed with a show of enthusiasm to take a gitar part.

"Why Piemur, I thought sure you'd take a drum part," said Menolly, her expression so bland that he nearly rose to her bait.

Piemur restrained an urge to kick her in the shins and smiled sweetly at her instead. "You heard today what the drummers think of me," he replied so demurely that Menolly chortled until her eyes filled.

As the harpers filed out of the Hall for the Gather, Sebell fell in step with Piemur.

"Heard anything of interest?"

"Who talks during the day's heat?" asked Piemur with heartfelt disgust. He suspected that Sebell had known about desert daytime indolence.

"You'll notice the change in them now, and you'll only need to do the dance turns. If I gauge the Gather right," said Sebell, glancing ahead at Menolly's slender figure in harper blue, "they'll keep her singing until she's hoarse. They always do."

Piemur glanced swiftly at Sebell, wondering if the journeyman was aware of showing his feelings for the harper girl so openly.

The first dance turn was the longest and most energetic. The crisp night air stimulated the dancers' gyrations until they were energetic beyond Piemur's credence. Quite a transformation from the languid manners of the afternoon. Then, as Bantur, Deece, Strud and Menolly remained on the platform to sing, Sebell nodded to Piemur to work his way from the square's attentive audience toward the smaller groups of men, drinking tubes in hand, conversing in quiet tones.

The subdued level, Piemur decided, was out of courtesy to the singers and their audience, but it made it hard for him. He was about to give up when the word "Oldtimers" caught his ear. He sidled closer to the group and, in the light of the glow baskets, recognized two as seaholders, a miner, a smith and an Igen holder.

"I don't say it was them, but since they've gone south, we've had no more unexpected demands," said the smith. "G'narish may also be an Oldtimer, but he follows Benden's ways. So it had to have been Oldtimers."

"Young Toric often sends his two-master north for trade," said one of the seaholders, in a voice so confidential that Piemur had to strain to catch the words. "He always has, and my Holder sees no harm in it. Toric's no dragonman, and those that stayed south with him don't fall under Benden's order. So we trade. He may bargain close, but he pays well."

"In marks?" asked the Igen holder, surprised.

"No. Barter! Gemstones, hides, fruit, such like. And

once"—here Piemur held his breath for fear of missing the confidential whisper—"nine fire lizard eggs!"

"No?" Envy as well as surprised interest were expressed in that startled reply. The seaholder quickly gestured the man to keep his tone down. "Of course," and there was no disguising the bitter jealousy, "they've all the sand beaches in the world to search in the south! Any chance . . ."

The fascinating conversation broke off as another seaholder joined them, an older man, and possibly superior to the gossiping seaman, for talk turned to other things, and Piemur moved on.

Then Menolly began to sing alone, the other harpers accompanying her. All conversations died as she sang, with what appeared to Piemur to be incredible aptness, the "Fire Lizard Song."

Her voice was richer now, Piemur noticed with a critical ear, the tone better sustained. He couldn't fault her musical phrasing. Nor should he be able to after three Turns of severe instruction by Master Shonagar. Her voice was so admirably suited to the songs she sang, he thought, and more expressive than many singers who had even better natural voices. As often as Piemur had heard the "Fire Lizard Song," he found himself listening as intently as ever. When the song ended, he applauded as vigorously as everyone else, only then aware that he had been equally captivated. Putting words to music was not Menolly's only talent; she put her music in the hearts and minds of her listeners, too.

While her enrapt audience started shouting for their favorite tunes, she beckoned Sebell to the platform, and they sang a duet of an eastern sea hold song, their voices so well blended that Piemur's respect and admiration for his fellow harpers reached unprecedented heights. Now, if only his voice turned tenor, he might have the chance to sing with . . .

He played three more dance turns, but Sebell had been correct: the Igen gatherers wanted Menolly whenever she would favor them with song. Piemur also noticed that for every solo she sang, there was at least one group song and a duet including the Igen harpers. Clever of her to forestall ill-feeling. Too bad such discretion did not translate into his particular problem with the drum apprentices!

Whether it was because he'd had a sleep in the afternoon or because the desert air was particularly bracing, Piemur was never sure, but it was only when he noticed the thinning of the crowd around the dance area, and the increased number of people rolled up in their blankets in the Gather tents, that he began to feel fatigue. He looked around then for Sebell and Menolly. When he saw nothing of them, he finally sought a weary, yawning Strud, who advised him, with a grin, to find a corner and get some sleep, if he could.

It had been easy enough to sleep that afternoon, but now, with no heat to lull him, the things he had heard— music as well as malice—danced about in his mind. One positive fact emerged: the Oldtimer's descent on the miner in Fort Hold was not an isolated incident. He also knew that while G'narish, Igen's Oldtime Weyrleader, was respected, Igen Holders would have given much to be beholden to Benden instead.

A sharp peck on his ear woke him, and he had a momentary fright before he focused his eyes on Rocky's cocked head and heard the reassuring soft chirrup. Someone was snoring lustily beside him, and Piemur's back was warm. He cautiously eased away from this unknown sleeper.

Rocky chirped again and, hopping off his shoulder, walked a few paces away with exaggerated steps before looking back at Piemur. He wanted Piemur to come with him, and while his eyes were not red with hunger, they were whirling fast enough to indicate some urgency.

"I don't need a drum to get your message," Piemur said under his breath as he moved further away from his snoring bed companion. He really must have been tired to sleep through that sort of racket.

Rocky landed on his right shoulder, poking at his cheek to force his head left. Piemur obediently ducked under the tent flap and, in the glows that were shedding a subdued waning light on the sands before Igen Hold, he saw the dark bulk of a dragon and several figures.

Rocky called in a sweet light voice and then took off toward the group. Piemur followed, yawning and shivering in the chill pre-dawn breeze, wishing he had some klah. Especially if the presence of a dragon meant he had to go *between*; he was cold enough already.

The dragon was not Lioth, as he'd half expected, but a brown nearly as big as the Fort Weyr dragon. It had to be Canth. And it was, for as he neared the group, he saw the scars on F'nor's face from the dreadful, near-fatal scoring he'd taken on his famous jump to the Red Star.

"C'mon, Piemur," called Sebell. "F'nor's here to take us to Benden Weyr. Ramoth's latest clutch is Hatching."

Piemur started to whoop with joy, then bit his tongue, choking off his jubilation. Bad enough he'd been to a Gather, but when Clell and that lot heard he'd been to a Benden Hatching, his life wouldn't be worth a wax mark! He saw in the same instant that the others were expecting him to react with appropriate anticipation and, loudly damning his changing voice, he affected as genuine a smile as he could manage. The groan that escaped him as he climbed to Canth's back was for the inexorable forces he couldn't resist rather than the physical effort. He endured in silence Sebell's teasing about the miseries of an apprentice's life, and then Menolly's for his silence, which she attributed to either hunger or sleepiness.

"Never mind, Piemur," she said with an encouraging smile, "there's bound to be some klah left in the pot for you at Benden Weyr." She peered down at his face. "You are awake, aren't you?"

"Sort of," he said, yawning again, then added for her benefit, "I just can't take it in that me, Piemur, gets to go to a Benden Weyr Hatching!"

Should he ask Menolly not to tell the Drum Master and Dirzan? Could he ask her to say he'd been left at Igen Hold until they could collect him? No, he couldn't, because she'd want to know why. And he couldn't tell her because that would mark him a blubber-baby, bleater, bab-blemouth. There had to be some way he could settle Clell and Dirzan by himself!

Despite his misgivings, Piemur succumbed to the fear-charged thrill of Canth's initial vault into the air, the sensation of being pressed down, the breathlessness as the huge wings beat powerfully, and he felt the effort of Canth's neck muscles under his buttocks. It wasn't quite as scarey flying in this predawn darkness because he didn't know how far he was above the ground, particularly since his face was turned away from Igen Hold's fading lights;

but he caught his breath in a spurt of pure terror as F'nor gave Canth the audible request to take them *between* to Benden Weyr. He was again alone in the intense, sense-deprived, utter cold, and then, before the cold could sink to his bones, they had emerged into the brightening day, momentarily suspended above the massive Bowl of Benden Weyr.

He'd been to Fort Weyr once, by cart, with a group of harpers, when Ludeth, the Weyrqueen, had her first queen egg hatching. He'd thought that Fort was huge, but Benden seemed much bigger. Perhaps because he was seeing it from dragonback, perhaps because of the light, touching the far edges of the Bowl, gilding the lake. Perhaps it was because this was Benden, and Benden figured so hugely and importantly in his eyes, and the eyes of everyone else on Pern.

Without Benden and her courageous leaders, Pern might have been half-destroyed by Thread.

Another dragon appeared in the air just above them, and instinctively Piemur ducked, hearing Menolly laugh at his reflex. A third and then a fourth dragon arrived even as Canth began to glide down to the bowl floor. By the time Piemur could slide from Brown's shoulder to the ground, he marveled that the dragons hadn't collided midair, appearing as they had with such startling frequency.

Beauty, Kimi, Rocky and Diver popped in above Menolly's head, caroling with excitement, and suddenly they were joined by five other fire lizards Piemur had never seen before. When Menolly muttered worriedly about feeding fire lizards before they disrupted the Weyr, F'nor laughingly told them to find Mirrim. She was likely to be supervising breakfast in the kitchen caverns. Sebell's nudge in his ribs reminded Piemur to thank the brown rider and his dragon. Then the three harpers made their way across the Bowl to the brightly lit cavern.

The enticing aromas of fresh klah and toasted cereals quickened their steps, Menolly leading the way toward the smallest hearth, away from the bustle and hurry of weyrfolk at the larger fires.

"Mirrim?" she called, and the girl at the hearth turned, her face lighting as she recognized the new arrivals.

"Menolly! You came! Sebell! How are you? What have

you been up to recently to get so tanned? Who's this?" Her smile disappeared as she noticed Piemur bringing up the rear, as if such a scruffy apprentice shouldn't be in such good company.

"Mirrim, this is Piemur. You've heard me speak of him often enough," said Menolly, putting her hand on Piemur to draw him forward and closer to her, the intimacy a guarantee of him to Mirrim. "He was my first friend at the Harper Hall, as you were mine here. We've all been at the Igen Gather. Baked yesterday, frozen this morning, and very hungry!" Menolly let her tone drift upward plaintively.

"Well, of course, you're hungry," said Mirrim, breaking off her stern appraisal of Piemur to turn to the hearth. She filled cups and bowls and set them out on one of the small tables with such alacrity that Piemur changed his first, unflattering impression of her. "I can't stop long with you. You know how things are at the Weyr when there's a Hatching; so much to do. The important details you really have to see to yourself to be sure they're done right." She flopped gracelessly into a chair with an exaggerated sigh of relief to underscore the weight of responsibility on her shoulders. Then she ran both hands through the fringe of brown hair on her forehead, ending the gesture with pats at the near plaits that hung down her back.

Piemur eyed her with a certain skeptical cynicism but, when he realized that Menolly and Sebell took no notice of her mannerisms and had sought out her company from everyone in the busy cavern, he came to the reluctant conclusion that there must be more to her than was obvious.

Beauty landed on Menolly's shoulder just then, chirruping with some petulance, her eyes whirling reddishly. Diver swooped to Menolly's other shoulder just as Kimi landed on Sebell's. Rocky, to Piemur's intense delight, came to roost on his.

"I thought that was Rocky," Mirrim said, pointing accusingly at Piemur as if he oughtn't to have a fire lizard anyhow.

"It is," said Menolly with a laugh, "but Piemur helps me feed him every day so Rocky's just reminding us he's hungry, too."

"Why didn't you say they hadn't been fed?" Mirrim

bounced to her feet, scowling with disapproval. "Really, Menolly, I'd've thought you'd take care of your friends first. . . ."

Sebell and Menolly exchanged guilty smiles as Mirrim stalked off to a table where women were cutting up wherries for the Hatching Feast. She returned with a generous bowlful of scraps, three fire lizards hovering anxiously above her. She shooed them away, reminding them with gruff affection that they'd already been fed. To Piemur's relief, because he was developing an antipathy to her manner, Mirrim was called away to one of the main hearths. Rocky poked his cheek imperiously, and Piemur concentrated on feeding him.

"Is she a good friend of yours?" Piemur asked when the first edge of fire lizard hunger had been eased.

Sebell laughed, and Menolly made a rueful grimace.

"She's very good-hearted. Don't let her ways put you off."

Piemur grunted. "They have."

Sebell laughed again, offering Kimi a large chunk of meat so he could get a swallow of his klah while she struggled to chew. "Mirrim does take a bit of getting used to but, as Menolly says, she'll give you the shirt from her back . . ."

"Complaining all the time, I'll wager," Piemur said.

Menolly's expression was solemn. "She was fosterling to Brekke, and Manora's always said that it was Mirrim's devoted nursing that helped Brekke live after her queen was killed."

"Really?" That did impress Piemur, and he looked for Mirrim among the knot of women by the hearth as if this disclosure had caused her to change visibly.

"Don't, please don't judge her too quickly, Piemur," said Menolly, touching his arm to emphasize her request.

"Well, of course, if *you* say so . . ."

Sebell winked at Piemur. "She says so, Piemur, and we must obey!"

"Oh, you," and Menolly dismissed Sebell's teasing with a scowl of irritation. "I just don't want Piemur jumping to the wrong conclusion on the basis of a few moments' meeting—"

"When everyone knows," and Sebell rolled his eyes ceilingward, "that it takes time, endurance, tolerance and luck to appreciate Mirrim!" Sebell ducked as Menolly threatened him with her spoon.

They had finished feeding the fire lizards and sent them out to sun themselves when Mirrim popped up before them again, exhaling a mighty sigh.

"I don't know how we're going to get everything finished in time. Why those eggs have to be so awkward in their timing. Half the western guests will be dead of sleep and need breakfast. . . . See?" She waved toward the entrance where dragons were depositing more passengers. "There's so much to be done. And I particularly want to get to this Hatching. Felessan's a candidate today, you know."

"So F'nor told us. I could manage the breakfast hearth, Mirrim," said Menolly.

"Just set us a task," said Sebell, throwing his arm across Piemur's shoulders, "and we'll do our best to assist."

"Oh, would you?" Suddenly the affected manners dropped, and Mirrim's scowl gave way to an incredulous smile of relief, illuminating her face and making her a very pretty girl. "If you would just set up those tables," and she pointed to stacks of trestles and tops, "that'd be the greatest help!"

She was again summoned across the cavern and dashed off with a smile of such unaffected gratitude that Piemur stared after her in astonishment. Why did the girl act oddly? She was much nicer when she was just herself!

"So, Felessan stands on the Hatching Ground," said Sebell. "I missed that this morning."

"Sorry, thought I'd told you," said Menolly, rising to clear the table of their dishes. "I wonder if he'll Impress."

"Why shouldn't he?" asked Piemur, startled by her doubt.

"He may be the son of the Weyrleaders, but that doesn't necessarily mean he'll Impress. Dragon choice can't be forced."

"Oh, Felessan'll Impress," said a dragonrider, approaching the small hearth, two others just behind him. "Are you tending the pot, Menolly?"

"And a good day to you, T'gellan," Menolly said with a pert smile for the bronze rider as she poured klah for him.

"How's yourself, Sebell?" T'gellan went on, seating himself on the bench and gesturing to the other riders to join him.

"Hard put upon," said Sebell in a long-suffering tone that sounded suspiciously like an imitation of Mirrim. "We just got organized to set up the tables. C'mon, Piemur, before Mirrim lays about us with her ladle."

Because Menolly had so stoutly championed Mirrim, Piemur kept an eye out for the girl as he and Sebell arranged the additional tables. He spotted Mirrim dashing from one hearth to another, called to assist in trussing wherries for roasting, herdbeasts for the spit. He watched her organize one group of youngsters to peel roots and tubers and another to laying the tables with utensils and platters. He decided that Mirrim had not been puffing up her responsibilities.

Menolly, too, was kept busy, feeding dragonriders and their sleepy-eyed passengers, dragged from their beds for the imminent Hatching.

Sebell and Piemur had just set up the last table when a faint hum reached their ears. Fire lizards reappeared in the cavern, the high notes of their chirruping a countercadence to the low bass throb of the humming dragons.

Mirrim, divested of her apron and brushing water stains from her skirt, came dashing toward them.

"C'mon, Oharan promised to save us all seats by him," she cried and led the way across the Bowl at a run.

The Weyr Harper had kept them places in the tiers above the Hatching Ground, though, he informed them, his life had been threatened by Holders and Craftmasters. Piemur could see why as he settled down, for this was a splendid position, in the second tier, close to the entrance so that the view of the entire Ground was clear. There was no queen egg for Ramoth to guard, so the Benden queen dragon was standing to one side of the ground, Lessa and F'lar on the ledge above her. Occasionally the enormous golden dragon looked up at her weyrmate, as if seeking assurance or, Piemur thought, consolation, since the eggs she had clutched were shortly to be taken from her care. The notion amused Piemur, for he'd never have ascribed maternal emotions to Benden's preeminent queen dragon. Certainly Ramoth with her yellow flashing eyes and restless foot-shifting, wing-rustling, was a far picture from the gentle concern female herdbeast or runners showed their offspring.

A blur of white, seen from the corner of his eye, drew Piemur's attention to the Hatching Ground entrance. The candidates were approaching the eggs, their white tunics fluttering in the light morning breeze. Piemur suppressed his amusements as the boys, stepping further on the hot sands, began to pick up their feet smartly. When they had reached the clutch, they ranged themselves in a loose semi-circle about the gently rocking eggs. Ramoth made a noise like a disapproving growl, which the boys all ignored, but Piemur noticed that the ones nearest her edged surreptitiously away.

A startled murmur ran through the audience as one of the eggs rocked more violently. The sudden snapping of the shell seemed to resound through the high-ceilinged cavern, and the dragons on the upper ledges hummed more loudly than ever with encouragement. The actual Hatching had begun. Piemur didn't know where to look because the audience was as fascinating as the Hatching: dragonriders' faces with soft glows as they relived the magic moment when they had Impressed the hatchling dragon who became their life's companion, minds indissolubly linked. On other faces was hope, breathless and incredulous, as guests and parents of the candidates waited for the moment when their lads would be chosen, or rejected, by the hatchlings. Fire lizards, respectfully quiet, perched on many shoulders in the Ground. And Piemur, who could never aspire to Impress a dragon, was reminded of that unfilled promise, that he would have a fire lizard one day. He wondered if Menolly remembered her promise to him. Or if he'd ever have the opportunity to remind her of it.

"There's Felessan," said Menolly, nudging him sharply with her elbow. She pointed to a leggy figure with such a luxuriant growth of dark curling hair that his head seemed oversized.

"He doesn't even look nervous," said Piemur, as he noted the signs of apprehension in other candidates who shifted uneasily or twitched unnecessarily at their tunics.

A concerted gasp directed their attention from Felessan, and they saw that several more eggs were rocking violently as the hatchlings struggled to be free. Abruptly an egg split open, and a moist little brown dragon was spilled to his feet on the hot sands. Dragging his fragile-looking damp wings on the ground, he began to lunge this way and that, calling piteously, while the adult dragons crooned encouragement, reinforced by Ramoth's half-hum, half-howl.

The boys nearest the dragonet tried to anticipate his direction, hoping to Impress him, but he lurched out of their immediate circle, staggering across the sands, his call plaintive, desperate until the next group of boys turned. One, prompted by some instinct, took a step forward. The little brown's cries turned joyous, he tried to extend his wet wings to bridge the distance between them, but the boy rushed to the dragon's side, caressing head and shoulders, patting the damp wings while the little hatchling crooned with triumph, his jeweled eyes glowing the blue and purple of love and devotion. The day's first Impression had been made!

Piemur heard Menolly's deep and satisfied sigh and knew that she was reliving the moment she had Impressed her fire lizards in the Dragon Stones cave three Turns ago. He was again assailed by a deep stab of envy. When would he rate a fire lizard?

Excited cries brought his attention back to the Hatching Ground as more eggs cracked, exposing their occupants.

"Watch Felessan, Piemur! There's a bronze near him . . ." cried Mirrim, grabbing Piemur's arm in her excitement.

"And two browns and a blue," added Menolly, scarcely less excited as she canted her body in a mental effort to direct the little bronze toward Felessan. "He deserves a bronze! He deserves one!"

"Only if the dragon wants him," said Mirrim sententiously. "Just because he's the Weyrleader's son—"

"Shut up, Mirrim," said Piemur, exasperated, clenching his fists, urging the Impression to occur.

Felessan was aware of the bronze's proximity, but so were a handful of other candidates. The little creature, rocking unstably on his wobbly legs, seemed not to see any of them for a moment. Then the wedge-shaped head fell forward and got buried in the sand as his hind legs overbalanced him. It was too much. Felessan gently righted the little beast and then stood transfixed, the expression on his exultant face plainly visible to his friends as Impression was made.

Ramoth's bugle astonished everyone into a long moment of silence; but it was no wonder, Piemur thought, that F'lar and Lessa were embracing each other at the sight of their one child Impressing a bronze!

The excitement was over too soon, Piemur thought, just moments later. He wished that all the eggs hadn't hatched at once, so this dizzy happiness could be extended. Not that there wasn't some disappointment and sadness, too, because far more candidates were presented to the eggs than could Impress. Only one little green had not Impressed, and she was mewling unhappily, butting one boy out of her way, lurching to another and peering up into his face, obviously searching for just the right lad. She had worked her way toward the tiers, despite the efforts of the remaining candidates to attract her attention and keep her well out into the Ground.

"Whatever is the matter with those boys?" demanded Mirrim, frowning with anxiety over the little green's pathetic wandering. She stood up, gesturing peremptorily to the candidates to close around the little green.

Just then the creature began to croon urgently and made directly for the steps that led up to the tiers.

"What is possessing her?" Mirrim asked no one in particular. She looked behind her accusingly, as if somehow a candidate might be hiding among the guests.

"She wants someone not on the Ground," rang a voice from the crowd.

"She's going to hurt herself," said Mirrim in an agitated mutter and pushed past the three people seated between her and the stairs. "She'll bruise her wings on the walls."

The little green did hurt herself, slipping off the first step and banging her muzzle so sharply on the stone that she let out a cry of pain, echoed by a fierce bugle from Ramoth who began to move across the sands.

"Now, listen here, you silly thing, the boys you want are out there on the Ground. Turn yourself around and go back to them," Mirrim was saying as she made her way down the steps to the little green. Her fire lizards, calling out in wildly ecstatic buglings, halted her. She stared for a long moment at the antics of her friends, and then, her expression incredulous, she looked down at the green hatchling determinedly attacking the obstacle of steps. "I can't!" Mirrim cried, so panic-stricken that she slipped on the steps herself and slid down three before her flailing hands found support. "I can't!" Mirrim glanced about her for confirmation. "I'm not supposed to Impress. I'm not a candidate. She can't want *me*!" Awe washed over the consternation on her face and in her voice.

"If it's you she wants, Mirrim, get down there before she hurts herself!" said F'lar, who had by now reached the scene, Lessa beside him.

"But I'm not—"

"It would seem that you are, Mirrim," said Lessa, her face reflecting amusement and resignation. "The dragon's never wrong! Come! Be quick about it, girl. She's scraping her chin raw to get to you!"

With one final startled look at her Weyrleaders, Mirrim half-slid the remaining steps, cushioning the little green's chin from yet another harsh contact with the stone of the step.

"Oh, you silly darling! Whatever made you choose me?" Mirrim said in a loving voice as she gathered the green into her arms and began to soothe the hatchling's distressed cries. "She says her name is Path!" The glory on Mirrim's face caused Piemur to look away in embarrassment and envy.

For one brief moment, Piemur had entertained the bizarre notion that maybe the little green dragon had been looking for him. A deep sigh fluttered through his lips, and a hand was laid gently on his shoulder. Schooling his expression, he turned to see Menolly watching him, a deep pity and understanding in her eyes.

"I promised you Turns ago that you'd have a fire lizard, Piemur. I haven't forgotten. I will keep that promise!"

As one they turned their heads back to watch Mirrim fussing over her Path, her fire lizards hopping on the sands, chattering away as if welcoming the little green in their own fashion.

"Come on, you two," said Sebell, as Mirrim began to encourage Path to walk out of the Hatching Ground. "We'd better see Master Robinton. This is going to cause problems." The last he said in a low voice.

"Why?" asked Piemur, making sure they weren't overheard. But everyone was filing out of the tiers now, eager to congratulate or condole. "She's weyrbred."

"Greens are fighting dragons," began Sebell.

"In that case, Mirrim's well paired, isn't she?" asked Piemur with droll amusement.

"Piemur!"

At Menolly's shocked remonstrance, Piemur turned to Sebell and saw an answering gleam, though the journeyman turned quickly and started down the steps.

"Sebell's right, though," Menolly said thoughtfully as they started across the hot sands, quickening their pace as the heat penetrated the soles of their flying boots.

"Why?" asked Piemur again. "Just because she's a girl?"

"There won't be as much shock as there might be," Sebell went on. "Jaxom's Impression of Ruth set a precedent."

"It's not quite the same thing, Sebell," Menolly replied. "Jaxom is a Lord Holder and has to remain so. And then the weyrmen did think the little white dragon mightn't live. And now he has, it's obvious he's never going to be a full-sized dragon. Not that he's needed in the Weyrs, but Mirrim is!"

"Exactly! And not in the capacity of green rider."

"I think she'd make a good fighting rider," said Piemur, keeping the comment carefully under his breath.

When they located Master Robinton, he was already earnestly discussing the matter with Oharan.

"Completely unexpected! Mirrim swears that she hadn't been in the Hatching Ground at all when the candidates were familiarizing themselves with the Eggs," Master Robinton told his craftsmen. Then he smiled. "Fortunately, with F'lessan Impressing a bronze, Lessa and F'lar are in great spirits." Now he shrugged, his grin broadening. "It was simply a case of the dragon finding her own partnership where she wanted it!"

"As Ruth did with Jaxom!"

"Precisely."

"And that is the Harper message?" asked Sebell, glancing about the Bowl where knots of people surrounded weyrlings and dragonets.

"There doesn't seem to be any other explanation. So let

us drink and be merry. It's a good day for Pern! And I'm terribly dry," said the Masterharper as the Weyr Harper solemnly proffered a cup of wine. "Oh thanks, Oharan. Must be the heat of the Hatching Ground or the excitement. I'm parched. Ahhhh." The Harper's sigh was of relief and pleasure. "A good Benden vintage . . . ah, an old one, the wine has a mellowness, a smoothness . . ." He glanced about him as his audience waited expectantly. Oharan's hand casually covered the seal of the wineskin. The Harper took another judicious sip. "Yes, indeed. I have it now. The pressing of ten Turns back, and furthermore . . ." he held up a finger, ". . . it's from the northwestern slopes of upper Benden."

Oharan slowly uncovered the seal, and the others saw that the Harper had been absolutely correct.

"I don't know how you do it, Master Robinton," said Oharan, having hoped to confound his master.

"He's had a lot of practice," said Menolly at her driest, and they all laughed as Master Robinton started to protest.

They had time for a quiet glass before the admiring guests had exhausted all the possible things one could say to a newly impressed pair. Then the Weyrlingmaster took his charges off to the lake where the newly hatched would be fed, bathed and oiled, and the guests began to drift toward the tables, seating themselves for the feasting that would follow.

Master Robinton led his craftsmen in a rousing ballad of praise to dragons and their riders before he joined the Weyrleaders and their visiting Lord Holders. Oharan, Sebell, Menolly and Piemur did the courtesy round to the tables where the parents of new dragonriders were seated, singing requests. Menolly's fire lizards sang several songs with her before she excused them, explaining that they were far more interested in the new dragons than singing for mere people. Then she got involved with a group from the crafthall at Bitra, and the other three harpers left her explaining how to teach fire lizards to sing as they continued the rounds.

The tradition was that a harper's song deserved a cup of wine. Chatting as they drank, Sebell and Oharan took turns directing conversation where they wished it: Mirrim's unexpected Impression.

There was, to be sure, considerable surprise that Mirrim had done so, but most of those queried found it to be no large affair. After all, they said, Mirrim was weyrbred, a fosterling of Brekke's, had Impressed three of the first fire lizards to be found at Southern, so her unexpected rise to dragonrider was at least consistent. Now Jaxom, who had to remain Lord of Ruatha, was a different case entirely. Piemur noticed that everyone was a good deal interested in the health of the little white dragon and, while they wished him the best, were just as pleased that he'd never make a full-sized beast. Evidently that made it easier for people to accept the fact that Ruth was being raised in a Hold instead of a Weyr.

Holdlessness was a topic to which conversations returned time and again that evening. Many lads, growing up in land crafts, would not find holdings of their own when they were old enough. There simply weren't any old places left. Could not more of the mountainous regions of the far north be made habitable? Or the remote slopes of High Reaches or Crom? Piemur noted that Nabol, which actually had tenable land uncultivated, was never cited. What about the marshlands of lower Benden? Surely with such a competent Weyr, more holds could be protected. Occasionally Piemur, standing or sitting at the edges of groups, would overhear fascinating snatches and try to make sense out of them. Mostly he discarded them as gossip, but one stuck in his tired mind. Lord Oterel had been the speaker. He didn't know the other man, though his lighter clothes suggested he came from the southern part of Pern. "Meron gets more than his share; we go without. Girls impress fighting dragons, and our lad stands on the Ground. Ridiculous!"

Piemur found it getting progressively harder to rise from one table and move to another. Not that he was drinking any wine; he had sense enough not to do that. He just seemed to be more tired than he ought to be; if he could just put his head down for a few moments.

He was scarcely conscious of the cold of *between*, only annoyed because he was being forced to walk when he wanted to sit down. He did recall some sort of argument going on over his head. He could have sworn it was Silvina giving someone the very rough edge of her tongue. He was mercifully grateful that finally he was permitted to stretch out on a bed, feel furs pulled over his shoulders, and he could give in to the sleep he craved.

The bell woke him, and his surroundings confused him. He looked about, trying to figure out where he was, since he certainly wasn't in the drum apprentices' quarters. Further he was on a rush bag on a floor—the floor in Sebell's room, for the clothes Sebell had been wearing for the past two days were draped on a nearby chair, his flying boots sagging against each other by the bed. Piemur's empty clothes had been neatly piled on his boots at the foot of the rush bag.

The bell continued to ring, and Piemur, keenly aware of the emptiness of his belly, hastily dressed, paused long enough to splash his face and hands with water in case anyone, like Dirzan, wanted to fault him on cleanliness and proceeded down the corridor to the steps and the dining hall. He was just turning into the hall when Clell and the other three came in the main door. Clell flashed a look at the others and then strode up to Piemur, grabbing him by the arm roughly.

"Where've you been for two days?"

"Why? Did you have to polish the drums?"

"You're going to get it from Dirzan!" A pleased smirk crossed Clell's face.

"Why should he get it from Dirzan, Clell?" asked Menolly, quietly coming up behind the drum apprentices. "He's been on Harper business."

"He's always getting off on Harper business," replied Clell with unexpected anger, "and always with you!"

Piemur raised his fist at such insolence and leaned back to make the swing count in Clell's sneering face. But Menolly was quicker; she swung the apprentice about and shoved him forcefully toward the main door.

"Insolence to a journeyman means water rations for you, Clell!" she said and, without bothering to see that he'd continued out of the hall, she turned to the other three who gawked at her. "And, for you, too, if I should learn of any mischief against Piemur because of this. Have I made myself perfectly clear? Or do I need to mention the incident to Master Olodkey?"

The cowed apprentices murmured the necessary assurances and, at her dismissal, lost themselves in the throng of other apprentices.

"How much trouble have you been having in the drum-heights, Piemur?"

"Nothing I can't handle," said Piemur, wondering when he could get back at Clell for that insult to Menolly.

"Water rations for you, too, Piemur, if I see so much as a scratch on Clell's face."

"But he . . ."

Bonz, Timiny and Brolly came flying into the hall at that point and hailed Piemur with such evident relief that, after giving Piemur a long, forbidding glance, Menolly went off toward the journeyman's tables. The boys demanded to know where he'd been and he was to tell them everything.

He didn't. He told them what he felt they should know as far as the Igen Hold Gather was concerned, an innocuous enough tale. And he could, and did, describe in great detail the Impression of Path to Mirrim. The bare bones of that unexpected event was already the talk of the Hall, and Piemur had heard the public version so often that he knew he wasn't committing any indiscretion. He was careful to play down, even to his good friends, the circumstances that had brought him to Benden Weyr at such an auspicious occasion.

"No dragonrider was going to take me, an apprentice harper, all the way back to the Hall when there was a Hatching, so I had to stay."

"C'mon, Piemur," said Bonz, thoroughly disgusted with his indifference, "you can't ever get me to believe that you didn't enjoy every moment of it."

"Then I won't. 'Cause I did. But I was just bloody lucky to be at the Igen Gather right then. Otherwise I'd've been back polishing the big drums yesterday!"

"Say, Piemur, you getting on all right with Clell and those others?" asked Ranly.

"Sure. Why?" Piemur kept his voice as casual as he could.

"Oh, nothing, except they're not mixers, and lately, they've been sort of asking about you in a funny sort of way." Ranly was worried, and from the solemn expressions on the other faces, he had confided their concern.

"You just haven't been the same since your voice changed, Piemur," said Timiny, blushing with embarrassment.

Piemur snorted, then grinned because Timiny looked so uncomfortable. "Of course, I'm not, Tim. How could I be? My voice is changing, and the rest of me, too."

"I didn't mean that . . ." and Timiny faltered in a muddle of confusion, looking at Bonz and Brolly for help to express what puzzled them all.

Just then the journeyman rose to give out the day's assignments, and the apprentices were forced to be quiet. Piemur held his breath, hoping that Menolly had not made Clell's discipline a public one and felt relieved when it was obvious that she hadn't. He was going to have enough trouble with Clell as it was. Not that he worried about the apprentice going hungry. He'd seen the other three secreting bread, fruit and a thick wherry slice to smuggle out to him.

As the sections dispersed for their work parties, Piemur went to the drumheights, wondering exactly what awaited him. He was not surprised to find that the drums had been left for him to polish, or that Dirzan grumbled about his absence because how could he learn enough to be a proper drummer. And it was only to be expected that there was no word of praise from Dirzan when he came out measure perfect on all the sequences Dirzan asked him. What Piemur wasn't prepared for was the state of his belongings when Dirzan dismissed him. He got the first whiff when he opened the door to the apprentices' room. Despite the fact that both windows were propped wide open, the small room smelled like the necessary. He opened the press for clean clothes and realized where the worst of the offending stench lay. He turned, half-hoping this was all, but as he ran his hand over his sleeping furs they were disgustingly damp.

"Who's been . . ." Dirzan came striding into the room, finger and thumb pinching his nose against the odor.

Piemur said nothing, he merely let the soiled clothing unroll and held the furs up so that the light fell on the long, damp stain. Dirzan's eyes narrowed, and his grimace deepened. Piemur wondered what annoyed Dirzan more: that Piemur's unexpectedly long absence had made the joke more noisome than necessary, or that here was proof positive that Piemur was being harassed by his roommates.

"You may be excused from other duties to attend to this," said Dirzan. "Be sure to bring back a sweet candle to clear the odor. How they could sleep with that . . ."

Dirzan waited until Piemur had cleared the noxious things from the room, and then he slammed the door with such force that the journeyman on watch came to see what was the matter.

With everyone scattered for work sections, Piemur managed to get to the washing room without being stopped. He was so furious he wouldn't have trusted himself to answer properly if anyone had asked him the most civil of questions. He slapped the furs, hair side out into the warm tub, sprinkling half the jar of sweetsand on the slowly sinking bedding. He shook the half-hardened stuff out of his clothing into the drain, and then, with washing paddle, shoved and prodded the garments to loosen the encrustations. If there were stains on his new clothes, he'd face a month's water rations but he'd pay them all back, so he would.

"What are you doing in here at this time of day, Piemur?" asked Silvina, attracted by the splashing and pounding.

"Me?" The force of his tone brought Silvina right into the room. "My roommates play dirty jokes!"

Silvina gave him a long searching look as her nose told her what kind of dirty jokes. "Any reason for them to?"

In a split second Piemur decided. Silvina was one of the few people in the Hall he could trust. She instinctively knew when he was shamming, so she'd know now that he was being put on. And he had an unbearable need and urge to release some of the troubles he had suppressed. This last trick of the apprentices, damaging his good new clothes, hurt more than he had realized in the numbness following his discovery. He'd been so proud of the fine garments, and to have them crudely soiled before he'd worn some of them enough to acquire honest dirt hit him harder than the slanders at his supposed indiscretions.

"I get to Gathers and Impressions," Piemur drew a whistling breath through his teeth, "and I've made the mistake of learning drum measures too fast and too well."

Silvina continued to stare at him, her eyes slightly narrowed and her head tilted to one side. Abruptly she moved beside him and took the washpaddle from his hand, slipping it deftly under the soaking furs.

"They probably expected you back right after the Igen Gather!" She chuckled as she plunged the fur back under the water, grinning broadly at him. "So they had to sleep in the stink they caused for two nights!" Her laughter was infectious, and Piemur found his spirits lifting as he grinned back at her. "That Clell. He's the one who planned it. Watch him, Piemur. He's got a mean streak." Then she sighed. "Still, you won't be there long, and it won't do you any harm to learn the drum measures. Could be very useful one day." She gave him another long appraising look. "I'll say this for you, Piemur, you know when to keep your tongue in your head! Here, put that through the wringer now and let's see if we've got the worst out!"

Silvina helped him finish the washing, asking him all about the Hatching and Mirrim's unexpected Impression of a green dragon. And how did he find the climate in Igen? It was as much a relief for him to talk to Silvina without restraint as to have her expert help in cleaning his clothes.

Then, because she said nothing would be dry before evening, she got him another sleeping fur, and a spare shirt and pants, commenting they they were well-enough worn not to cause envy.

"You'll mention, of course, that I tore strips out of you for ruining good cloth and staining fur," she said with a parting wink.

He was halfway out of the Hall when he remembered the need for a sweet candle and went back for it, bearing her loud grumbles to the rest of the kitchen with fortitude.

Afterward, Piemur thought that if Dirzan had ignored the mischief the way Piemur intended to, the whole incident might have been forgotten. But Dirzan reprimanded the others in front of the journeymen and put them on water rations for three days. The sweet candle cleared the quarters of the stench, but nothing would ever sweeten the apprentices toward Piemur after that. It was almost as if, Piemur thought, Dirzan was determined to ruin any chance Piemur had of making friends with Clell or the others.

Though he did his best to stay out of their vicinities, he was constantly having benches shoved into his shins in the study room, his feet trod on everywhere, his ribs painfully stuck by drumsticks or elbows. His furs were sewn together three nights running, and his clothes were so frequently dipped in the roof gutters that he finally asked Brolly to make him a locking mechanism for his press that he alone could open. Apprentices were not supposed to have any private containers, but Dirzan made no mention of the addition to Piemur's box.

In a way, Piemur found a certain satisfaction in being able to ignore the nuisances, rising above all the pettiness perpetrated on him with massive and complete disdain. He spent as much time as he could studying the drum records, tapping his fingers on his fur even as he was falling asleep to memorize the times and rhythms of the most complicated measures. He knew the others knew exactly what he was doing, and there was nothing they could do to thwart him.

Unfortunately, the coolness he developed to fend off their little tricks began insidiously to come between him and his old friends. Bonz and Brolly complained loudly that he was different, while Timiny watched him with mournful eyes, as if he somehow considered himself responsible for Piemur's alterations.

Piemur tried to laugh it off, saying he was drum happy.

"They're putting on you up in the drumheights, Piemur," said Bonz glowering loyally. "I just know they are. And if Clell—"

"Clell isn't!" Piemur said in a tone so fierce that Bonz rocked back on his heels.

"That's exactly what I mean, Piemur!" said Brolly, who wasn't easily intimidated by a boy he'd known for five Turns and still topped by a full head. "You're different and don't give me that old wheeze about your voice changing and you with it. Your voice is settling. You haven't cracked in days!"

Piemur blinked, mildly surprised at the phenomenon of which he'd been unaware.

"It's too bad. Anyhow, Tilgin's got the part down . . . finally, and it wouldn't sound the same with you as baritone," Brolly went on.

"Baritone?" Piemur's voice broke in surprise and, when he saw the disappointment on his friends' faces, he started to laugh. "Well, maybe, and then, maybe not."

"Now you sound like Piemur," said Bonz, shouting with emphasis.

Isolated as he'd been in the drumheights, Piemur had easily managed to forget the fast approaching feast at Lord Groghe's and the performance of Domick's new music. Two sevendays had passed since the Benden Hatching, and he'd been too engrossed with his own problems to give much attention to extraneous matters. His friends now underlined the nearness of the Feast, and he was sure that he couldn't escape attending it and wondered how he could. He'd prefer to be out of Fort Hold altogether on the night of the performance because, sure as eggs cracked, he'd have to go to it.

Then it occurred to him that he hadn't been on any trips with Sebell and Menolly lately. He forced himself to laugh and joke with his friends in a fair imitation of his old self, but once back in the drumheights, while he stood his afternoon watch, he began to wonder if he'd done something wrong at Benden Weyr or Igen Hold. Or if, by any freak chance, Dirzan's tittle-tattle had affected Menolly's opinion of him. Come to think of it, he hadn't seen Sebell at all of late.

The next morning, when he was feeding the fire lizards with her, he asked her where the journeyman was.

"Between you and me," she said in a low voice, having seen Camo occupied with the greedy Auntie One, "he's up in the Ranges. He should be back tonight. Don't worry, Piemur," she said, smiling. "We haven't forgotten you." Then she gave him a very searching look. "You haven't been worried, have you?"

"Me? No, why should I worry?" He gave a derisive snort. "I put my time to good use. I know more drum measures than any of those dimwits, for all they've been mucking about up there for Turns!"

Menolly laughed. "Now you sound more like yourself. You're all right with Master Olodkey then?"

"Me? Sure!" Which, Piemur felt, was not stretching the truth. He was fine with Master Olodkey because he rarely came in contact with the man.

"And that rough lad, Clell, he's not come back at you for the other day, has he?"

"Menolly," said Piemur, taking a stern tone with her, "I'm Piemur. No one gets back at me. What gave you such a notion?" He sounded as scornful as he could.

"Hmmmm, just that you haven't been as—well . . ." and she smiled half-apologetically. "Oh, never mind. I expect you can take care of yourself any time, anywhere."

They continued feeding the fire lizards, and Piemur wished heartily that he could tell Menolly the real state of affairs in the drumheights. But what good would it do? She could only speak to Dirzan, who would never accept Piemur for any reason. Asking Dirzan to discipline the other apprentices for what was only stupid petty narking wouldn't help. Piemur could see clearly now that his well-founded reputation for mischief and game playing were coming back at him when he least expected, or even less, deserved it. He'd no one but himself to fault, so he'd just have to chew it raw and swallow! After all, once his voice settled, he'd be out of the drumheights. He could put up with it because he'd have the odd Gather out with Sebell and Menolly.

Chapter 5

That afternoon a drum message came in from the north. Piemur was in the main room diligently copying drum measures that Dirzan had set him to learn by evening, although he already knew them off rhythm perfect. He translated the message as it throbbed in.

"Urgent. Reply required please. Nabol." To himself Piemur smiled as the rest of the message pounded on, because he had the sudden suspicion that the Nabol drummer had begun with those measures to soften the arrogance of the main message. "Lord Meron of Nabol demands the immediate appearance of Master Oldive. Reply Instantly." Had the drummer added "grave illness," the signal "urgent" would have been appropriate.

Piemur continued his copying smoothly, aware of the eyes of the other apprentices on him. Let them think that he understood little beyond the first three measures, which was about all they'd know.

Rokayas, the journeyman on duty, came into the room a moment later.

"Who's running messages today?" he asked, the thin, folded sheaf of the transcribed message in his hand.

The others all pointed to Piemur, who immediately put his pen down and rose to his feet. The journeyman frowned.

"You were on yesterday."

"I'm on today again, Rokayas," said Piemur cheerfully and reached for the sheaf.

"Seems to me you're always on," Rokayas said, holding the message away from Piemur as he glared suspiciously at the others.

"Dirzan said I was messenger until he said otherwise," said Piemur, shrugging as if it were a matter of indifference to him.

"All right, then," and the journeyman surrendered the message, still eyeing the other four boys, "but it seems queer to me you're always running!"

"I'm newest," said Piemur and left the room. He was rather pleased that Rokayas had noticed. Actually he didn't mind because he got a brief respite from the sour presence of the other apprentices.

He dashed down the three flights of steps in his usual fashion, one hand lightly on the stone rail, plummeting down as fast as he could go. He burst out into the courtyard, automatically glancing about. The raking team was at work. He waved cheerfully to the section leader and then took the main steps to the Hall three at a time. His legs must be getting longer, he thought, or he was improving his stride because he used to be able to leap only two.

Slightly puffed, he tapped politely at Master Oldive's door and handed over the message, wheeling instantly so that no one could say he'd seen the message.

"Hold a moment, young Piemur," said Master Oldive, unfolding the sheaf and frowning as he read its contents. "Urgent, is it? Well, it could be, at that. Though why they wouldn't in courtesy send their watch dragon. . . . Ah well. Nabol hasn't one, has it? Reply that I'll come, and please ask Master Olodkey to pass the word to T'ledon that I must prevail on his good nature for passage to Nabol! I shall go straight to the meadow to wait for him."

Piemur repeated the message, using Master Oldive's exact phrasing and intonation. Released by the healer, he sped back across the court with another wave to the section leader. He was halfway up the second flight when he felt his right foot slide on the stone. He tried to catch himself, but his forward motion and the stretch of his legs were such that he hadn't a hope of saving himself from a fall. He tried to grab the stone railing with his right hand but it, too, was slick. He was thrown hard against the stone risers, wrenching thighs and hips, cracking his ribs painfully as he slid. He could have sworn that he heard a muffled laugh. His last conscious thought as his chin hit the stone and he bit his tongue hard was that someone had greased the rail and steps.

His shoulder was roughly shaken, and he heard Dirzan's irritated command to wake-up.

"What are you doing here? Why didn't you return immediately with Master Oldive's request? He's been waiting in the meadow. You can't even be trusted to run messages!"

Piemur tried to form an excuse, but only a groan issued from his lips as he groggily tried to right himself. He was dimly conscious of aches and pains all over his left side and sore stiffness across his cheek and under his skin.

"Fell on the steps, did you? Knocked yourself out, huh?" Dirzan was unsympathetic, but he was less rough-handed as he helped Piemur turn and sit on the bottom step.

"Greased," Piemur mumbled, waving with one hand at the steps while with the other he cushioned his aching head to reduce the pounding in his skull. But every place he touched his head seemed to ache, too, and the agony was making him ill to his stomach.

"Greased! Greased?" Dirzan exclaimed in acid disbelief. "A likely notion. You're always pelting up and down these steps. It's a wonder you haven't hurt yourself before now. Can't you get up?"

Piemur started to shake his head, but the slightest motion made him feel sick to his stomach. If he had to spew in front of Dirzan, he'd be doubly humiliated. And if he tried to move, he knew he would be ill.

"You said it was greased?" Dirzan's voice came from above his head. The agitated tone hurt Piemur's skull.

"Step there and handrail . . ." Piemur gestured with one hand.

"There's not a sign of grease! On your feet!" Dirzan sounded angrier than ever.

"Did you find him, Dirzan?" Rokayas called. The voice of the duty journeyman made Piemur's head throb like a message drum. "What happened to him?"

"He fell down the steps and knocked himself *between*." Dirzan was thoroughly disgusted. "Get up, Piemur!"

"No, Piemur, stay where you are," said Rokayas, and his voice was unexpectedly concerned.

Piemur wished he wouldn't shout, but he was very willing to stay where he was. The nausea in his belly seemed to be echoed by his head, and he didn't dare so much as open his eyes. Things whirled even with them shut.

"He said it was greased! Feel it yourself, Royakas, Clean as a drum!"

"Too clean! And if Piemur fell on his way back, he was *between* a long time. Too long for a mere slip. We'd better get him to Silvina."

"To Silvina? Why bother her for a little tumble? He's only skinned his chin."

Rokayas' hands were gently pressing against his skull and neck, then his arms and legs. He couldn't suppress a yelp when a particular painful bruise was touched.

"This wasn't a little tumble, Dirzan. I know you don't like the boy . . . but any fool could see he's hurt. Can you stand, Piemur?"

Piemur groaned, which was all he dared to do or his dinner would come up.

"He's faking to get out of duty," Dirzan said.

"He's not faking, Dirzan. And another thing, he's done too much of the running. Clell and the others haven't moved their butts out of the drumheights the last two sevendays I've been on duty."

"Piemur's the newest. You know the rule—"

"Oh, leave off, Dirzan. And take him from the other side. I want to carry him as flat as possible."

With Dirzan's grudging assistance, they carried him down the stairs, Piemur fighting against his nausea. He was only dazedly aware that Rokayas shouted for someone to fetch Silvina and be quick.

They were maneuvering him up the steps to the Main Hall, toward the infirmary, when Silvina intercepted them, asking quick questions, to which she got simultaneous answers from Dirzan and Rokayas.

"He fell down the stairs," said Rokayas.

"Nothing but a tumble," said Dirzan, overriding the other man. "Kept Master Oldive standing in the meadow . . ."

Silvina's hands felt cool on his face, moved gently over his skull.

"He knocked himself *between*, Silvina, probably for a good twenty minutes or more," Rokayas was saying, his urgent tone cutting through Dirzan's petulant complaint.

"He claimed there was grease!"

84

"There was grease," said Silvina. "Look at his right shoe, Dirzan. Piemur, do you feel nauseated?"

Piemur made an affirmative sound, hoping that he could suppress the urge to spew until he was in the infirmary, even as a small spark of irreverence suggested that here was a superb opportunity to get back at Dirzan with no possible repercussions.

"He's jarred his skull, all right. Smart of you to carry him prone, Rokayas. Here, now, set him down on this bed. No, you fool, don't sit him. . . ."

The tipping of his body upward triggered the nausea, and Piemur spewed violently onto the floor. Miserable at such a lack of control, Piemur was also powerless to prevent the heaving that shook him. Then he felt Silvina's hand supporting his head, was aware that a basin was appropriately in position. Silvina spoke in a soothing tone, half-supporting his trembling body as he continued to vomit. He was thoroughly exhausted and trembling when the spasms ended and he was eased back against a pile of pillows and could rest his aching head.

"I take it that Master Oldive has already gone off to Nabol?"

"How did you know where he went?" demanded Dirzan, irritably astonished.

"You are a proper idiot, Dirzan. I haven't lived in the Harper Hall all my life without being able to understand drum messages quite well! Not to worry," she said, and now her fingertips were delicately measuring Piemur's skull inch by inch. "I can't feel a crack or split. He may have done no more than rattle his brains. Rest, quiet and time will cure that thumping. Yes, Master Robinton?"

Silvina's hands paused as she tucked the sleeping fur about Piemur's chin.

"Piemur's been hurt?" The Harper's voice was anxious.

As Piemur turned to one elbow, to acknowledge the Harper's entrance, Silvina's hands forced him back against the piled pillows.

"Not seriously, I'm relieved to say, but let's all leave the room. I'd like a word with these journeymen in your presence, Master Robin—"

The door closed, and Piemur fought between the over-

85

whelming desire to sleep and curiosity about what she had to say to Dirzan and Rokayas in front of the Masterharper. Sleep conquered.

Once she'd closed the door, Silvina gave vent to the anger she'd held in since she'd first glimpsed the gray pallor of Piemur's face and heard Dirzan's nasal complaints.

"How could you let matters get so out of hand, Dirzan?" she demanded, whirling on the astonished journeyman. "What sort of prank is that for apprentices to try on anyone? Piemur's not been himself, but I put that down to losing his voice and adjusting to the disappointment over the music. But this . . . this is . . . criminal!" Silvina brandished Piemur's begreased boot at Dirzan, backing the astonished journeyman against the wall, oblivious to Master Robinton's repeated query about Piemur's condition, to Menolly's precipitous arrival, her face flushed and furrowed with anxiety, and to Rokayas' delighted and amused observation.

"Enough, Silvina!" The Masterharper's voice was loud enough to quell her momentarily, but she turned to him with an injunction to keep his voice down. Please!

"I will," said the Harper in a moderate tone, keeping Silvina turned toward him, and away from the subject of her ire, "if you will tell me what happened to Piemur."

Silvina let out an exasperated breath, glared once more at Dirzan and then answered Master Robinton.

"His skull isn't cracked, though how it wasn't I'll never know," and she exhibited the glistening sole of Piemur's boot, "with stair treads coated with grease. He's bruised, scraped and shaken, and he's definitely suffering from shock and concussion. . . ."

"When will he recover?" There was an urgency behind the Harper's voice that Silvina heard. Now she gave him a long keen look.

"A few days' rest will see him right, I'm sure. But I mean rest!" She crossed her hands in a whipping motion to emphasize her verdict, then pointed to the closed infirmary door. "Right there! Nowhere near those murdering louts in the drumheights!"

"Murdering?" Dirzan gasped an objection to her term.

"He could have been killed. You know how Piemur

climbs steps," she said, scowling fiercely at the journeyman.

"But . . . but there wasn't a trace of grease on those steps or the railing. I tested them all myself!"

"Too clean," said Rokayas, and earned a reprimanding glare from Dirzan. "Too clean!" Rokayas repeated and then said to Silvina. "Piemur's decidedly odd man. He learns too quickly."

"And spouts off what he hears!" Dirzan spoke sharply, determined that Piemur should share the responsibility for this untoward incident.

"Not Piemur," Silvina and Menolly said in one breath.

Dirzan sputtered a moment. "But there've been several very private messages that were all over the Hall, and everyone knows how much Piemur talks, what a conniver he is!"

"Conniver, yes," said Silvina just as Menolly drew breath to defend her friend. "Blabberer, no. He's not been saying more than please and thank you lately either. I've noticed. And I've noticed some other things happening to him that ought not to have! No mere pranks for the new lad in the craft, either!"

Dirzan moved uneasily under her intense stare and looked appealingly toward the Masterharper.

"How much of drum message has Piemur learned in his time with you?" asked the Harper, no expression in voice or face other than polite inquiry.

"Well, now, he does seem to have picked up every measure I've set him. In fact," and Dirzan admitted this reluctantly, "he has quite a knack for it. Though, of course, he's not done more than beat the woods or listen with the journeyman on duty." He glanced at Rokayas for support.

"I'd say Piemur knows more than he admits," said Rokayas in a droll tone, grinning when Dirzan began to mouth a denial.

"It'd be like Piemur," said Menolly with a grin and then, touching Silvina's arm, "does he need someone with him right now?"

"Rest and quiet is what he needs, and I'll look in on him every little while."

"Rocky could stay," Menolly said. The little bronze fire

lizard put in an immediate appearance, chittering worriedly to find himself in such an unexpected place.

"I won't deny that would be sensible," said Silvina, glancing at the closed door. "Yes, that would be very wise, I think."

Everyone watched as Menolly, stroking Rocky gently, told him that he should stay with Piemur and let her know when he spoke. Then she opened the door just enough to admit the little fire lizard, watched as Rocky settled himself quietly by Piemur's feet, his glistening eyes on the boy's pale face.

"Rokayas, would you help Menolly collect Piemur's things from the drumheights?" asked the Harper. His voice was mild, his manner unexceptional but, unmistakably his attitude informed Dirzan that he had misjudged Piemur's standing in the eyes of the most important people of the Hall.

Dirzan offered to do the small task himself, and was denied; offered to help Menolly, who awarded him a cool look. He desisted then, but the set look to his mouth and the controlled anger in his eyes suggested that he was going to deal sternly with the apprentices who had put him in such an invidious position. When he was unexpectedly placed on duty for the entire Feastday, he knew why the roster had been changed. He also knew better than to blame Piemur.

Once Menolly and the journeymen had left them, Robinton turned again to Silvina, showing all the anxiety and concern he had kept hidden.

"Now, don't you worry, Robinton!" Silvina said, patting him on the arm. "He's had a frightful knock on his skull, but I could feel no crack. Those scrapes on chin and cheek'll mend. He'll be stiff and sore from the bruising, that's certain. If you'd only asked me," and Silvina's manner indicated that she'd have her say any road, "I'd have said there were much better uses for Piemur than message drumming. He's been a changed lad since he went to the heights. Not a peep of complaint out of him, but it's as if he wouldn't speak for fear of saying something that was the least bit out of line. And then Dirzan has the nerve to say that Piemur babbled drum messages!"

They were at the Harper's quarters now, and Silvina waited until they were within before she had her final words. "And don't I know what he'd never whsipered!"

"And what would that be?" Robinton eyed her with wry amusement.

"That he brought the masters' stones down from the mine, and something else happened that day to keep him overnight, which I haven't discovered as yet," she added with a sigh of regret as she seated herself.

Robinton laughed then, rubbing his fingers gently on her cheek before he came around the table and poured wine, looking at her as he suspended the wine skin above a second glass. She nodded agreement. She needed the wine after the excitement and worry over Piemur, and with the little bronze watching the boy, she didn't need to hurry back.

"The whole accident is my fault," said the Harper after a long sip of wine. He seated himself heavily. "Piemur *is* clever, and he *can* keep his tongue still. Too still for his own good health, I see now. He hasn't hinted of any trouble in the drumheights to either Menolly or Sebell. . . ."

"They'd be the last he'd tell, except for yourself, of course." Silvina gave a snort. "I only knew about it after the Impression at Benden. The others . . ." and Silvina wrinkled her nose in remembered distaste, ". . . treated his new clothes. I came upon him washing them, or I'd never have known either." She chuckled with such malice the Harper had no trouble following her thought.

"They did it while he was at Igen Hold, not knowing about the Impression?" He joined in her laughter, and Silvina knew that she'd restored his perspective of the unfortunate affair. "And to think that I placed him in the drumheights to safeguard him! You're sure he's sustained no lasting hurt?"

"As sure as I can be without Master Oldive to confirm it." Silvina spoke tartly for Master Oldive's attendance on that worthless Lord of Nabol when he was urgently needed in the Hall aggravated her intensely.

"Yes, Meron!" The Master Harper sighed again, one corner of his expressive mouth twitching with irritation and an inner perplexity.

"The man's dying. Not all of Master Oldive's skill can save him. And why bother with Meron? He's better dead after all the harm he's done. When I think that Brekke's queen might still be alive today . . ."

"It's his dying that will cause even more trouble, Silvina."

"How?"

"We can no more have Nabol Hold in contention than we can Ruatha Hold—"

"But Nabol has a dozen heirs of full blood—"

"Meron won't name his successor!"

"Oh." Silvina's exclamation of startled comprehension was followed quickly by a second of utter disgust. "What more could you expect of that man? But surely steps can be taken. I doubt that Master Oldive would scruple against . . ."

Master Robinton held up his hand. "Nabol has been cursed with Holders either too ambitious, too selfish, or too incompetent to render it in any way prosperous . . ."

"To be sure, it's not the best of Holds, stuck in the mountains, cold, damp, harsh."

"Quite right. So there's little sense in forcing combat on the full-Blooded heirs when one might just end up with another unsympathetic and uncooperative Lord."

Silvina narrowed her eyes in thought. "I make it nine or ten full-Blooded close male heirs. Those daughters of Meron's are too young to be married, and none of them will ever be pretty, taking after their sire as they all seem to have had the misfortune to do. Which of those nine—"

"Ten . . ."

"Which would get the most support from the small holders and crafthalls? And how, pray tell, does Piemur fit into . . . ah, but, of course." A smile smoothed Silvina's frown, and she raised her glass to toast the Harper's ingenuity. "He did well then at Igen Hold?"

"Indeed he did, though Igen's a loyal group under any circumstances."

Silvina caught his slight emphasis on the word "loyal," and scrutinized his thoughtful face. "Why 'loyal'? And to whom? Surely there's no more disloyalty to Benden?"

Robinton gave a quick negative shake of his head. "Several disquieting rumors have come to my notice. The most worrying, the fact that Nabol abounds with fire lizards . . ."

"Nabol has no shoreline and scarcely any friends in Holds that do acquire what fire lizards are found."

Robinton agreed. "They have also been ordering, and paying for, large quantities of fine cloth, wines, the delicacies of Nerat, Tillek and Keroon, not to mention every sort of mongery from the Smithcrafthall that can be bought or bartered, quantities and qualities enough to garb, feed and supply amply every holder, cot and hold in Nabol . . . and don't!"

"The Oldtimers!" Silvina emphasized that guess with a snap of her fingers. "T'kul and Meron were always two cuts from the same rib."

"What I cannot figure out is what besides fire lizards the association gains Meron . . ."

"You can't?" Silvina was frankly skeptical. "Spite! Malice! Scoring off Benden!"

Robinton reflected on that opinion, turning his wine glass idly by the stem. "I'd like to know . . ."

"Yes, you would!" Silvina grinned at him, tolerance for his foibles as well as affection in her glance. "You and Piemur are paired in that respect. He has the same insatiable urge to know, and he's a dab hand at finding out, too. Is that why you want his head mended? You're sending him up to Candler at Nabol Hold?"

"No . . ." and the Harper drawled the word, pulling at his lower lip. "No, not directly to Nabol Hold. Meron might recognize him: the man's never been a fool, just perverted in principle."

"Just?" Silvina was disgusted.

"I'd like to know what's going on there."

"Today is not likely to be the last time Meron summons Master Oldive. . . ." she said, raising her eyebrows suggestively.

Robinton brushed aside the notion. "I hear that a Gather's been scheduled at Nabol on the same sevenday as Lord Groghe's. . . ."

"Isn't that just like Meron."

"Consequently, no one would expect Hall harpers to be in attendance," and Robinton ended his sentence on an upswing of tone, eyeing Silvina hopefully.

"The boy'll be fit enough for a Gather, and undoubtedly it's kinder to send him away from the Hall on that particular day. Tilgin's come along amazingly."

"Could he do aught else?" asked Robinton with real humor in his voice, "with both Shonagar and Domick spending every waking moment with him?"

Chapter 6

Piemur drifted in and out of sleep for the rest of that day and most of the next, immeasurably reassured and comforted by the presence of Rocky or Lazy and Mimic who spelled the bronze fire lizard.

If Menolly's fire lizards were with him, he reasoned, during the moments he drifted into consciousness, then Master Robinton couldn't be annoyed that he'd been stupid enough to fall and hurt himself just when the Harper needed him. For that was how Piemur construed the Harper's urgent query about his injury. He fretted, too, about what Clell and the others might do with his possessions until he saw his press against the wall beside his bed.

The first time Silvina appeared with a tray of food, he didn't feel like eating.

"You're not likely to be sick again," she told him in a low but firm voice, settling on his bed to spoon the rich broth into him. "That was due to the crack you gave your head. You need the nourishment of this broth, so open your mouth. Too bad we can't numbweed the inside of your head, but we can't. Never thought to see the day *you* weren't ready to eat. Now, there's the lad. You'll feel right as ever in a day or two more. Don't mind if you seem to want to sleep. That's only natural. And here's Rocky to keep you company again."

"Who's been feeding him?"

"Don't sit up!" Silvina's hand pressed him back into the half-reclining position. "You'll spill the broth. I suspect Sebell gave Menolly a hand. Not to worry. You'll be back at that chore soon enough!"

Piemur caught at her skirt as she made a move. "There was grease on those steps, wasn't there, Silvina?" Piemur had to ask the question, because he couldn't really trust what he thought he'd heard.

"Indeed and there was!" Silvina frowned, pursing her lips in an angry line. Then she patted his hand. "Those little sneaks saw you fall, scampered down and washed the grease off the steps and handrail . . . but," she added in a sharper tone, "they forgot there'd be grease on your boot as well!" Another pat on his arm. "You might say, they slipped up there!"

For a moment, Piemur couldn't believe that Silvina was joshing him, and then he had to giggle.

"There! That's more like you, Piemur. Now, rest! That'll set you right quicker than you realize. And likely to be the last good rest you'll get for a while."

She wouldn't say more, encouraging him to go back to sleep, and slipping out of the room without giving him any hint to the plans for his future. If his things were here, he didn't think he'd be going back to the drumheights. Where else could he be placed at the Hall? He tried to examine this problem, but his mind wouldn't work. Probably Silvina had laced that broth with something. Wouldn't surprise him if she had.

Complacent fire lizard chirpings roused him. Beauty was conferring with Lazy and Mimic, who were perched on the end of the bed. No one else was in the room, and then Beauty disappeared. Shortly, while he was fretting that no one seemed to be bothering about him, Menolly quietly pushed the door open, carrying a tray in her free hand. He could hear the normal sounds of shouting and calling, and he could smell baked fish.

"If that's more sloppy stuff . . ." he began petulantly.

" 'Tisn't. Baked fish, some tubers, and a special bubbly pie that Abuna insisted would improve your appetite."

"Improve it? I'm starving."

Menolly grinned at his vehemence and positioned the tray on his lap, then seated herself at the end of the bed. He was immensely relieved that Menolly had no intention of feeding him like a babe. It had been embarrassing enough with Silvina.

"Master Oldive checked you over last night when he returned. Said you undoubtedly have the hardest head in the Hall. And you're not going back to the drumheights." Her expression was as grim as Silvina's had been. "No," she added when she saw him glance at his press, "no more pranks. I checked. And I checked with Silvina to be sure all your things are accounted for." She grinned, then, her eyes twinkling. "Clell and the other dimglows are on water rations, and they won't get to the Gather!"

Piemur groaned.

"And why not? They deserve restriction. Pranks are one thing, but deliberately conspiring to injure—and you could have been killed by their mischief—is an entirely different matter. Only . . ." and Menolly shook her head in perplexity, ". . . I can't think what you did to rile them so."

"I didn't do anything," Piemur said so emphatically that he slopped the water glass on his tray.

Rocky chirped anxiously, and Beauty took up the note in her trill.

"I believe you, Piemur." She squeezed his toes where they poked up the sleeping furs. "I do! And, would you also believe, that that's why you had trouble? They kept expecting you to *do* some typical Piemur tricks, and you were so busy behaving for the first time since you apprenticed here, no one could credit it. Least of all Dirzan, who knew all too much about you and your ways!" She gave his toes another affectionate tweak. "And you, bursting your guts with discretion to the point where you didn't tell me or Sebell what you bloody ought to have. We didn't mean for you to stop talking altogether, you know."

"I thought you were testing me."

"Not that hard, Piemur. When I found out what Dirzan . . . no, eat all your tubers," and she snatched from his grasp the plate with the still bubbling pie.

"You know I only like 'em hot!"

"Eat all your dinner first. You'll need your strength, and wits. You're to go with Sebell to Nabol Hold for Meron's Gather. That'll get you away from here during Tilgin's singing, though he has improved tremendously—and no one at Nabol will be expecting any extra harpers. Not that they've all that much to sing about in Nabol Hold anyhow."

"Lord Meron's still alive?"

"Yes." Menolly sighed with distaste, then cocked her head slightly. "You know, your bruises might just come in very handy. They're just purpling beautifully now, so they won't have faded. . . ."

"You mean," and Piemur affected a tremulous whine in his voice, "I'm the poor apprentice lad whose master beats up on him?"

Menolly chuckled. "You're on the mend."

Late that evening, a dust-grayed, raggedly dressed man peered around the door and shuffled slowly into the room, never taking his eyes from Piemur's face. At first, Piemur thought that the man might be a cotholder, looking for Master Oldive's quarters on the Hall's social level; but the fellow, though initially hesitant and almost fearful in his attitude, altered perceptibly in manner and stance as he came closer to the bed.

"Sebell?" There was something about the man that made Piemur suspicious. "Sebell, is that you?"

The dusty figure straightened and strode across the floor, laughing.

"Now I'm sure I can gain a discreet arrival at the Nabol Hold Gather! I fooled Silvina, too. She says you still have some rags that will be appropriate to the status of a rather stupid herder's boy!"

"Herder's boy?"

"Why not? Kum in handy, like, tha' knowin' the way from tha' bluid, like." As Sebell affected the speech mannerisms of the up-range herders, he became completely the nondescript person who had first entered the infirmary.

Despite his chagrin at being told to resume a role he'd hoped never to play again, Piemur was enchanted by the journeyman's dissembling. If Sebell would do it, so would he.

"Master Robinton's not angry with me, is he?"

"Not a mite." Sebell shook his head violently for emphasis. Kimi swooped in, scolding because Sebell had made her wait outside. Then his expression became serious, and he waggled a finger at Piemur. "However, you will have to watch your step with Master Oldive. We've sworn blue to him that this isn't going to be an energetic adventure for you. Even heads as hard as yours must be treated with caution after such a fall. So, instead of hiking you in from Ruatha Hold as I'd planned," and Sebell gave a mock scowl at Piemur's burst of laughter, "N'ton will drop you off at dawn in the valley before Nabol Hold. Then we'll proceed at a proper pace with beasts suitable for sale at the Nabol Gather."

"Why?" asked Piemur bluntly. Discretion had got him nothing but misery, confusion and unwarranted accusations. This time he would know what he was about.

"Two things," Sebell said without so much as a pause for consideration. "If it's true that there are more fire lizards in Nabol Hold than—"

"Is that what they meant?"

"Is that what who meant?"

"Lord Oterel. At the Hatching. I overheard him talking to someone . . . didn't know the man . . . and he said, 'Meron gets more than he ought and we have to do without.' Didn't make sense then, but it would if Lord Oterel was talking about fire lizards. Was he?"

"He very likely was, and I wish you'd mentioned that snip of talk before."

"I didn't know you'd want to know, and it made no sense to me then." Piemur ended on a plaintive note, seeing Sebell's frown of irritation.

The journeyman smiled a quick reassurance. "No, you couldn't've known. Now you do. We know that Lord Meron had his first fire lizards from Kylara nearly four Turns ago, so they could have clutched at least once, possibly twice. And he'd've made certain he had control of the distribution of those new eggs. Nonetheless, he has distributed more in Nabol than we can account for. What is equally important is the amount of other supplies that are being brought into the Hold and . . . disappearing!

"Meron's trading with the Oldtimers?"

"Lord Meron, lad you don't forget the title even in your thoughts . . . and yes, that's the possibility."

"And he's getting whole clutches of fire lizard eggs for trading for 'em? As well as the eggs of his original pairs?" Piemur was assailed by a variety of emotions: anger that Lord Meron of Nabol Hold was getting more than a fair share of the fire lizard eggs when other, more worthy persons, Piemur included himself, ought to have a chance to Impress the precious creatures; a righteous indignation that Lord Meron (and he slurred the title into an insult in his thoughts) was deliberately flouting Benden Weyr by trafficking in any way with the Oldtimers; and an intense excitement at the possibility that he, Piemur, might help discredit further this infamous Lord Holder.

"Those are two of the main things to listen for. The third, which is the most important in some ways, is which of Lord Meron's male heirs would be most acceptable to craft and cot."

"He is dying then?" He'd been sure that the message to Master Oldive was spurious.

"Oh, yes, a wasting disease." Sebell's grin was malicious, and there was an unpleasant gleam in his eyes as he met Piemur's astonished gaze. "You might say, a very proper disease to fit Lord Meron's . . . peculiar ways!"

Piemur would have liked to have particulars, but Sebell rose.

"I must be away now, Piemur. You're to rest, without getting into any mischief."

"Rest? I've been resting—"

"Bored? Well, I'll ask Rokayas to give you drum measures to learn. That ought to ease your boredom without taxing your strength." Sebell laughed at Piemur's snort of dismay.

"As long as it's Rokayas."

"It will be. *He's* of the mind that you learned a great deal more than Dirzan believes."

Piemur grinned at the subtle question in Sebell's words, but before he could retort, the door was closing behind the journeyman and Kimi, who fluttered above him. Piemur hugged his knees to his chest, rocking slowly on his tail bones as he thought over all that Sebell had confided to him. And tried to figure out what it was Sebell hadn't told him.

One thing Sebell hadn't mentioned was how cold and how dark it would be when N'ton collected him before dawn. Menolly with Beauty and Rocky had roused him from a fitful sleep, for he'd been afraid he'd oversleep and consequently spent a restless night. He could sense Menolly's amusement as the two of them, guided by the encouraging chirrups of the fire lizards, stumbled across the dark courtyard toward the Gather meadow. Then Lioth turned his brilliant jewel-faceted eyes in their direction, and they moved more confidently forward.

Menolly giggled as she boosted Piemur up to catch the fighting straps, and then he felt N'ton's downstretched hand and was aided into position. He heard her softly wish him luck, then she blended into the shadows, her actual position discernible only by four points of light that were fire lizard eyes.

"D'you want the fighting strap about you, Piemur? Night flying unnerves a lot of people."

Piemur wanted to say yes, but instead took a good hold on the leathers that encircled Lioth's neck. He replied that since this was only a short trip, he wouldn't need them. Then clutched convulsively as Lioth sprang upward. They were above the rim of Fort Hold's fireheights before Piemur caught his breath. N'ton gave the bronze dragon the audible command to Nabol, and Piemur knew he screamed into the nothingness of *between*. He choked off the noise as he felt the change from intense cold and blackness to frosty chill and the faint lightening in what must be the eastern sky.

Two whirling points of light danced above N'ton's left shoulder, and a fire lizard's complacent chirp informed Piemur that N'ton's bronze, Tris, had turned to look at him. Then Lioth swerved and Piemur's fingers became numb as he increased the pressure on the straps, unconsciously leaning backward against the angle of descent into darkness. Tris chirruped encouragingly, as if he were completely aware of Piemur's internal confusion. Piemur prayed fervently that Tris wouldn't inform N'ton of how scared he was. Abruptly the bronze dragon backwinged and settled with the lightest of bumps in black shadow.

"Lioth says there are people not far down the road, Piemur," said N'ton in a low voice. "Give me your flying gear."

"Isn't it Sebell?" asked Piemur, shedding helmet and jacket and thrusting them blindly toward N'ton.

"Lioth says no, but Sebell is not far behind. He hears Kimi."

"Kimi?" Piemur's surprise made him speak louder than he intended, and he winced at N'ton's warning.

"You forget," whispered N'ton, "Sebell can bring Kimi because fire lizards are so common here in Nabol. Or so we're led to understand." Displeasure colored the Fort

Weyrleader's amendment. Then Piemur felt the strong gloved hand curl about his wrist, and he obediently threw his right leg back over Lioth's neckridge, sliding down the massive shoulder, aware as he slipped beyond N'ton's guiding hand, that the dragon had cocked his leg to allow an easier slope of descent. He let his knees take the shock of his landing and patted Lioth's shoulder, wondering as he did so if that were bold of him.

"Good luck, Piemur!" N'ton's muted voice just reached his ears.

He stepped back, turning his head against the shower of dust and sand as the huge bronze launched himself skyward.

Once his eyes were accustomed to the variations of black and dark gray, Piemur located the winding road and whistled softly as he realized how accurately the dragon had landed in the one flat area big enough to accommodate him. Piemur's respect for draconic abilities rose to new heights.

He heard now the occasional sound of voices and saw the erratic wavering of light from the glowbaskets of the leading file. A creaking of wheeled carts and the familiar *sluff-sluff* of plate-footed burden beasts reached his ears. He looked about him for a place to hide. He had a choice of boulders and ledges, and found a shielded spot that faced the track but gave him a clear view of the dimly seen exit. He curled up small, hugging knees to chest, secure in the belief that he couldn't be seen.

A chirrup disabused him of that notion and, startled, he glanced up and saw three pairs of fire lizard eyes gleaming at him.

"Go away, you silly creatures. I'm not even here!" To prove this, he closed his eyes and concentrated on the awful nothingness of *between*.

The fire lizards responded with an agitated chorus.

"What's the matter with them?" a gruff male voice called over the creaking of cartwheels and the shuffling sound of the burden beasts.

"Who knows? Who cares? We'm most to Nabol now!"
Piemur redoubled his efforts to think of nothing, and heard the faint flutter of fire lizards taking flight. To think of nothing took more effort than to concentrate on

something. A great many carts, too, Piemur thought, for a Nabol Gather when there was another, better one at Fort Hold. He opened his eyes now and saw the flicker of winging fire lizards in the gathering daylight, and the point-lights of their eyes in gloom. And these were carters? Small holders? The anger that injustice roused warmed Piemur long after the caravan and the comfort of their glow-baskets passed from his angle of vision.

The cold dawn wind rose, and Piemur wished that Sebell would put in his promised appearance. He ought to have asked N'ton if Lioth had seen Sebell as he glided to his landing. Then Piemur chided himself that this was scarcely the first time he'd waited on his lonesome in the dark of dawn. He'd done his watches with his father's herds. Of course, there'd usually been someone sleeping in the cot within voice range during those long, slow hours. What if something had happened to Sebell? Or he was delayed? Should Piemur go on to Nabol by himself? And how was he to return to the Harper Hall? He'd forgotten to ask N'ton that, presuming it was the Fort Weyrleader who'd collect him. Or was he to be collected? Did Sebell plan to sell those suitable beasts of his during the Gather? Or would they have to herd them back whence they'd come? There was a great deal that Sebell hadn't told him in spite of the journeyman's candid explanation about their surreptitious appearance at Nabol Hold.

Piemur relieved his anxieties by remembering that he wasn't going to have to attend the Fort Hold festivities, or listen to Tilgin sing music that Domick had written for *him*. He sighed, depressed that he wasn't going to be singing the role of Lessa, that he wasn't still comfortably in his bed in the senior apprentices' dormitory, waking to anticipate the applause of Lord Groghe's guests, the accolades of his friends and Domick. And quite likely Lessa's approval, since the Weyrwoman was Lord Groghe's special guest today.

Here he was, cold, miserable, and uncomfortably aware that he hadn't had so much as a cold cup of klah before he was bundled onto a dragon's back and dumped here to await a man who might not arrive for hours if he was walking a herd of beasts in from Ruatha Hold all by himself!

And when they found out what they'd come to discover and returned to the Harper Hall, what would Piemur do tomorrow?

He grinned, hugging his knees in smug satisfaction, remembering Rokayas' surprise the day before when he had perfectly dead-sticked the complicated message Rokayas had thought up to test his knowledge of the drum language. Piemur was almost sorry he wouldn't be—

He groped on the ground beside him and found a rock, gave it an experimental whack against the boulder that sheltered him. The resultant sound echoed about the small valley. Piemur found another rock and, rising, went to the now visible track. He beat the rocks together in the monotone code for "harper," adding the best for "where," grinning as the sharp staccato sounds reverberated. He repeated the two measures, then waited. He beat his measures again to give Sebell time to find his own rocks. Then in the pause he heard distantly a muffled reply: "journeyman comes."

Immeasurably relieved, Piemur was wondering whether to proceed down the track and intercept Sebell when he heard a "stay" as the message was repeated. He was a bit daunted by the "stay" and restlessly scuffed at the loose gravel on the track. Surely Sebell wasn't far away. What did it matter if Piemur did go to meet him? But the message had been clear—"stay"—and Piemur decided that Sebell must have a reason, other than obedience to Master Oldive's instruction about Piemur's dented head.

Sullenly, Piemur resumed his position behind the boulder. And none too soon. He heard then the sharp clatter of hooves against stone, the jangle of metal against metal, and a rumble of encouraging shouts. A fair of fire lizards arrowed out of the graying southern skies, heading straight up the track. Piemur thought of cold *between*'s nothingness, as the fire lizards, intent on keeping ahead of the swiftly pacing riders, swept on. The ground beneath Piemur's rump trembled with the runners' passage.

There was so much dust raised that Piemur couldn't be sure how many rode by, but he estimated a dozen or more. A dozen riders with a full fair of fire lizards escorting them?

Again anger consumed Piemur. He knew that he wouldn't have resented this latest concentration of fire lizards, obviously companioning holders prosperous enough to own fast pacers, if the earlier caravan hadn't been just as well favored with the creatures. It wasn't fair. He agreed wholeheartedly with Lord Oterel! There were many, too many fire lizards abroad in Nabol.

He was so incensed over such inequity, since the caravaners obviously hadn't appreciated the capabilities of the little creatures, that at first he didn't hear the *shluff-shluff* of the approaching herd.

Kimi's quizzical cheep nearly frightened him out of his wits. She cheeped again, apologetically, and her eyes whirled a little faster as she peered at him from the top of the boulder.

"Well?" asked Sebell, appearing around one side. "You took me too literally."

"They all have fire lizards," cried Piemur, too indignant to make polite greeting.

"Yes, I had noticed."

"I don't mean that lot," and Piemur jerked his thumb in the direction of the riders. "There was a caravan that had two or three full fairs—"

"Did they see you?" asked Sebell, suddenly wary.

"The fire lizards did, but no human paid any attention to their alert!" Then Piemur caught sight of the beasts that Sebell had herded and whistled.

"So? They meet with your approval?"

The leader had ambled past, eyes half-closed against the dust, and the rest, nose to the tail in front, with eyes fully closed, followed. Piemur counted five: all were well-fleshed, with good, thick, furry hides, moving steadily without a stumble, which meant their feet were sound.

"You'll sell them all right," said Piemur.

"Happen Ah will!" said Sebell in proper accent and, passing his arm about Piemur's shoulders, urged him ahead of the herd. "Here," and Sebell passed Piemur a padded flask. "It should still be hot. I only broke camp when Kimi told me Lioth had flashed by."

Piemur mumbled his gratitude for the klah, which was hot enough to warm his belly. Then Sebell handed Piemur a dried meat roll of the sort that was standard journey rations, and Piemur began to view the imminent day in a much improved frame of mind.

As soon as he'd finished eating, he voluntarily dropped back to the apprentice's uncomfortable position at the end of the single file. He'd be properly coated with dust by the time they arrived at Nabol Hold.

The first thing Piemur did when they got to the Gather meadow was head toward the nearest watering trough, fighting against his thirsty charges for a space at the edge. He also remembered exactly where to pinch their noses to make them turn from him.

"Ar, lad, let th'beasts drink deep farst!" Sebell unceremoniously hauled him away, his voice angry, though his eyes twinkled as he warned Piemur to play the proper part.

"Ar, sor, tongue that dry can't move."

Two young boys were approaching the trough with pails, but they waited, as custom dictated, until the beasts had drunk their fill and the cold mountain water flowed clear again. Piemur and Sebell then herded their charges toward the area of the meadow set aside for animal sales. The Hold Steward, a pinch-faced man with a runny nose, all but pounced on them, demanding the Gather fee. Sebell immediately protested the amount, and the two set to haggling. Sebell brought the fee down a full mark before he surrendered his token, but he didn't protest when the Steward waved them contemptuously toward the smallest enclosure at the end of the rank. Piemur was about to object when Sebell's hand closed warningly on his shoulder. Looking at the journeyman in surprise, Piemur saw the imperceptible jerk of his head over his shoulder. Piemur waited a few discreet seconds and then casually glanced about him. Three men had started to follow them toward their allotted space. A thrill of fear made Piemur catch his breath until he recognized the unmistakable herder gait and knew these were prospective buyers.

"Tol'ya Ah'd suitable beasts, di' Ah no?" drawled Sebell under his breath.

"Ar, an yull drink th' profit again, like as not," replied Piemur in a sullen tone, but his shoulders shook with the effort to control his amusement. He hadn't a single doubt in his mind that Sebell would also play the happy drunken herdsman to perfection. And manage to say without offense what would be impossible for a sober man anyplace.

They got the beasts enclosed, and Piemur was sent with a worn mark of the Herdsman's Crafthall to haggle for fodder. He managed to save an eighth on the dealing, which he pocketed as any apprentice would. Sebell was already deep in bargain with one of the men while the others were examining the beasts with pinch and prod. Piemur wondered where under the sun Sebell had managed to acquire such proper mountain-bred creatures, with rock-worn hooves and shaggy coats. He could no more account for the good flesh on them after this long winter than the prospective buyers, so he hunkered down and listened to Sebell's explanation.

Trust a harper to weave words well, and Piemur's respect for the journeyman increased proportionately to the elaborations of the tale he told. Sebell would have his audience believe that he merely used an old trick handed down from grandsire to grandson: a combination of herbs and grasses sweetened with just the right amount of berries and well-moistened dried fruits. He also said that he and his did without sometimes to improve their beasts, and Piemur promptly sucked in his cheeks to look suitably haggard. He saw the eyes of the men linger on his bruises, showing yellow on his chin and cheek, while Sebell rambled on about his holders scrambling up and down the southern face of his hold hill to find the sweet new grasses that produced such spectacular results.

The earnest knot of listeners attracted more who stood respectfully back but close enough to hear. What Piemur couldn't figure out was that, while the beasts had very old marks of Ruathan breeding, the secondary marks were also well-worn. Then he was annoyed with himself: Sebell must have pulled this sort of stunt before. Undoubtedly somewhere in Ruatha was a cotholder who kept a few special beasts for the Harper Hall's convenience. He began to relax and enjoy Sebell's tale-spinning thoroughly.

The sun was well over the mountains by the time Sebell had struck hands on the bargains—for there were three. One man bought three of the beasts, and the others one apiece, at what Piemur knew was a bloody good price. He wondered if that had covered their original purchases and their keep. Appropriately sober-faced during the bargaining, Sebell permitted pleasure to glow on his dirt-smeared face as he carefully stowed the mark pieces in his belt pouch while the beasts were prodded away by their new owners.

"Didn't think I'd make that much, but the trick always works!" said Sebell in a low mutter to Piemur.

"Trick?"

"Sure," said Sebell softly as he patted dust from his clothing. "Arrive dusty, early, with the well-fleshed beasts, and they're on to you fast, hoping you're tired enough to be stupid."

"Where did you get 'em?"

Sebell flashed Piemur a grin. "Craft secret. Get along with you now," and he gave Piemur a wink and a rough shove. "See t'Gather!" he added in a louder tone. "Ah find thee when Ah wish to go."

This wasn't much of a Gather, Piemur decided when he'd done one round of the small nestle of stalls. They didn't even have bubbly pies at the baker's, and the Crafthalls had obviously sent very junior men to represent them. Still, a Gather was a day to be enjoyed, and not many were held at Nabol even when restdays were Thread-clear, so the Nabolese were making as much of the occasion as they could.

The wineman was doing a brisk trade by the time Piemur returned that way. He squatted at the corner of the stand, munching slowly away at another meatroll, listening to comments and noticing with deep chagrin and a growing wrath how many fire lizards flitted about, resting for a moment on the stall tops, wheeling up in fairs to dance in the air a bit before settling on their friends' shoulders or on a new position where they could overlook. At first Piemur tried to convince himself that he was only seeing the same group again and again. He did notice that most were greens with a sprinkling of brown and blues—the lesser fire lizards. When he saw bronzes, they were always on the shoulder or arm of the more prosperously dressed. Yet no matter how Piemur argued the matter in his mind, it was clear that Nabol Hold boasted more fire lizards than he had seen even at Benden Weyr during the Impression.

Suddenly a phrase stood out from the murmurous conversation about the winestand.

"There'll be a few more happy holidays today, I hear!"

Piemur turned to scratch his shoulder fiercely and located the man who had spoken from his knowing smirk, a smith from his clothing. His companion, a miner by his shoulder badge, was nodding in comprehension.

"Nabol don't take proper care of 'em, he don't. Three never shelled. My master was fair upset about that. Means to have three more today or his name's not Kaljan."

"Is that so?" The smith bobbed his head up and down to show regret. "We'd one that didn't hatch, too, but no joy did we get above! Eggs we was promised and eggs we was given. Up to us to care for 'em proper enough to make 'em hatch. That one," and his head jerked toward the Hold cliff to indicate Lord Meron, "enjoys putting a snake among the wherries!" He snorted derisively. "Happen it's his only pleasure now."

Both men guffawed with malicious delight.

"Happen we'll not need to worry about him much longer, I hear tell." The smith winked broadly at the miner.

"Couldn't be soon enough for me. Well, see you at the dancing?"

"Going so soon?"

"Had my glass. Must get back."

The disappointment in the miner's face made Piemur think that the smith's departure was precipitous. Going to tell his master about the eggs that were up at the Hold, was he? Piemur decided to tag along.

Eggs handed out in quantities, eggs that had been badly handled and wouldn't hatch. Unless . . . and Piemur reflected over something that Menolly had said about fire lizard eggs. Green fire lizards laid eggs as well, having been fertilized by a mating flight with a blue or brown, sometimes even a bronze. But green fire lizards were stupid: they'd lay a clutch, ten at the most, Menolly said, and leave them with such a shallow covering of beach sand that they were easy prey to wild wherries or sand snakes. Very few green-laid clutches survived to Hatch. Which, as Menolly had succinctly stated, was just as well or Pern would be up to the eyeballs in little green fire lizards.

Piemur wondered if anyone in Nabol realized that a deception was being practiced on them, and green fire lizard eggs were what were dispersed so lavishly. Then he realized that he'd lost sight of the smith and, cursing his inattentiveness, began to retrace his steps, turning with assumed idleness to peer between the stalls. He spotted the smith, urgently speaking to a man with a smithmaster's badge and, as the man reacted to his journeyman's excited words, his master's chain sparkled. Piemur managed to duck away as both men suddenly turned toward him. When they had passed him on their way to the Hold, Piemur followed, restlessly scanning faces in the hopes that he might see Sebell and tell him what he'd overheard. Sebell might wish to investigate.

As the two smiths turned from the Gather area toward the Hold, Piemur had to pause or be noticeable. The smiths strode purposefully up the ramp toward the main Hold gates. They were challenged by the guard and, after some moments of arguing, the guard summoned another from the gatehouse and sent him to the Hold with the smithmaster's message.

While the messenger was gone, two men emerged from the Hold, well wrapped in their cloaks, though the air had lost its chill. Something about the way they walked, carefully; the way they carried their heads, proudly; the way they nodded and smiled at the guards, smugly; and most of all the way they pointedly avoided contact, struck Piemur as significant. He continued to watch them as they turned toward the Gather meadow. As they approached him he caught sight of their figures in profile and realized that each man carried something hidden in his cloak, held tight against his side. It couldn't have been a large object. But, thought Piemur, putting expression, manner and profile together, an egg pot wouldn't be large. He wanted to follow the men to see if his suspicion was correct, but he also didn't want to leave the Hold until the message from the smithmaster had been answered.

A new party, holders by the look of them, now made themselves known to the guards and were admitted, to the angry chagrin of the smithmaster. Then three carts, heavily laden to judge by the straining of the burden beasts struggling up the ramp, forced the smithmaster to one side. The guard waved the carts toward the kitchen courtyard. The last cart jammed a wheel against the ramp parapet, the driver thudding his stick against the burden beast's rump.

"Wheel be jammed," yelled Piemur, not liking to see any animal beaten for what was not its fault.

He jumped forward to help guide the carter. The man now backed his stolid beast, swinging its head left. Piemur, setting his shoulder to the tailgate, gave a push in the proper direction. He also tried to peek under the covering to see what on earth was being delivered to the Hold on a Gather day when most business was done in the Gather meadow. Before he could get a good look, the cart had picked up speed as it reached more level ground.

He was past the guards, arguing with the smith and paying no more attention to the procession of carts. Ducking quickly to the side of the cart away from the carter, Piemur gained access to the Hold proper.

As the carts rumbled on into the kitchen court, Piemur rapidly wondered how he could turn this opportunity to advantage and remain in the Hold after the carters had unloaded and left. Certainly if he was actually in the Hold, he might find out more than he could possibly learn wandering about the Gather. If nothing else he could discover what the carter had delivered.

Then he spied a line of coveralls bleaching in the spring sun. He darted over and removed one, ignoring the slight dampness as he slipped it over his head. Kitchen drudges were never noted for cleanliness, and once the beast dirt and stains on his tunic were covered, the dust on his boots and trousers would be unremarkable.

"Hey, you!" Piemur tried to ignore the call, but it was repeated and could only be directed to him. He turned toward the speaker, affecting a stupid expression. "I mean you, with the empty arms!"

Obediently he trudged back to the carter, who slung a heavy sack across his back. At that point, the kitchen steward bustled out to supervise, and Piemur, bent double under the sack, passed him without a glance. The steward alternated between chivvying his drudges out to help unload, and the carter for his ill-timed arrival. The carter replied with equal heat that he had heavy carts and slow beasts and had had to give way and eat dust from those hurrying to this bloody Gather. Meron ought to be pleased he'd got here within the day allotted, much less at an earlier hour.

The steward hushed him and began shouting orders, ordering Piemur on to the back storerooms. Piemur got inside the kitchen, not knowing where the stores rooms were, so, making a business of wiping his face and easing his shoulders, he waited until someone brushed past him and turned down the proper corridor.

"Don't know where Ah'm t' put more as is plenty here a'ready," muttered the drudge as Piemur followed him.

"A-top them others?" suggested Piemur helpfully.

In the dim light of waning glows, the Nabolese peered at Piemur. "Never saw you afore."

"Nor you haven't," Piemur agreed amiably. "Sent from t'Hold to help in kitchen for t'Gather."

"Oh!" And the sly gleam in the man's eyes suggested to Piemur that he had just let himself in for the worst and dirtiest of the chores about a Hold on a Gather day when the Lord was feasting guests.

Haste appeared the vital factor in unloading the carts, so Piemur didn't see many of the seals on the sacks, barrels and boxes he humped out of sight. But he saw enough to realize that the delivery came from a variety of sources: tanner, weaver, smithcraft for the heaviest boxes, wine from many of the yards, but none, he was pleased to note, from Benden. When the last bundle was stowed in the now-bulging stores rooms, Piemur's sigh of relief was echoed by Besel, the sly drudge, who had managed to stay close to him during the unloading. Piemur had no sooner lowered himself to a sack to rest than the man snatched him to his feet.

"C'mon, we've no time to rest t'day."

Nor did Piemur, who was set first to scrape out ashes from the secondary hearths and then to gutting beasts and wild fowl, thankful that he'd watched Camo often enough at that task to know the tricks. He scoured extra plates, encrusted with the dirt and grime of Turns, until his fingers shriveled. When he'd done that, and peeled a dragonload of tubers, he was allowed a breather so long as he kept one of the five spits turning.

Chaos broke loose when the Hold Steward arrived to inform the kitchen that Lord Meron chose to eat in his own quarters and these were to be prepared while he walked the Gather.

The kitchen steward obsequiously took the change of order, having only that hour completed the feast arrangements in the Great Hall. The moment the heavy door had swung shut on the Hold Steward's back, however, he burst into obscenities that won him Piemur's astounded approval.

If Piemur had thought he'd worked hard already, he was soon disabused of that notion by the rate at which he was sent flying about the kitchen to collect cleaning and polishing tools and preparations. Then he was sent on ahead with Besel and a woman to start cleaning the Lord's rooms. Already weary from an early rising and more hard labor than he'd known since he'd left his native cothold, Piemur tried to cheer himself by imagining Master Oldive's reaction to his "quiet day" at Nabol Gather.

"Who'd a thought he'd walk t'Gather?" the woman was saying as they trudged up the steep steps from the main hall to Meron's apartment.

"Had to. Didncha hear what they be saying at Gather? Meron dead a'ready and none know his heir. Some as want to turn Gather Day into Duel Day."

That remark set both Nabolese into cackles of laughter, and Piemur wondered if he could be ignorant enough of Hold problems to ask why they were so amused.

"Ah saw 'em comin' in, Ah did," said Besel, again with that sly, knowing expression on his face. "Ev'ry one of 'em was with 'im some time t'day, they was. Outsides with him now, shouldn't wonder."

"He'll have his li'l game wi'em, he will, each thinking he's been named," said the woman and dug her elbow into Besel's ribs which sent them both off into malicious laughter again.

"Hope it's not just us as has to do all the cleaning here," Besel said, putting his hand on the door handle. "Hasn't been done in . . . faugh!" He turned his head away, coughing against the stench that wafted out to them from the opened door.

As the smell reached Piemur's nostrils, sweet, cloying,

sickening, he felt his stomach turn in protest and tried not to inhale. He hung back, hoping the fresher air of the corridor would cleanse the room of its stink.

"Here, you get in and open shutters. You're used to stinking messes, guttingman." Besel grabbed Piemur roughly by the arm and propelled him violently into the room.

How Piemur managed not to vomit from the odor of the room before he reached the shutters and flung them open, he didn't know. He half-threw his body up the deep sill, gasping in fresh, cool air.

"Other windows, too, boy," ordered Besel from the doorway.

Piemur filled his lungs and opened the other windows, staying by the last until the chill air dissipated the odors of decay and illness. And Lord Meron's heirs had had to attend him in this funking atmosphere? Piemur spared them a moment of sympathy.

Then Besel shouted for him to go into the other rooms and open them up to air properly. "Else no one'd eat his food, like as not, and we'm to clean up their messes."

The foul odor hung heaviest in the last of the four large rooms that comprised the Lord Holder's private apartments in Nabol. It was then that Piemur blessed the happenstance that had sent him in here ahead of the others. Reposing on the hearth were nine pots of exactly the size in which fire lizard eggs were placed to keep warm and harden. Mastering his urge to gag, Piemur ducked across the room to investigate. One pot was set slightly apart from the others and, lifting the lid, Piemur scraped enough sand away to see the mottled shell before he covered it carefully over. He took a quick look at the contents of the first pot in the other group. Yes, the egg was smaller and of a different hue. He'd wager every mark he owned that the separate pot contained a fire lizard queen egg.

Quickly he switched pots. Shielding his actions with his body in case Besel ventured this far to check on him, he dumped the sand with deft speed into the cinder shovel, removed the egg and shoved it up under his coverall and into his shirt above his belt. Poking among the cinders, he selected one that had a slightly rounded end and neatly inserted it into the egg pot, replaced sand and lid and stood the rifled pot back in line, straightening up just as the woman crossed the threshold.

"That's the lad, tend the fire first. And you'll need to bring up more blackrock from the yard. *He* likes his warmth, he does." She cackled again as she roughly pushed carven chairs out of her way to sweep under the worktable. "To be sure, he'll feel the cold soon enough, he will!"

Besel joined in her laughter.

The fire was hot as Piemur shook the grate free of ashes, and his face burned by the time he had cleared the debris. The heat also warmed the egg, lying against his ribs.

"Hurry it up, you guttingman," said Besel when Piemur began to lug the heavy ash bucket out. "No slouching, or I'll take me hand to you." He raised a big fist and Piemur ducked away, feeling the egg pinch his skin and worried he might crack it prematurely.

As he strained with the heavy bucket down the long steps, he wondered how ever was he going to keep the egg safe. Certainly not on his person. And he'd have to keep it warm, too. As well as in someplace to which, in his guise as a lowly guttingman, he'd have easy access.

The solution came to him just as he was about to dump the ashes. He checked the swing of the bucket and glanced about the ashpit. Then very carefully, he emptied the ashes in a pile just to the left of the ashpit opening. Anyone emptying ashbuckets tended to fling the contents to the back wall where the cinders spread downward from the top of the accumulated pile. The molding on either side of the opening kept ashes from tumbling back into the court-yard until the pit was full. Its capacity was by no means reached at this moment. With his booted toe, Piemur made a small depression in the warm ashes, quickly inserted the egg, covering it first with warm ashes, then with a coating of cold cinders to insulate it. Glancing at the sun as he filled his bucket with fresh blackstone from the dump next to the ashpit, Piemur saw that the sun was lowering. Which was a mercy he thought, lugging the blackstone back into the Hold, because he wondered if he'd manage to last through the most arduous day of his life.

They'd have the Feast soon; more than likely as soon as Lord Meron returned to his freshened quarters. What caused that noxious stink? Certainly not Master Oldive's medicines, for the healer believed in fresh air and freshening herbs, which at their worst were pungent but could not cause the odor in Lord Meron's rooms. No matter. Once the Lord and his guests were served, the drudges would get what remained on the serving platters and that would mean everyone could relax for a while. He could, perhaps, sneak away then, before Sebell got anxious. And did he have a lot to tell Sebell!

Half the workers in the Hold were now running up and down the steps, pursued by the strident voice of the Hold Steward who had arrived to direct the freshening. Piemur was promptly given another ashbucket to empty and fill with blackrock. On his way back through the kitchen this time, he sneaked a breadroll, which heartened him considerably.

By some miracle, they were just about finished when a messenger arrived from the guard to say that Lord Meron and his guests were returning. The Steward shoved and pushed everyone out, even to the point of collecting abandoned cleaning tools. As the last of the drudges scurried back into the kitchen, the laughter of the returning Gatherers was heard at the Hold doors.

Piemur had to assist the cook turn the roast for carving, and nearly had his fingers sliced thinner when the cook caught him taking bits that dropped to the table. Then he had to mash endless kettles of tubers. As fast as a dish was served up and garnished, it was despatched above. At one point, Piemur thought he might be sent, but it was decided he was much too dirty to carry food. Instead he was sent to the bowels of the Hold for more glowbaskets as Lord Meron complained that he couldn't see to eat. Piemur had to make three trips to satisfy the need. By that time, the platters were coming back to the kitchen. The drudges and lesser stewards stripped food off as it passed them by. The kitchen began to quiet as mouths were stuffed too full to permit speech. Piemur managed to secure a meat-rimmed bone and, grabbing a handful of the sliced breads, he retired to the darkest corner of the huge room to eat.

He applied himself ravenously to his food, having decided to leave as quickly as possible now. The sun had set during the furor of serving the feast, so he had the cover of darkness to retrieve his egg. And he'd have the excuse for the guards, if they stopped him, that he was finished with his duties. Lord Groghe always gave his drudges time to attend the Gather dancing. Piemur was looking forward to encountering Sebell again. He might not have heard much to the point of which heir the Hold staff preferred, but he had proof that Lord Meron was getting far more fire lizard eggs than a small Hold like Nabol ought to receive; that his stores rooms were full of more supplies than he and his could ever use in a full pass much less a Turn.

Hungry though he was, Piemur couldn't finish all the meat on the bone. He was too tired to eat, he thought, and before he did collapse from exhaustion, he'd better retrieve the egg and slip out to meet Sebell. How he longed for his bed at the Harper Hall.

The regular kitchen drudges were too busy grumbling about the poor selection left for them to eat and how much those blinking guests were eating and drinking to notice Piemur's deft exit.

He took possession of the precious egg, warm to the touch, and wrapping it carefully in a wad of rags, thrust the bundle once again under his tunic. He jauntily approached the main gates, whistling deliberately off key.

"And where do you think you're going?"

"T'Gather," Piemur replied as if this was all too obvious.

He was as surprised by the man's guffaw as he was by being swung around and roughly propelled back the way he had come.

"Don't try that one on me again, guttingman!" called the guard as the force of his push sent Piemur stumbling across the cobbles, trying not to fall and damage the egg. He stopped in the darkest shadow of the wall and stood fuming over this unexpected check to his escape. It was ridiculous! He couldn't think of any other Hold in all Pern where the drudges were denied the privilege of going to the Hold's own Gather.

"G'wan back to the ashes, guttingman!"

It was then that Piemur realized his coverall, none too clean in the light, was still visible in the shadows, so he slunk past the opening into the kitchen court. Out of sight, he stripped off the betraying coverall and flung it into a corner. So he wasn't allowed to leave, was he?

Well, the guests would have to be passed. He would simply bide his time and slip out of Nabol Hold the same way he'd gotten in.

Taking heart in that notion, he looked about him for a suitable place to wait. He should remain in the courtyards, where he would hear the commotion of leave-taking. He'd better not return to the kitchens, or he'd be put to work again. His roving eye caught the blackness that was the ash and blackstone pits, and that solved his problem. Keeping to the shadows, he made his way to this least likely of all hiding spots and settled on the spongy surface at the right hand side of the opening to the ashpit. Not the most comfortable place to wait, he thought, removing a large cinder shell from under his tail bone before he achieved some measure of comfort. The night wind had picked up a bit, and he felt the chill when he poked his nose over the coping. Ah well, he shouldn't have long to wait. He doubted anyone would tolerate Lord Meron's smell longer than absolutely necessary.

He was awakened from a fitful doze by the sound of shouting and much running about in the main courtyard, and then a nearer, more frightening clamor in the kitchen itself. Above the shouts and slammings, he heard a pathetic wail.

"Ah dunno 'im. Ah tell yuz. First time today Ah saw 'im. Said he was here to help t'Gather, and we needed help."

Trust Besel to clear himself of any blame, thought Piemur.

"Sir, gate guard says a boy answering his description tried to pass out to the Gather awhile back. He couldn't say if the drudge carried anything about him. Wasn't looking for stolen items."

"Then he didn't leave?" The voice was a snarl of fury.

Lord Meron? wondered Piemur. And then realized that the unexpected had happened. The substitute in the egg pot had been discovered. There'd be no way he could creep out of this Hold in the shadow of departing guests. With the way men were dashing about lighting up every crook and corner of the courtyards, he'd be lucky to remain undiscovered. Some eager soul would certainly think to prod a spear through the ashpit just on the off-chance . . .

especially if Besel remembered that he'd emptied ash buckets and might have hidden the egg there.

Frantic now, Piemur glanced up at the walls about him. Carved from the cliff itself, they were, and he could never climb straight up unseen. He caught sight of a rectangular darkness just above his head to the left of the ashpit. A window? To what? This side of the kitchen was devoted to stores rooms, but what window. . . . The stores rooms were backed from the corridor side. No searcher would believe him able to open locked doors without a key. Which the kitchen steward kept on a chain about his waist at all times. He couldn't ask for a safer hiding place. And if he closed the window behind him . . .

He had to wait until the kitchen courtyard had been thoroughly searched . . . except for the garbage and ashpits. The shout went up that the thief must be hiding in the Hold. The searchers swarmed back inside, and he leaped to the top of the ashpit wall. His fingers just reached the ledge of the window. Taking a deep breath, Piemur gave a wriggling jump and succeeded in planting both hands over the sill. It took every sinew in his body to secure that awkward and painful grip. He felt as if he'd scraped the skin from all his fingers as he clung and worked his body up until his elbows had purchase on the sill. With another mighty wriggle and kick, he managed to propel himself up and over, falling on his head on the topmost sack. Groaning at the pain of that contact, he twisted about, and reaching up, drew the shutter tightly but quietly across, barring the window. Then he felt the egg to be sure his fall had done it no harm.

He tried to imagine this room from the perspective of the door side, but all the stores rooms had seemed the same. He crouched in terror as he heard shouting in the corridor. Someone rattled the bolts of the door.

"Locked tight, and the steward has the keys. He can't be here."

They might just take a look, thought Piemur, when they didn't find him anywhere else. He crawled cautiously over the stacked bundles until he found one with enough slack at the top to admit him. He opened the thong, and just as he was crawling in, wondered how under the sun he was going to tie it up again, the switching at the side began to give in his hands. Smiling happily at such a solution, he rapidly undid the stitching down the side. Crawling out, he retied the knot about the mouth of the sack, then slid through the undone seam, which, once inside, he could do up, slowly but enough to pass a cursory inspection. It was hard to do, feeding the thick thread through the original holes from the inside, and his hands and fingers were cramped when he finally accomplished the feat.

He was in a sack of cloth bales and, despite the cramped confines, he was able to wiggle down between bolts so that he was standing on the bottom of the sack and both he and the egg were cushioned on all sides by the material.

Between fatigue and the scant supply of air in the sack, he found his eyes drooping, and surrendering to the combination of exhaustion and safety, he fell fast alseep.

He was roused briefly when the door was unlocked and thrown open. But the inspection was cursory, since the Hold Steward kept insisting that the doors had been locked since the morning and he wouldn't let them poke any spears lest they harm the contents of the bales.

"He could have hid in the glow room. He was sent there several times."

The door was duly shut and locked.

Piemur was conscious of more activity, but his sleep was so deep that he wasn't certain later whether he dreamed the noise or not. He wasn't even conscious of being moved or of the cold of *between*. What woke him was a strange difficulty with breathing, a sense of heat and the terror of suffocating in his own sweat.

Gasping, he tore at the thread he had reworked, hard to undo with moist trembling hands that had no strength, and with sight impeded by perspiration pouring down his forehead.

Even when he had forced a small hole in the sack, he still couldn't seem to breathe. Weeping in terror, even to the point of forgetting the egg that had brought him to this extremity, he squirmed out of the sack to discover himself in a small space among other sacks. The heat was unbearable, but caution returned and he listened for any sounds. Instead of noise, his senses reported sun-heated material and hides, sun-warmed metal, and the sour sweat of hot wine.

He tried to shove the nearest sack away from him and couldn't shift it. Feeling the contents, he realized that it was metal. Twisting around, he tested the sack above him and gave an experimental heave. It moved, and a whoosh of slightly cooler air rewarded his efforts. Dragging breath into his lungs, he waited until his heart stopped its frantic pounding. And then, belatedly remembering the egg, he felt the rags about the precious burden. It seemed to be whole, but he didn't have sufficient space to get it out and look. He gave another shove at the upper bale with no success. Angling so that his shoulders were against the un- yielding metal, he levered his feet and pushed as hard as he could. It moved farther, and he saw a crack of sky so bril- liantly blue that he gasped at the color.

It was then that he realized he wasn't in Nabol Hold any longer. That the heat was not due to the unventilated stores room beyond Lord Meron's kitchen, but the sun pouring down from southern skies.

Once he was able to breathe easily, Piemur became aware of other discomforts: parched mouth and throat, a stom- ach gnawing with emptiness, and a head that banged with a distressingly keen ache.

He repositioned himself and shoved the sack a little fur- ther to one side. Then he had to rest, panting with the exertion as sweat trickled down inside his clothes. He had made enough space to take a look at the egg, and he fum- bled under his tunic for it with trembling hands. It was warm to his touch, almost hot, and he worried that an egg could be overheated. What had Menolly said about the temperature required by hatching eggs? Surely beach sands under the sun were hotter than his body. He could see no fracture marks on the shell and fancied he felt a faint throbbing. Probably his own blood. He squinted at the blue sky, which meant freedom, and decided not to put the egg back in his tunic. If he held it in front of him, then it didn't matter how he twisted and squeezed his body past the sacks and bales, the egg would take no harm and there was no way it could fall far.

When he was breathing more easily, he gathered his

body, egg-holding hand above his head, and began to squirm upward. Just as he thought he was free, the sack behind him settled agonizingly on his left foot, and he had to put the egg down to free himself.

Bruised—torn in muscle, skin and nerve—Piemur slowly dragged himself out of the carelessly piled goods. He lay stretched flat, mindful that he might be visible. The unshielded sun baked his dehydrated and exhausted body as he listened beyond the pounding of his heart and the thudding of blood through his veins. But he heard only the distant sound of voices raised in laughing conversation. He could smell salt in the air and the odd aroma of something sweet, and perhaps, overripe.

His tired mind could not recall much of what he'd heard of the Southern Weyr. Vague flashes of people saying you could pick fresh fruit right off the trees reassured him. A breeze fanned his face, bringing with it the smell of baking meats. Hunger asserted itself. He licked his dried, cracking lips and winced as the salt of his sweat settled painfully in the cuts.

Cautiously he raised his head and realized that he was at the top of a considerable mound that was braced against the stone walls of a structure of some height. To one side there was open space, to the other the crushed green of leaves and fronds, half-trapped by the bales. He inched himself cautiously toward the foliage, the egg considered at each movement. But even with caution his heart all but stopped when his motion caused one of the bundles to settle abruptly with what seemed to him a lot of unnecessary noise.

He listened intently for a long moment before continuing his crawl toward the foliage. Now, if he could climb up that tree . . . One look at the horny bark decided him against that. His hands were sore, scratched and bleeding from past efforts. He was about to crawl down the mound instead when something orangey caught his eye. A round fruit slowly swayed just above his head. He licked his dry lips and swallowed painfully against the parched tissue of mouth and throat. It looked ripe. He reached out, scarcely believing his luck, and the fruit rind dented softly at his touch.

Piemur did not remember picking the fruit: he did remember the incredibly delicious, wet, tangy taste of the orange-yellow meat as he tore juicy segments out of the rind and crammed them into his moisture-starved mouth. The juice stung his cracked lips, but it seemed to revive the rest of him.

It was while he was licking his fingers clean of the last of the fruit that he noticed the change in the laughing and talking. The noise was coming nearer, and he could hear individual phrases.

"If we don't get some of that stuff under cover, it'll be ruined," said a tenor voice.

"I can smell the wine, in fact, and that better be taken out of the sun or it will be undrinkable," said a second male voice with some urgency.

"And if Meron's ignored my order for fabric *this* time . . ." The woman's sharp alto left the threat unspoken.

"I made it a condition of that last shipment of fire lizard eggs, Mardra, so don't worry."

"Oh, I won't worry, but Meron will."

"Here, this one bears a weaver's seal."

"At the very bottom, too. Who piled this so carelessly?"

Piemur, scurrying down the other side as fast as he could, felt the shiver as someone began tugging at the sacks in the front. Then he was sliding and grabbed the egg more tightly, exclaiming as he hit the ground with a thud. Immediately three fire lizards, a bronze and two browns, appeared in the air about him.

"I'm not here," he told them in a soundless whisper, gesturing urgently for them to go away. "You haven't seen me. I'm not here!" He took to his heels, his knees wobbling uncertainly, but as he lurched down a faintly outlined path leading away from the voices and the goods, he thought so fiercely of the black nothingness of *between* that the fire lizards gave a shriek and disappeared.

"Who's not here? What are you talking about?" The strident tones of the woman's voice followed Piemur as he careered away.

When he could run no more for the stitch in his side and the lack of breath, he dared no more than pause until he'd gotten his wind. He did stop longer when he came to a stream, rinsed his mouth out with the tepid water and then splashed it about his heated face and head.

A noise, to his apprehensive mind like the querying note of a fire lizard, set him off again, after nearly falling into the stream. He plunged on, tripped twice, curling his body each time as he fell to protect the egg; but the third time he fell, he had reached the end of his resources. He crawled out of the line of the faint path to a place well under the broad leaves of a flowering bush and probably slept even before his labored breathing quietened.

Chapter 7

Sebell had not really worried about Piemur throughout the Gather day as he wandered—or staggered—about in his assumed role of wine-happy herdsman. And when word flashed through the crowds that Lord Meron was to walk the Gather, Sebell had no time to look for his apprentice. He had to concentrate on listening to the mutterings about Lord Meron and his curious generosity with fire lizard eggs that only hatched greens.

If Lord Meron's appearance gave the lie to rumors that the man was dead or dying, it was apparent to Sebell's sharp eyes that the Lord Holder needed the support of the two men who walked beside him, arms linked in his. Some of his heirs, Sebell heard whispered in glum and disgusted tones.

When the roasted beasts were being sliced for distribution to the Gather crowd, Sebell did begin to search for Piemur. Surely the boy wouldn't miss free meat at Lord Meron's expense. Not that the beasts were juicy, probably the oldest creatures in the Hold herds, Sebell thought, endlessly chewing on his portion. He had placed himself at an end table about the Gather square where Piemur ought to be able to see him.

By the time the dancing started, Sebell began to worry. N'ton would be returning for them at full dark, and he didn't want to impose on the bronze dragonrider by requiring him to wait about or return at a later time.

It was then that Sebell wondered if Piemur had somehow gotten into trouble and maybe left the Gather area. But, if Piemur had gotten into trouble, surely he would have set up a howl for Sebell to rescue him. Perhaps he had only crawled away for a nap. He'd had an early rising and he might not be completely recovered from his fall. Sebell sent Kimi about the Gather to see if she could locate the boy, but she returned, cheeping anxiously at her failure. He sent her then to the allotment, in case Piemur had gone there to wait. When that errand too was fruitless, Sebell appropriated a handy, fast-looking runner beast from the picket lines and made his way to their original meeting place, on the off-chance that Piemur had returned there, to wait for him and N'ton.

Though Sebell searched the valley carefully, he found no trace of his young friend. He was forced to admit that something had indeed happened to Piemur. He couldn't imagine what, nor why Piemur, or whoever the lad might have crossed, had not sent for him as Piemur's master.

He sped back to the Hold, retied his borrowed mount, and reached the Gather just as news of the theft of the queen egg rippled through the crowds. Feelings were mixed as that news spread; anger from those who had received lesser eggs, and amusement that someone had outsmarted Lord Meron. By the time Sebell got to the Hold gates, no one was being allowed in or out. Glowbaskets shone on empty courtyards, and every window of the Hold was brilliant with light. Sebell watched with the rest of the curious gatherers while even the ash and refuse pits were searched. Wagers were being laid that somehow Kaljan the Miner had managed to steal the egg.

Sebell was there when the minemaster was escorted by guard into the Hold after the man's baggage was thoroughly searched. An order was circulated, and additional guards posted, to prevent anyone's leaving the Gather. Sebell positioned himself along the ramp parapet leading to the Hold, where Piemur could easily spot him in the light from the Hold's glows. Surely if the boy had only fallen asleep, the noise would rouse him.

It was only when word filtered through the crowd that some unknown drudge had made off with the precious egg that Sebell came to the startling conclusion that that drudge could have been Piemur. How the boy had managed to enter the guarded Hold, Sebell couldn't figure out, but trust Piemur to find a way. Certainly it was like the boy to steal a fire lizard egg, given the opportunity. A queen egg at that! Piemur never did anything by halves. Sebell chuckled to himself and then sent Kimi flying with the other agitated fire lizards to see if she could discover where Piemur was hiding.

She returned and conveyed to Sebell that she couldn't get close to Piemur. It was too dark and too full. When Sebell questioned her for details, she grew distressed and repeated the image of darkness and her inability to reach the boy.

The frenzy of the search mounted. Guards were now dispatched on fast runners up every road leading from the Hold to find any travelers journeying from the Gather. Sebell sent Kimi to the valley to warn N'ton away in case the bronze rider was awaiting them. When Tris accompanied her back, Sebell knew that his warning had been timely. Tris chittered at him and then settled beside Kimi, giving Sebell the opportunity to send the fire lizard to bring N'ton should he be needed.

Both moons had risen by now, adding their soft light to the glows, but despite the fact that the guards endlessly searched and researched the Hold and yards, their efforts proved vain. Delighted with Piemur's elusiveness, Sebell settled himself to wait out the night in the shadowy corner of the first cot below the ramp. He had a good view of the guards and, by carefully looking over the ramp wall, could see most of the courtyard.

He was roused from a half-doze by the shouts and angry muttering as the guards prodded those who had lingered about the gates back down toward the Gather area.

"Go on now," the guards kept saying. "Go to your cots or your allotments. You'll be allowed to leave in the morning. No need to linger here. Go on with you, now!"

The moons had set, and gone, too, were all the glowbaskets that had illuminated the courtyards. Even the Hold was in darkness, though some light seeped through the shutters of the Lord Holder's apartments on the first level. Curling himself into a tight ball in the shadows, Sebell hid his face and hands and ordered Kimi to tell Tris to be quiet and for both to keep their eyes closed.

When the guards disappeared, he wondered what was happening. The Hold was virtually unguarded as well as unlit. Was this some sort of trap to catch Piemur? Or should Sebell take advantage of this opportunity and sneak into the Hold? Kimi rattled her wings in alarm, and through narrow slits her eyes gleamed yellow with worry. Tris, too, stirred nervously.

Then Sebell picked up from Kimi's mind the image of dragons; furthermore, dragons that neither fire lizard knew! Just as that image faded in his mind, Sebell heard the sound of dragon wings. Gliding from the northern shadows of the Hold cliff, he saw the black bulks of four dragons, wing on wing. Two settled neatly into the kitchen courtyard while the other pair landed in the main yard. Sebell heard hushed commands and then an unusual, muted hubbub. Grunts and muffled oaths punctuated the activity. Sebell was considering moving out of his protective shadows for a better view when he heard a heavy groan, the unmistakable scrabble of talons on stone, and the equally identifiable swhoosh of mighty wings making a powerful downstroke.

In the one band of light in the kitchen courtyard he saw the belly of a heavily laden bronze dragon struggling to rise, his sides bulging. No sooner had the first one cleared, than the second dragon launched himself skyward. The two in the main courtyard moved to the kitchen yard. More activity ensued, conducted with hoarse whispers and low voiced commands.

All during this, Kimi and Tris shivered, clinging to Sebell in a fashion they had never exhibited in the vicinity of other dragons. It took no great effort for Sebell to conclude that he had witnessed Lord Meron delivering goods to the Oldtimers from the Southern Weyr. That queen fire lizard egg had probably been prepayment for whatever the dragons had lugged away.

Sebell heard the sound of low voices coming from the direction of the Gather, and he hastily nipped back to his dark corner, warning the two fire lizards to close their eyes as he hid his face and hands again.

After moments of boot scuffing and muttered phrases, there was silence. Cautiously raising his head, he saw that the guards were back in position and that the glowbaskets again glowed on ramp and Hold walls, illuminating the roads leading up to the Hold. He was trapped in his shadowy corner. Nor did he dare to send Kimi or Tris from him, for their flight would surely be noticed when there wasn't another fire lizard to be seen. With a sigh, he settled himself as comfortably as he could, Kimi draped warmingly about his shoulders, and Tris curled at his side.

He couldn't have slept very long before he was rudely awakened by the boom of the message drums. "Urgent to the Healer! Lord Meron very ill. Masterharper required. Urgent! Urgent! Urgent!"

Had they then caught Piemur and, recognizing him, summoned Master Robinton to account for the misbehavior of one of his apprentices? Lord Meron would like nothing better than to be able to humiliate Master Robinton, for any censure of the Masterharper would also touch the Benden Weyrleaders, whom Lord Meron hated. Oh, well, if that were the case, at least the boy had been found. Sebell felt certain that Master Robinton could handle Lord Meron's accusations. And yet, why was Master Oldive so urgently required? No Hold drummed that measure unless the emergency was critical.

The Hold's fire lizards had been awakened by the boom of the big message drums and now wheeled about in the glowlight. Sebell unwrapped Kimi's tail from his neck, and holding her slender body in his hands, compelled her to look at him while he gave her directions to Menolly. He thought hard about clean clothes and imaged himself dressed in harper blue. Kimi chirruped understandingly and, after stroking his chin with her head, launched herself up. Tris chirped questioningly, tugging at Sebell's sleeve. N'ton would be a good ally, but strictly speaking the Fort Weyrleader had no genuine business here since Nabol was beholden to T'bor of the High Reaches Weyr. So Sebell looked deeply into Tris's lightly whirling eyes, thought hard that N'ton need not come to the valley, and sent the little brown back to his friend at Fort Weyr.

The message drum boomed a repeat, emphasizing again the urgency. Sebell strained his ears for the relay drums at the next point, but a handful of guards quick-stepped down the road toward the Gather and their passing masked the distant sounds.

Dawn was just breaking when Sebell, scanning the lightening skies, saw a dragon emerge. As the creature circled gracefully down, Sebell was relieved to note the silhouettes of four riders. He was perplexed because the dragon's spiraling descent would not put the party in the Hold's courtyard, where logically they would be expected to land. Abruptly, Kimi appeared in the air above him, chittering excitedly and darting off toward the Gather meadow. Her mind pictured Menolly. When Sebell did not move quickly enough to please her, she hovered at his shoulder and tugged at his dirty tunic, darting off again toward the meadow.

"I understand, of course. I'm tired, that's why I'm slow, Kimi," he said. Sticking to the shadows, he skirted the cot and started down the deserted road until he was far enough away from the guards. Then he picked up his feet and ran down the deserted road toward the new arrivals. He reached them just as the blue dragon left.

"Ah, Sebell," said the Masterharper, for all the world as if he were welcoming his journeyman into his rooms at the Harper Hall instead of surreptitiously meeting on a dark meadow in early dawn. "Menolly, hand him his clothes. He can tell us what has been happening while he changes. Is Lord Meron so desperately ill?"

"Probably. Of temper if nothing else," replied Sebell, stripping off his tunic and getting a shower of dust and grit in his hair and face. "He walked the Gather last evening . . ."

"He what!" exclaimed Master Oldive, cocking his head up at Sebell in surprise.

"He had to. And then someone stole a fire lizard queen egg from the hearth of his bedroom . . ."

"No?" Laughter as well as amazement colored the Harper's exclamation.

"Piemur?" asked Menolly at the same moment. "Is that why he isn't with you?"

"Is that why I've been summoned? To witness the punishment of a thieving apprentice?" Master Robinton was no longer amused.

"I don't know, Master. Kimi located Piemur in the Hold, but she couldn't explain where, said she couldn't get to him because it was too dark. I know the guards spent hours searching the Hold. Presumably they know it better than Piemur could. But—" Sebell paused. "I'm bloody certain they would have made some sort of commotion if they had found him and recovered that egg."

"Nothing would give Lord Meron more satisfaction than to force me to punish an apprentice thieving in his Hold."

"The message clearly states that Lord Meron is ill," said Master Oldive. "If he was foolhardy enough to walk his Gather and then agitate himself over the loss of a queen egg, he could indeed be very ill in his condition."

"It's accepted fact among the Nabolese," said Sebell, gratefully throwing aside his herdsman's cracked boots, which had rubbed his heels raw, "that the man's dying." He glanced up at Oldive and saw the Healer's head move affirmatively.

"Did you find out whom the Nabolese prefer as heir?" asked Master Robinton.

"A grand-nephew, Deckter. A carter who runs a steady business between Nabol and Crom. He's got four sons that he keeps firmly in line. He's not a friendly man, but he's got the grudging respect of those who know him." Sebell had finished dressing and now gestured the group toward the Hold. "I have also discerned that there are more fire lizards in and about Nabol than there ought to be. Most of them . . ." and he paused to give his words more weight, ". . . are green."

"Green?" Menolly swung on him in surprise.

"Yes, green."

"You mean," Menolly went on, "he's been distributing eggs from green fire lizard clutches? Why, the bloody beast!"

"On top of that insult, a lot of the eggs don't hatch at all, so you can imagine how little his generosity endears Lord Meron to the recipients," Sebell added grimly. "Of more importance," and Sebell held up his hand to forestall her angry words, "just after moonset, four dragons landed right in the courtyards and lifted off again so heavily laden you could hear their wings creaking!" Sebell grinned at the expressions of shock from his companions. "Further, Kimi didn't know those dragons and their presence frightened her."

"Now that is the most interesting piece of news you've given me," remarked the Master Harper.

He said no more because they had reached the foot of the ramp to the Hold and the group of men waiting there

129

impatiently rushed down to meet them. Sebell recognized the Hold's harper, Candler, and the healer, Berdine. Of the other three, he recognized the two men who had supported Lord Meron on his Gather walk. The fatter man barged straight up to the Harper.

"Master Robinton, I am Hittet, of the Blood, and you simply must assist us. The situation must be clarified with all possible dispatch. As I'm sure Master Oldive will tell you, there is no time to be lost. . . ." The others exclaimed in support of his words. "I fear that after the alarms and excitements of this night, the poor man cannot long survive. But come, we must hurry." Then he took the Harper by the arm and urged him toward the Hold.

"Alarms and excitements? Ah, yes, you had a Gather yesterday. . . ." Master Robinton was saying.

"I can't thank you enough for responding, Master Oldive," said Berdine falling in step with the Healer as the others followed Hittet and Master Robinton across the Court. "I know you said that there was nothing more you could do for Lord Meron, but the truth of the matter is that he has sadly taxed what strength was left him. I warned him, oh I did most explicitly, that he ought not walk the Gather, but he was adamant. Had to reassure his holders. I think that would have been safe enough, but then he insisted on having guests in his apartments . . . so much excitement. And then, to discover the queen egg had been stolen!" Berdine fluttered his hands in distress. "Oh my, oh my. I was beside myself trying to calm him. He wouldn't take that draught you left me for such an emergency. He became utterly uncontrollable when they couldn't find that wretched drudge who'd stolen the egg—"

"Journeyman Berdine," said Hittet in chilling tones, whipping about to stare warningly at the healer.

That interruption was timely made, for none of the Nabolese saw the looks of relief that the harpers exchanged.

"A drudge stealing an egg?" asked the Harper, as if he didn't believe his ears.

"Yes, if you must know," began Hittet, still glaring at the indiscreet healer. "Lord Meron was recently given a clutch of fire lizard eggs, one of which was thought to be a queen egg. He naturally took the best care of such prizes, kept them on his own hearth. He has had a lot of experience with fire lizards, you see. He was to distribute the eggs to deserving people as the high point of the Gather Feast. When his rooms were being freshened, one of the kitchen drudges had the audacity to steal the queen egg. How, we can't yet understand. But it's gone, and that wicked lad is somewhere in the Hold." Hittet's tone augured ill for Piemur when he was found.

None of the Nabolese noticed Beauty, Zair and Kimi peeling off from airy escort and darting out an open window as the group traversed the Main Hall. Sebell gave Menolly's hand a reassuring squeeze. She didn't look at him, but her lips curved slightly in a smile of relief.

"You can appreciate how upset Lord Meron was when the theft was discovered, and I fear this, and our pressing him to name an heir, resulted in his collapse," Hittet was saying to Master Robinton.

"Collapse?" Master Oldive looked sternly at Berdine, who immediately got his tongue twisted, trying to vindicate himself to his craft's Master. Master Oldive now brushed past Hittet and Master Robinton and, with the still apologetic Berdine on his heels, ran up the steps with no regard to his physical handicap or dignity.

Master Robinton also quickened his pace until the fat Hittet was forced to run to keep up. Sebell and Menolly deliberately slowed, to give their fire lizards a chance to range through the Hold and locate Piemur.

"If you could know how good it is to see a friendly face," said Candler, quite willing to match their laggard advance to the Lord's apartments. "If anyone can make that dreadful man see reason, it's Master Robinton. Lord Meron won't name an heir. That's why he collapsed, to avoid it. He was furious about the egg theft, to be sure, but while they were searching, he was more like himself— totally disagreeable and planning all kinds of fiendish punishments when they caught the drudge. Frankly, Sebell, he wants the Hold in contention. You know how he hates Benden. And now," and Candler laughed sourly, "none of the relatives who've been badgering him to name one of them wants to be the heir. I don't know why. They changed their tune abruptly this morning. Just as well." Candler snorted with disgust. "Any one of the lot would create disorder in next to no time."

"Changed their minds early this morning, did they?" said Sebell, grinning at Menolly.

"Yes, and I can't figure out why. Every single one of them has done all he could to secure the nomination. Now . . ."

"I'd heard that Deckter was an honest man."

"Deckter?" Candler swung toward Sebell in surprise. "Oh, the carter." He gave a mirthless laugh. "I suppose he could be considered an heir, couldn't he? Grand-nephew, isn't he? Forgot about him. Which is probably Deckter's doing. Said he could make more money carting than he could holding. He's probably right. How'd you know about him?"

"Looked up the Nabol bloodline."

Beauty flitted back, skimming so close to Candler that he ducked. Rocky, Zair and Kimi followed her, all chittering in some distress. All had the same message: Piemur was not in the Hold. Sebell and Menolly exchanged glances.

"Would he have hidden somewhere outside?" Menolly asked.

Sebell gave a quick shake of his head. "Kimi couldn't find him."

"Rocky and Beauty have been much closer to Piemur than Kimi."

"Can't hurt to try!"

"Piemur?" asked Candler, mystified by this cryptic exchange.

"I've reason to believe that the theft was accomplished by Piemur," said Sebell. He and Menolly gave their fire lizards new instructions and watched them dart out the Hold door.

"Piemur? But I remember Piemur. The boy with the fine soprano. I didn't see him anywhere—" Candler broke off and pointed at Sebell. "You *were* there when Lord Meron walked the Gather. The very drunken herdsman. I thought there was something familiar about him. It was you! Well. And Piemur here, too? On harper business? I thought it odd for one of Meron's drudges to have so much initiative.

Well, I'll tell you one thing, Piemur is not in this Hold."

"How could he have gotten out?" asked Sebell. "I was just beyond the ramp all night. Even if I didn't see him, Kimi would have."

They had reached the Lord's apartments now, and Candler opened the door, gesturing them to precede him.

"What's that smell?" asked Menolly softly, grimacing in distaste.

"Smell? Oh, you get used to it. Disgusting, I know, but it has something to do with Lord Meron's illness. We try to mask it," and Candler gestured to the sweet candles alight in containers about the room. "I often think that it's only justice," he added in a careful whisper, "for the suffering he's given others, but it's a terrible way to die."

"I thought Master Oldive had given him . . ." Sebell began.

"Oh, he has. The strongest there is, according to Berdine. But the medicine only dulls the pain."

The doors to the next two rooms were open, and the harpers could see the clusters of men standing about, in silence, all avoiding each other's gaze. Suddenly, in the third room, there was a brief flurry as the Harper appeared at the door to the Lord's private room.

"Sebell!" Master Robinton's calm request carried clearly, and everyone turned to watch the journeyman hurry to his master's side. "Please send a drum message to Lords Oterel, Nessel and Bargen, and to Weyrleader T'bor. Would they please attend us here at Nabol immediately. Double urgency on the beat, please."

"Yes, sir," said Sebell with such unexpected vigor that Master Robinton gave him a mild second look. But Sebell turned on his heel and walked swiftly out of the apartments, motioning as he passed them for Candler and Menolly to come with him. "I don't know why I didn't think of it earlier, Menolly. *If* Piemur got out of the Hold and is hiding somewhere in the hills, he'll surface to a drum message aimed at him. Lead us to your drumheights, Candler."

The big message drums needed only to be uncovered. Sebell stood for a moment, beaters poised over the taut hide as he composed his message. The opening roll boomed across the valley, the urgent measure following as the last echoes died. Then Sebell, eyes half-closed in concentration, beat out the recipients' names, the Harper's request, and the urgent measures once again to insure immediate reply and attention. Menolly positioned herself at the window then, ears straining to catch the pass-along roll from the next drumheights.

"There it is from the east," she told the two men. "What's wrong with the northern listeners? Still asleep? Ah, there they are."

"Candler, any chance of some food?" Sebell asked the Hold Harper. "We'd best wait here for replies."

"Yes, let's eat here where the air is clear," said Menolly, with a shudder as she thought of the thick, distasteful odor in Lord Meron's rooms.

"Of course, of course. I apologize for not offering sooner." Candler was away down the stairs.

Sebell picked up the sticks again and beat a quick measure. "Apprentice. Report. Urgent." He waited a few breaths and then repeated the measure.

"If he's anywhere between here and Ruatha or Crom, he'll hear that," Sebell said, carefully replacing the drumsticks on their hooks before he joined Menolly at the window.

Her face was sad and her brows constricted in a tiny frown as she gazed across the huddle of cots below the Hold ramp and over the disorganized Gather square, still tenanted by those unwillingly held over by the emergency. Few sounds wafted to their ears at this height, and the scene was unrealistically calm.

"Don't fret over Piemur, Menolly," Sebell said, trying to sound more lighthearted than he felt. "He has a knack of landing on his feet." He smiled down at her, allowing himself the luxury of putting his arm lightly about her shoulders.

"Except when the steps are greased!" Menolly's voice had an angry edge, and he gripped her shoulder reassuringly.

"Look at it this way: just see how that misadventure has worked to his advantage. He's got out of the drumheights and acquired himself a queen fire lizard egg. For all we know, he may meet us at the Hold gates with it, smiling in that ingenuous fashion of his, when you and I know he's as devious as Meron!"

"I wish I could believe you, Sebell," Menolly said sighing heavily, but she leaned trustingly against him for his comfort. "If he was anywhere in the vicinity, Beauty and Rocky ought to have found him."

"He's somewhere," replied Sebell firmly, and daring more than ever, he gave her a quick hug, turning abruptly from her as he caught her startled look. "The wretch!" he added, more of a growl than a comment. At that moment, they both heard the message drum roll across the mountains, and Sebell hastily strode back to the drums.

Candler arrived just as Sebell beat "receive" for the last of the messages. The Nabol Harper was panting with the exertion of his climb, for he carried not only a well-laden tray, but a full wine skin slung over his shoulder. The three harpers had time to make a leisurely meal before the first of the visitors arrived. The harpers then escorted the Lord Holders and T'bor to the Master Harper.

Sebell almost gagged and lost his breakfast when he brought Lords Holder Nessel and Bargen into Lord Meron's inner room. Menolly was already there with Lord Oterel and Weyrleader T'bor. He saw her mouth working to control the revulsion she was obviously feeling. Only Candler seemed impervious to the odor.

Although Sebell had seen Lord Meron the day before, he was appalled by the change in the man propped up in the bed: the eyes were sunken, pain had lined his face deeply, his skin was a pale yellow, and his fingers, plucking nervously at the fur rug that covered him, were claws with hanging bags of flesh between the knuckles. It was as if, Sebell thought, all life was centered in those hands, feebly holding onto life through the hair of the fur.

"So, I'm granted my own private gather, is that it? Well, I've no welcome for any of you. Go away. I'm dying. That's what you all wished me to do these past Turns. Leave me to it."

"You've not named your successor," said Lord Oterel bluntly.

"I'll die before I do."

"I think we must persuade you to change your mind on that count," said the Masterharper in a quiet, amiable tone.

"How?" Lord Meron's snarl was smug in his self-assurance.

"There is friendly persuasion. . . ."

"If you think I'll name a successor just to make things easy for you and those dregs at Benden, think again!" The force of that remark left the man gasping against his props, one hand feebly beckoning to Master Oldive, whose attention was on the Harper.

". . . Or unfriendly persuasion," continued Master Robinton as if Lord Meron hadn't spoken.

"Ha! You can do nothing to a dying man, Master Robinton! You, Healer, my medicine!"

Master Robinton lifted his arm, effectively barring Berdine from approaching the sick man.

"That's precisely it, my Lord Meron," said the Harper in an implacable voice, "we can do . . . nothing . . . to a dying man."

Sebell heard Menolly's catch of breath as she understood what Master Robinton had in mind to force this issue with Lord Meron. Berdine started to protest, but was silenced by a growl from Lord Oterel. The healer turned appealingly to Master Oldive, whose eyes had never left the face of the Harper. Although Sebell had known how desperately Master Robinton wished for a peaceful succession in this Hold, he had not appreciated the steel in his pacific Master's will. Nabol Hold must not come into contention, not with every Holder's younger sons eager and willing to fight to the death to secure even as ill-managed a Hold as this. Such fighting could go on and on, until no more challengers presented themselves. What little prosperity Nabol enjoyed would have been wasted in the meantime with no one holding the lands properly.

"What do you mean?" Meron's voice rose to a shriek. "Master Oldive, attend me. Now!"

Master Oldive turned to the Lords Holder and bowed. "I understand, my Lords, that there are many seeking my aid at the Hold gates. I will, of course, return when my presence is required here. Berdine, accompany me!"

When Lord Meron screamed for the two healers to halt, to attend him, Master Oldive took Berdine by the arm and firmly led him out, deaf to Meron's orders. As the door closed behind him, Meron ceased his entreaties and turned to the impassive faces that watched him.

"You wouldn't? Can't you understand? I'm in pain. Agony! Something inside is burning through my vitals. It won't stop until it's eaten me to a shell. I must have medicine. I must have it!"

"We must have the name of your successor." Lord Oterel's voice was pitiless.

Master Robinton began to name the male relatives, his voice expressionless as he intoned the list. When he had completed it, he recited it again.

"You've forgotten one, Master," Sebell said in a respectful tone. "Deckter."

"Deckter?" The Harper turned slightly toward Sebell, his brows raised in surprise at being corrected.

"Yes, sir. A grand-nephew."

"Oh." The Harper sounded surprised, at the same time dismissing the man with a flick of his fingers. He repeated the list to Lord Meron, now mouthing obscenities as he writhed on his bed. Deckter was added as an afterthought. Then the Harper paused, looking inquiringly at Lord Meron, who responded with another flow of invective, demanding Oldive's presence at the top of his voice. Again, the effort rendered him momentarily exhausted. He lay back, panting through his opened mouth, blinking to clear the sweat from his eyes.

"You must name your successor," said T'bor, High Reaches Weyrleader, and Meron's eyes rested on the man whose private grievance with him ran deepest. For it was Lord Meron's association with T'bor's Weyrwoman, Kylara, that had caused the death of both Kylara's queen dragon, Pridenth, and Brekke's Wirenth.

Sebell watched Meron's eyes widen with growing horror as he finally realized that he would have no surcease from the pain of his body until he did name a successor, confronted as he was by men who had excellent reason for hating him.

Sebell also noted that T'bor forgot to mention Deckter. So did Lord Oterel when he took his turn. Lord Bargen recited the name first, with a glance at Oterel for his omission.

Sebell knew he would always remember this bizarre and macabre scene with horror as well as with a certain awful respect. He had long known that Master Robinton would use unexpected methods to maintain order throughout

Pern and to uphold the leadership of Benden Weyr, but he had never expected such ruthlessness in the otherwise gentle and compassionate Robinton. He schooled his mind away from the stink and closeness of the room, from Meron's pain, by trying to appreciate the tactics that were being used as Lord Meron was deftly maneuvered into choosing the one man the others preferred among his heirs by their seeming to forget Deckter half the time. For a long while afterward, the flickering of glows would remind Sebell and Menolly of those eerie hours while Lord Meron tried to resist the will of his inflexible peers.

It was inevitable that Meron would capitulate: Sebell thought he could almost feel the pulsing of pain through the man's body as he screamed out Deckter's name, thinking he had chosen to displease the men who had so tormented him.

The instant he spoke Deckter's name, Master Oldive, who had gone no further than the next room, came to give the man relief.

"Perhaps it was a terrible cruelty to inflict on anyone," Master Oldive told the Lords when they left Meron in a drugged stupor, "but the ordeal has also hastened his end. Which can only be a mercy. I don't think he can last another day."

The other heirs, Hittet the most vocal, now barged in from the entry room, demanding to know why they had been excluded from their kinsman's presence, berating the Lord Holders and Master Robinton for this unconscionable delay and finally remembering to ask if Lord Meron had indeed named an heir. When they were told of Deckter, their reactions were compounds of relief, consternation, disappointment and then incredulity. Sebell extricated Menolly from the knot of chattering relatives and guided her to the steps down to the Main Hall and out of the Hold where they could breathe the fresh, untainted air.

A considerable and silent crowd lined the ramp, held back by the guards. At the sight of the two harpers, they began to shout for news. Was Lord Meron dead? What was happening to bring Lord Holders and the Weyrleader to Nabol?

As Sebell raised his hands for silence, he and Menolly

scanned the faces, looking for Piemur in that crowd. When he had their attention, Sebell told them that Lord Meron had named his successor. A curious rippling groan came from the crowd as if they expected the worst and were steeling themselves. So Sebell grinned as he called out Deckter's name. The multiple gasp of astonishment turned into a spate of relieved cheers. Sebell then told the head guard to send for the honored man, and half the crowd followed the messengers of this mixed fortune.

"I don't see Piemur," said Menolly in a low anxious voice, her eyes continually scanning. "Surely with us here, he'd come forward."

"Yes, he would. And since he hasn't . . ." Sebell looked about the courtyard. "I wonder . . ." As he twisted slowly in a circle, he realized that there would have been no way for Piemur to climb out of the Hold yards. Not even a fire lizard could claw its way up the cliff above the Hold's windows. Especially not in the dark and encumbered by a fragile fire lizard egg. His eyes were drawn by the ash and refuse pits, but he distinctly remembered their being vigorously spear-searched. His glance traveled upward and paused on the small window. "Menolly!" He grabbed her by the hand and started pulling her toward the kitchen yard. "Kimi said it was dark. I wonder what's . . ." In his excitement, Sebell reversed back to the guard, hauling the complaining Menolly with him. "See that little window above the ashpit?" he asked the guard excitedly. "What does it open on? The kitchen?"

"That one? Naught but a stores room." And then the guard clamped his teeth shut, looking apprehensively back to the Hold as if he had been indiscreet and feared reprisal.

His reaction told Sebell exactly what he needed to know.

"The supplies for the Southern Weyr were stored in that room, weren't they?"

The guard stared straight ahead of him, lips pressed firmly together, but the flush in his face was a giveaway. Laughing with relief, Sebell half-ran toward the kitchen yard, Menolly eagerly following him.

"You think Piemur hid himself among the stuff for the Oldtimers?" Menolly asked.

"It's the only answer that suits the circumstances, Menolly," said Sebell. He halted right in front of the ashpit and pointed to the wall that separated the two pits. "That wouldn't be too high a jump for an agile lad, would it?"

"No, I wouldn't think so. And just like Piemur! But, Sebell, that would mean he's in the Southern Weyr!"

"Yes it would, wouldn't it," said Sebell, unutterably relieved that the mystery of Piemur's disappearance could be explained. "C'mon. We'll send a message to Toric to be on the lookout for that rascal. I think Kimi knows Southern better than Beauty and Rocky."

"Let's send them all. Mine know Piemur best. Oh, just wait till I get my hands on that young man!"

Sebell laughed at Menolly's fierce expression. "I told you he'd land on his feet."

Chapter 8

The change in temperature roused Piemur, his mouth dry and sour, his body stiff. He couldn't think for a moment where he was or why he ached and his guts rumbled.

He sat bolt upright as he remembered and felt inside his tunic for the beragged egg. He tore the covering in his frenzy to check the precious shell and was trembling with relief when he touched its warm shape. The quick tropical dusk was nearly on him, the vivid glimmer of the sun coating the foliage about him with gold. He heard the lap of water and, peering toward the sound, realized that he was close to a beach. The call of a nest-homing wherry startled him as he crept stiffly from under his bush. He knew he'd have little time and light to settle the egg in warm sand for the night. He staggered to the beach, praying it would be a sandy one, crying out in relief when he saw that it was, dropping to his knees to burrow into the warm sand and bury the egg safely.

Wearily he built a pile of rocks to mark the spot and then pulled himself back to the jungle, using the light to locate a tree with orange fruit. The first few he batted down from the branches with a long stick were too hard to be edible, another fell with a liquid splot. He scooped up the overripe fruit and swallowed it down, grimacing at the slightly rancid taste. Then he managed, after several more attempts, to get two edible fruits. Barely satisfied, he propped himself against the tree's trunk and slept fitfully through the night.

Piemur stayed in that area all the next day, resting, washing his scratched and bruised self in the warm sea-water, rinsing out his stained and torn clothes. He had to seek the concealing shelter of the forest several times as first fire lizards and then dragons flew overhead. He was too close to the Weyr, he realized, and he would have to move on. But first, something to eat: more orange fruit and redfruit, which seemed to grow in profusion. He also picked up several dried hulls, one for carrying water and another for carrying his fire lizard egg buried in warm beach sand.

When he saw fire lizards and dragons returning to the Weyr, he waited for a spell before he retrieved his egg, packing it well in the hot sands, and headed westward, away from the Weyr.

Afterward, he never could figure out why he felt the Weyr and the Southern Hold were dangerous to him. He just felt he ought to avoid any contact with them, certainly until his egg had hatched and he had Impressed his own fire lizard. It wasn't logical, really, but he'd endured a harrowing experience, had already been in the role of the hunted, and so he continued to run.

The first moon rose early and full, lighting his way along the shore, up the rocky banks and steep sand dunes. He traveled on, occasionally eating fruit as he plodded and pausing three times for a small nap. But each time anxiety snapped him wakeful and set him on his way again.

The second moon rose, doubling the quantity of light but striking curious shadows against its companion that often made Piemur detour around rocks made gigantic by the mismatched illumination. He knew that strange things could happen to travelers under the double moons, but he persevered until both moons had set and the darkness forced him to seek refuge under the trees, where he'd be safely hid if he slept and dawn came before he knew.

He woke when a snake crawled over his legs, scraping against his bare skin where the trousers had been torn. He clutched feverishly at the egg, for snakes liked fire lizard eggs. The sand about his precious possession was cool and that brought him to his feet. He emerged onto a small cove, baking in a midmorning sun. He scooped out a hole and buried his egg, marking the spot with the upturned fruit shell ringed by beach stones. Then he returned to the jungle to seek his breakfast and water.

The diet of fresh raw fruit was affecting his digestion, and he spent some uncomfortable moments before he realized he would have to have something else to eat. He remembered what Menolly had said about fishing from her cave in the Dragon Stones, but he hadn't so much as a line. Then he noticed the thick vines clinging to tree trunks and viewed the thorns on the orange fruit trees with new sight. Using his belt knife and a little ingenuity, he shortly had himself a respectable fishing line. He baited his hook with a sliver of orange fruit, having nothing better.

The western arm of the cove had been swept into a long rocky hook and Piemur climbed and scrambled to the furthest point. Casting his hook and line into the foaming waves that lapped the base of the rock, he sat down to wait.

It was a long time before he had any luck in landing a fish, though he had pulls on several occasions that lost him his bait. When he finally hauled in a medium-sized yellowtail he had every right to be jubilant and think longingly of roast fish. But as he rose from his cramped position and turned, he realized he'd been very stupid. His rock was now isolated from the cove's arm by active surf. With a shock, he realized his second mistake: he had buried the egg in sands that would shortly be underwater. His yellowtail was considerably mangled by the time he had paddled, jumped and splashed ashore. His immersion in salt water had disclosed another shortsightedness on his part: his face, particularly his nose and the tips of his ears, had been badly sunburned, as well as the parts of his body showing through rents in his tunic.

He rescued his egg first, burying it in the shell with the hottest sands he could scoop about it. Then he hurried on to the next cove and a spot well above an obvious high-tide mark.

It took him time, too, to find rocks that would spark and light his fire of dried grasses and twigs. Eventually, he got enough of a blaze and he stretched the gutted yellowtail over the fire to broil, barely able to contain his impatient hunger until the meat darkened. Never had fish tasted so sweet and delectable! He could have eaten ten or twelve the same size and not had too much. He gazed longingly out at the sea, and to his disgust saw fish leaping out of the waters as if to tantalize him. Then he remembered that Menolly had said the best times to fish were sunrise and sunset or after a hard rain. No wonder he'd had such a wait, fishing at midday.

His face and hands burned now from too much sun, so he hiked deep into the woods that lined the beach, looking for fresh water, for ripe fruit, and seeing in the luxurious undergrowth, familiar, but oddly outsized, leaves of tuber plants. Experimentally he yanked on a handful of stems and up came a huge tuber root, which he dropped when he saw the small gray grubs that swarmed over it. But they disappeared quickly back into the rich loam, leaving clean the enormous white tuber. Suspiciously Piemur picked it up and examined it from all sides. It looked all right, even if it was much bigger than any tuber he'd ever seen. He was certainly hungry enough to eat all of it.

Taking it back to his dying fire, he fed the flame to a good height, washed the tuber in some of his precious fresh water, and sliced it thinly. He toasted the first slice on the end of his knife and broke off a tiny piece for judicious tasting. Maybe it was his hunger, but he decided he'd never tasted such a delicious tuber, crisp on the outside and just soft enough on the inside. He made quick work of cooking the remaining slices and felt immeasurably better.

Retracing his steps, he found tubers in quantity, but took only what he could carry.

When the tide had begun to recede from his boulder that evening, he splashed out to it again and was rewarded with several yellowtails of respectable size. He broiled two for his dinner, toasted another huge tuber and then undug his egg, arranging it in its carrying shell with plenty of warm sand.

He walked that night again until both moons had set. When he found a place to sleep on dried tree fronds, he arranged himself so that the rising sun would shine in his face and wake him. That way, he would be up in time to catch fish.

He followed this routine for two more days and nights, until the last night he realized that for some time he had seen no fire lizards nor dragons, nor any other living creature, except windborne wild wherries soaring high above the ground. He told himself that the next day, as soon as he found fresh water and a good cove with a wide sandy beach well above high-water markings with convenient fishing points, he would settle. The egg was perceptibly hardening and surely must be close to hatching time.

That evening he began to wonder why he had continued moving away from hold and Weyr. Of course, it was kind of fun, discovering each new cove and the vast stretches of sandy beach and rocky strand. To be accountable to no one except himself was also a new experience. Now that he had enough to eat and some variety of food, he was enjoying his adventure very much indeed. Why, he'd wager anything that he'd set foot on places no other person had ever trod. It was exhilarating to be first at something, instead of following others and doing just what every other apprentice had done before him Turn after Turn after Turn.

He fished in the morning, catching a packtail and being mindful of Menolly's experience with the tough, oily flesh as he gutted it. He smeared oil on face and body to ease the rough skin the sun had burned, reasoning that if Menolly had used fish oil for her fire lizards' flaking hides, it would do for his as well.

Retrieving and inspecting his precious egg, he was now certain it must be close to hatching, the shell was so rock hard. He packed it in the fruit shell with warm sand and proceeded westward, striking off through the shadier forest for a while.

At midmorning he stumbled out of the shade onto a wide expanse of gleaming white sand that forced him to squint against its glare. Shading his eyes, he saw a lagoon, partially sealed off from the sea by a jagged barrier of massive rocks, which must once have been the original coastline. Carefully climbing along that rocky arm, he could see all kinds of fish and crawlers in the clear water, trapped there after the higher tides had retreated. Just what he needed, his own private fishing pond. He retraced his steps and continued along the beach. Parallel to the point where the lagoon broke into the sea, he discovered a small stream emerging from the jungle, feeding into the lagoon. He followed it far enough up its course to clean water untainted by the sea.

He was jubilant and amazed that anywhere in this world of sun, sea and sand could exist that was exactly right to suit his requirements. And it was all his! Here he could stay until his egg hatched. And he'd better make the right preparations for that event now. It wouldn't do to miss

Impressing simply because he had no food for the hatch-ling.

He had seen neither fire lizards nor dragons in the sky for the past two days, so afterward he thought that might be why he had given no thought to Thread. In hindsight he realized that he had known perfectly well that Thread fell on the southern half of Pern just as it did in the North. His preoccupation with the fire lizard egg and his efforts to supply himself with food had simply divorced him from the concerns and memories of life in craft and hall.

He was fishing that dawn, lying prone on the grass pad he had made to protect his bare chest from the harsh rock surfaces when he experienced a sudden sense of alarm so intense that he glanced over his right shoulder and saw in horror the gray rain hissing into the sea not a dragon's length beyond.

He remembered later that he glanced for the reassuring sight of flaming dragons just before he realized that he was completely unprotected from Thread whether dragons were in the sky or not. That same instinct sent him plung-ing into the lagoon. Then he was in the midst of violent activity as half the fish in the ocean seemed to crowd against him, eager to consume the Thread that was diving to feed them. Piemur propelled himself up out of the wa-ter, flailing his arms to keep water about his body in the notion that water might protect him from Thread, as he gulped air into his lungs.

His shoulders wre stung while he fell back under the water. He pushed himself down, down again. But before long, he had to repeat the cycle of emerging, gulping air into his laboring lungs, then retreating to a depth that was free of viable Thread. He'd done this six or seven times before he realized that he couldn't sustain such activity for the length of Threadfall. He was dizzy with lack of oxy-gen, pinpointed by Threadscore that burned and stung in the salty water. Menolly had at least had a cave in which to shelter and. . . .

If he could find it, if it were sufficiently above the sur-face of the lagoon at this time of the tide, there was an overhanging rock. . . . He desperately tried to place its location on the lagoon arm the next time he surfaced, but he could barely see with eyes red and stinging. He was never sure in the mist of panic and anoxia how he found that meager shelter. But he did. He scraped his cheek, right hand and shoulder in the process, but when the redness cleared from his eyes, his nose and mouth were above water and his head and shoulders protected by a narrow roof of rock. Literally, just beyond the tip of his nose, Thread sheeted into the water. He felt fish bump and dive against him, sometimes sharply nibbling at his legs or arms until he flailed the attacked limb and the fish darted after their customary food.

Part of his mind knew when the menace of Thread had passed, but he remained where he was until the cloud of falling Thread moved beyond the horizon and the sun once more shone in unoccluded splendor on a peaceful scene. The terrified core of his soul, however, was slower to acknowledge that danger was over, and he remained in the shelter of the ledge until the tide had receded, leaving him stranded like a white fish on his portion of the reef.

Anxiety for his egg finally drove him from his sanctuary to check it in its beachy nest. The first scoop of sand he threw violently from him for it contained hundreds of the gray, squirming grubs. They reminded him so forcefully of Thread that he scrubbed his hands against his sides. Could Thread have penetrated the egg? He dug frantically until he reached it. He caressed the warm shell in relief. Surely it would hatch any time now!

Abruptly he hoped it wouldn't happen just now. He had no fish handy, and with their bellies full, he doubted if he'd catch any before sundown. If then. And how would he know precisely when the egg was going to hatch? Dragons always knew when a clutch was ready and warned their riders. Menolly said her fire lizards began to hum and their eyes whirled purple-red. He had no such forecasters to aid him.

Seized by a sense of urgency, he foraged in the jungle for vines to make another line and thorns from the fruit trees for hooks. But just to be safe, he gathered some fruit and some tough-shelled nuts. Hatchlings needed meat, he knew, but he supposed anything edible would be better than an empty hand.

It was while he was fitting the thorn hook into the end

of the vine that the impact of the day started to hit him. His fingers trembled so that he had to pause. He, Piemur of . . . well, he wasn't a herdsman's boy anymore, and he wasn't a harper's apprentice either . . . Piemur . . . Piemur of Pern. He, Piemur of Pern, he went on more confidently, had survived Threadfall holdless. He straightened his shoulders and smiled broadly as he glanced proudly across his lagoon. Piemur of Pern had survived Threadfall! He had overcome considerable obstacles to secure a queen fire lizard egg. It would hatch, and he would, at long last, have a fire lizard all his own! He glanced fondly at the mound in the sand that was *his* little queen.

Was he certain, though, that it was a queen? Doubt assailed him briefly. If it wasn't, it might be a bronze and that was every bit as good. But it had to be a queen egg, separated as it had been from the others warming by Lord Meron's fire.

Piemur chuckled at his own stupidity. He ought to have realized that Lord Meron would present the eggs as the climax to his feasting. Of course, the recipients would check, out of joy. Or maybe, out of distrust for Lord Meron's generosity. He really ought to have gotten out of the Hold before the feast had ended. How, he couldn't imagine, but he just might have done it if he'd tried. Certainly he wouldn't now be isolated on the Southern Continent. He put a final twist in the vine to hold the thorn hook firmly.

He gazed northward across the heat hazy sea in the general direction of Fort Hold and the Harper Hall. He'd been gone eight days now. Had they tried to find him at Nabol Hold? He was a bit surprised that Sebell hadn't sent Kimi or Menolly's Rocky to look. But then, how was anyone to know where he was? North or south? And fire lizards had to have directions, just like dragons. Sebell might not have learned that Lord Meron was dealing with the Southerners, or that there had been a collection that night.

A splash in the lagoon attracted his attention. The fish were back with the tide. He rose and made his way across the exposed rocks, affectionately patting the ledge that had sheltered him.

It took him longer than usual to catch a fish that evening. And he only landed a small yellowtail, too small to satisfy his hunger, much less provide for a voracious hatchling. Soon the rising tide would isolate him on this section of the lagoon so if he didn't hook shortly, he'd have to retreat to where the fishing was always poorer.

Controlling his impatience as best he could, for Piemur was certain that the fish heard sound, else why were they avoiding his hook, he also held his breath as he jerked his line in an imitation of live bait. That's when the curious noise came to his ears. He raised his head, looking about, trying to locate the source of that odd sound, so faintly heard above the lap of wave against rock. He scanned the skies, thinking there might be wild wherries or fire lizards above him. Or worse, dragonriders to whom he would be extremely visible, stretched along the reef rock.

It was the movement on the beach that caught his eye, more than placing the sound there. Just then the line in his hand jerked. In a panic of comprehension, he nearly let go but a reflex prompted him to haul the line in rapidly, rising to his feet as he did so, his eyes on the beach.

Something moved on the sand. Near his egg! A sandsnake? He picked up the first yellowtail, poked a finger in the gills of the hooked one, and made for the beach. Nothing was going to. . . .

Surprise and consternation halted him for one panic-filled instant as he saw the cause of the motion; a tiny glistening golden creature flapping awkwardly across the sands, piteously screaming. Wild wherries materialized in the sky, drawn by some uncanny magnet to this birth moment.

"All you have to do is feed a hatchling!" Menolly's calm advice rang in his ears as he stumbled across the sand and nearly fell on the tiny queen. He fumbled at his belt for his knife to cut up the fish. "Use pieces about the size of your thumb or else the hatchlings will choke."

Even as he tried to cut through tough fish scale, the little fire lizard darted forward, screaming with hunger.

"No. No. You'll choke to death," cried Piemur, pulling the fish tail from the fire lizard's grasp and hacking chunks from the softer flesh along the spine.

Shrieking with rage at being denied food, the little

queen began to tear at the fish flesh. Her talons were too birth soft to perform their function, so Piemur had time to slice suitable portions for her. "I'm slicing as fast as I can."

A race ensued then, between the hunger of the little queen and Piemur's knife. He managed to keep just a slice ahead of her voracity. When his knife opened the softer fish gut, she pounced, mumbling in her haste to consume it. Piemur wasn't certain if fish entrails, full of Thread no doubt, were a suitable diet for a newly hatched fire lizard, but it gave him time to cut more flesh.

He started on the second yellowtail, putting it first to occupy her while he hacked rapidly at the flesh. He knew one was supposed to hold the fire lizard while one fed it, to form the Impression, but he didn't see how he could contrive that until he had food enough to coax her into his hand.

Finished with the offal, she turned back to him, her rainbow eyes glaring at him as they whirled redly with hunger. She gave a scream, opened her still wet wings and dove on the small mound of fish pieces. He caught her first, holding her body firmly just under the wings and then proceeded to feed her piece by piece until she stopped struggling in his grasp. The edge of her hunger assuaged, she paused long enough to chew, and her voice took on a new, softer note. He loosened his hold and began to stroke her, marveling at the wiry strength in the slender body, at the softness of her hide, at the liveness of her, his very own fire lizard.

A shadow crossed them, and the queen raised her head and rasped out a warning.

He looked up and saw that the wherries had boldly circled down and were just above him, talons poised to grab. He waved his knife, the blade sparkling and glinting in the sun, frightening the wherries into wider, higher circles.

Wild wherries were dangerous, and he and the hatchling were unprotected on the open beach. He gathered her carefully into the crook of his arm, grabbed the line from which the fishhead still depended and started to run toward the jungle.

She shrieked in protest as he broke into a full run just as the wherry leader made its first pass. He sliced upward with his knife, but the wherry was clever and, adding its piercing scream to the fire lizard's, veered away from him. Holding the struggling queen against his chest, Piemur hunched his shoulders and concentrated on reaching the forest as fast as he could. He'd always prided himself on his speed: right now that ability had to save two lives.

He saw the shadow of another wherry dive at them and swerved to the left, grinning with satisfaction at its shrill call of anger when it was balked of its prey.

The queen's talons might not be dry but they scrabbled painfully against his bare chest as she struggled to grab the fishhead that dangled enticingly from the line in his hand. Piemur ducked right as he avoided a third wherry's dive, and the queen missed her lunge for the fishhead.

The fourth attack occurred so quickly that Piemur couldn't duck in time and felt a sharp pain as the wherry's talons scraped across his shoulders. Twisting upward, he slashed out with his knife, tripping as he did so and instinctively rolling to the right to protect his precious burden. He saw the wherries trying to veer fast enough to come at him on the ground, shrilling out that their prey had fallen and was at their mercy.

The little queen was now aware of their peril and slipping from his grasp, jumped to his shoulder, spreading her wings and screaming defiance at the attackers. She was so valiant, the little darling, so small in comparison to the wherries that her courage gave Piemur the impetus he needed. He scrambled to his feet, felt her cling to his hair, her tail tightly wound about his neck, continuing her stream of defiant cries as if by her fury she could repel their attackers.

Piemur ran then, pumping his legs as fast as he could, his lungs straining for breath to sustain the speed. He ran, expecting momentarily to feel the wherry talons rending his flesh. But abruptly their cries turned from triumph to fear. Piemur launched himself into the thick bushes, grabbing at his queen to keep her secure. Safe under the wide leaves and among the thick stalks, he turned to see what had frightened their pursuers. The wherries were flying away as fast as they could flap their wings, and he had to crane his neck eastward until he saw a flight of fire lizards arrowing in pursuit of the wherries. Just as he drew back under the concealing bush, he saw five dragons gliding above the sea.

His queen gave another cry, softer now, in protest that the fishhead still dangled beyond her reach. Afraid that somehow the dragons might hear her, he gave her the head, which she contentedly tore and consumed while Piemur watched the dragons circling the spot where she had lain enshelled. Without waiting to see if the dragons landed, Piemur pushed his way deeper into the jungle, trying to remember if Menolly had ever said anything about fire lizards tracing newly hatched ones.

But fire lizards only knew what they'd seen, and he'd been undercover by the time the winged rescuers had reached the lagoon area. The wherries' shrieks would have masked any sound she'd made, and as Piemur plunged past thorn trees and undergrowth, her cries became softer. Weariness overcame the last vestiges of her shelling hunger.

Piemur was more aware of her contentedness than his rasping breath as he continued to put as much distance between him and the lagoon, and possible discovery, while light remained to guide him in the murky jungle.

In the same hour Kimi returned with a message from Toric, answering the Harper's query about young newcomers in the southern settlement, the drum beat the news of Lord Meron's death.

"Eight days it's taken him to die," said the Harper on the end of a long sigh, "when Master Oldive thought one."

"Determined to disoblige us, I imagine," said Sebell, dismissing the man as he concentrated again on Toric's message. "No one has applied to him for shelter. There's been no outburst from the Weyr, which he's certain would have been made if a stowaway had been discovered. But that doesn't mean," said Sebell hurriedly, raising his hand to forestall Menolly's protest, "that Piemur didn't get there. Toric says that the Weyr has been barred to his holders for the last sevenday, but his fire lizards imaged a pile of strange shapes by the Weyrhold, so he suspects that a shipment has arrived from the north. They don't let the mere holders in the Weyr grounds to celebrate. So if Piemur smuggled himself out of Nabol Hold in one of the Oldtimers' sacks, he also got out of it and made himself scarce."

152

"Which is sensible of Piemur," said the Harper, idly twirling his wine glass with one hand. His face was expressionless, but his eyes moved restlessly with his thoughts. "Piemur would undoubtedly deem it discreet not to come to the Oldtimers' notice."

"At least not until that egg of his had hatched," added Menolly. She had so hoped that Piemur would have gone to Toric. She was certain he would know that Toric was friendly with the harpers. She turned to Sebell. "Candler will let us know the instant the other eggs from the clutch have hatched, won't he?"

"Yes, he said he would," the journeyman replied, but then he made a face, scratching his head. "But we don't know if that queen egg came from the same clutch as the others."

"But we do know the others weren't green's eggs; they were too big. And that's the only time scale we have to work with. I'm positive that Piemur won't attempt to seek anyone out until that egg has hatched and he's Impressed. I know I wouldn't if I were in Piemur's boots. Oh, I wish I knew if he were all right." She beat her thighs with her fists at her helplessness.

"Menolly," said the Harper soothingly, "you're not responsible for—"

"But I feel responsible for Piemur," she said, and then shot her Master an apologetic look for interrupting him so rudely. "If I hadn't encouraged his interest in the fire lizards, if I hadn't filled his ears with the pleasures they bring, he might not have been tempted to steal that egg and get himself into such a predicament." She looked up because both men started to laugh, and she exclaimed with exasperation at their callousness.

"Menolly, Piemur has been getting in and out of trouble since long before you arrived here," said Sebell. "You and your fire lizards calmed him down considerably. But I think you're right about Piemur not showing himself until Impression's been made. And Toric is on the alert for him. He'll show up."

"Meanwhile," said the Harper, rising from his chair and reaching for his flying gear, "I'd best go and assist the new Lord Deckter to secure his Hold."

Chapter 9

Afterward, Piemur wasn't certain why he had run from the dragonriders. He seemed to have been running from or to something ever since his voice had changed. In his panic, he supposed he aligned the Oldtime dragonriders with Lord Meron, and he did not want to encounter anyone connected with Lord Meron just then. Whatever, that night he plunged through the jungle until lack of breath, the painful stitch in his side and the darkness forced him to halt. Sinking to the ground, he rearranged his fire lizard comfortably and then fell asleep.

Just as the sun was rising the next morning, she awoke him, snappy with hunger. He eased the worst of her pangs and his own with fresh redfruit, cool from the night air and succulently sweet. Then he turned north, to make his way back to the beaches and fish for Farli, for that was the name he gave his little queen. Pushing his way through the underbrush, he tripped over a half-eaten runner beast carcass. Farli chattered with delight and ate flesh from bone, humming at him in pleasure.

"You'll choke like that," he said, and proceeded to hack smaller pieces, keeping about one knife slice ahead of her voracious appetite.

When Farli had curled herself about Piemur's neck, thoroughly sated, her belly bulging, he sliced more meat from the dead runner. He figured the creature must have been killed during Threadfall so the meat wouldn't as yet be tainted. Not only would it be a welcome change for him from fish, but red meat was better for Farli as well.

Comforted by her sleeping weight about his neck, Piemur found thick grasses and wove a rough envelope in which to carry the meat. He estimated he had enough for several meals for himself and Farli, but if he could cook it, the meat wouldn't spoil as quickly in the heat.

Continuing on a northwestern course back to the beach, he collected dry grass and sticks with which to build a fire. He was still heading generally north when he saw the unmistakable glint of water through the thinning trees to his left. He stopped, stared, unable to think how he could have mistaken his direction. A lake? However, if water was this close now. . . .

He pushed his way through the thinning screen of trees and bush and came out on a small rise. Below him were wide tidelands, which swept from the forest in an undulating grassy plain, broken by thick clumps of a gray-green bush. The plain continued on the other side of a broad river, which gradually widened until, in a distant point now hazy with heat, it must open its mouth into the sea. A breeze, scented with an oddly familiar, pungent odor, dried the sweat on his face. Squinting against the sunlight, Piemur could see herdbeasts grazing on the lush grass on both sides of the river. And yet there'd been Thread here the day before, and no dragonriders flaming to prevent the deadly stuff burrowing into the ground and eating the land barren.

As if to reassure himself, he poked at the soil with one of the sticks he'd collected, lifting up a clod of grass. Grubs fell from the roots, and Piemur was suitably awed by the abilities of those little gray wrigglies, which could, all by themselves, keep such an enormous plain free from the ravages of Thread. And those bloody Oldtimers hadn't so much as stirred from the Weyr during yesterday's Fall. They weren't proper dragonriders at all. F'lar and Lessa had been right to exile them here to the South, where the insignificant grubs did their work for them. Why, he could have been killed during that Threadfall, and not a dragonrider around to protect him. Not, Piemur honestly admitted, that he hadn't been well able to protect himself.

He gazed across the river, now noticing the swifter moving current that rippled toward the sea. He'd have fresh water for drinking here as well as a retreat from Thread. The jungle behind him would provide fruit and tubers; the meadow's inhabitants red meat for Farli. There was no need to trek to the sea again. He could stay here until Farli had lost the worst of her hatchling appetite. Then he'd better start back to the Southern Hold. If he was careful, he could avoid being noticed by the Oldtimers until he'd made contact with the holder . . . what was his name? He was certain he'd heard Sebell mention the man by name. Toric! Yes, that was it. Toric.

He set about making a rough circle of stones to protect his fire from the breeze, whistling softly. A fresh breeze brought him another whiff of that odor, sun-warmed and so puzzlingly familiar. Whatever it was must be down on the plain for the wind came from that direction. Leaving his meat to roast at his fire, Piemur made his way down the slope, looking about at the tiny blooms in among the grasses with Thread-pricked blades. He almost passed the first clump of bushes before he realized that their leaves were definitely familiar. Familiar, he thought as he reached out to touch one, but so much larger. He bruised the leaf as the final test and sure enough, had to jerk his hand back as his fingers smarted and then lost all feeling. Numbweed! The whole plain was dotted with numbweed bushes, growing bigger and fuller than any he'd ever seen in the north. Why, if you harvested even one side of this plain, you'd keep every Weyr on Pern in numbweed for the entire Pass. Master Oldive ought to know about this place.

A petulant squeak in his ear warned him that Farli had roused, probably smelling the roasted meat. He carefully broke off some large numbweed leaves, and wrapping their cut stems in a thick blade of grass, returned to the fire. When he had given Farli a few half-done pieces of meat, she was quite content to curl up for the rest of her nap. Then Piemur bruised a numbweed leaf between two flat, clean stones. He rubbed the wet side of the stones against his cuts, shivering at the slight sting of the raw numbweed before its anesthetic properties took effect. He was careful not to rub the stone too deep, for raw numbweed must be used sparingly or you could get horrible blisters and end up with scars.

As he settled by the fire to wait for his meat to cook, he knew he'd be sorry to leave here.

He said that to himself the next morning when he rose, and that evening when he curled up in the shelter he'd made for Farli and himself. He really ought to try to get word back to the Harper Hall.

Each day, however, found him too busy catering to the needs of a rapidly growing fire lizard to make provisions for a journey of possibly several days. He spent a whole day trying to catch a fish for the oils needed to soothe Farli's flaking skin.

Then Thread fell again. This time he was adequately prepared, and forewarned. Farli went hysterical with alarm, her eyes wheeling furiously with the red of anger as she rose on her wings and, shrieking defiance to the northeast, suddenly flicked out. When Piemur called her, she popped back in, scolded him furiously, and then disappeared. She had gone *between* before, inadvertently scared by some odd noise or other, so that it wasn't until she remained away for much longer than before that Piemur began to wonder what had frightened her. He looked northeast, noticing as his eyes swept across the plains, that the animals were all moving toward the river with considerable haste. The quick blossom of flame against the sky caught his eyes, and he saw, not only Thread's gray rain, but the distant motes of dragons.

He had made preparations against the next Fall of Thread, determined never to spend another eternity under a rock ledge. He had found a sunken tree trunk where the river flowed out of the forest. Diving into the water, he kicked down to the depth at which drowning Thread could no longer sting. There he hooked his arm around the tree trunk and poked back to the surface a thick reed, through which he then was able to breathe. It was not the most comfortable of hideaways, and fish constantly mistook his arms and legs for outsized Thread so he had to keep moving. Time, too, seemed motionless, and it felt like hours had passed before the impact circles of Thread on the water surface ceased. He was glad when with a mighty kick of his legs, he burst back into the air, nearly overturning a small runner. In fact the shallows seemed to be blanketed with animals. As if his eruption from the depths had been a signal, or perhaps his presence had frightened them, the creatures began to struggle toward the shore, shake themselves, and then rapidly take off down the plain. Some were bawling with pain, and he saw a number with bloody face scores where Thread had stung them. He also noticed some of the injured making to the numbweed brushes and rubbing against the leaves.

Piemur waded to the bank, calling for Farli as he sank to the solid ground. His arms and legs felt leaden from his efforts to discourage fish from eating him.

Farli burst into view just above him, chittering with relief and anxiety. She landed on his shoulder, wrapping her tail about his neck and stroking his cheek with her head, one paw wrapped around his ear, the other anchored to his nose. They comforted each other for a long moment. Then Piemur felt Farli's body go taut. She peered around his face and began to chatter angrily. Twisting about, at first Piemur saw nothing to alarm him. Farli loosed her hold on his nose, and he realized that she was pointing skyward. He saw the wherries then, circling high, and knew that something had not survived the Fall. If wherries were after it, it was something that would also feed him and his fire lizard.

Farli seemed as eager as he to beat the wherries to their victim, and she chattered encouragement as he found a stout stick and made his way up the riverbank.

Most of the creatures that had taken refuge in the river had disappeared, but he kept a wary eye for snakes and large crawlers that might also have found sanctuary in the river.

He saw the bulge of the fallen runner beast, half-hidden under a large numbweed bush. To his surprise, it heaved upward, its bloodied flank crawling with grubs. The poor thing couldn't still be alive? He raised his stick to put an end to the creature's pain when he realized that the movement came from under the animal, spasmodic and desperate. Farli hopped from his shoulder and chittered, touching a tiny protruding hoof that Piemur hadn't noticed.

It had been a female runner beast! With an exclamation, Piemur grabbed the hind legs and pulled the corpse from the youngster the female had given her life to protect from Thread. Bleating, it staggered to its feet, shedding a carpet of grubs, and hobbled the few steps to Piemur, its head and shoulders scored here and there by Thread.

Almost absently, Piemur stroked the furry head and scratched behind the ear cup, feeling its rough tongue licking his skin. Then he saw the long shallow scrape on the little beast's right leg.

"So that's why you didn't make it to the river, huh, you poor stupid thing?" said Piemur, gathering it closer to him. "And your dam sheltered you with her body. Brave thing to do." It bleated again, looking anxiously up at him.

Farli chirped and stroked her body against the uninjured leg before she moved on to start making a meal off the dead runner. With a sense of propriety, Piemur took the youngster off to the river to bathe its wound, treat it with numbweed and wrap it with a broad river plant to keep off insects. He tethered it with his fishing line and then went back to slice off enough meat for several meals. The wherries were closing in.

Farli was sated enough not to resist leaving the carcass. Nor did she object when Piemur carried little Stupid back to their forest shelter.

As Piemur settled down to sleep that night, he had Stupid curled tightly against him along his back and Farli draped across his shoulders. He had fully intended to use the interval between this Fall and the next to make his way to the Southern Hold, but he really couldn't leave Stupid, crippled as well as motherless. The leg would heal with care and rest. Once Stupid was walking easily, after the next Threadfall, he would definitely make tracks to Southern.

Despite the lateness of the hour, the Masterharper could see light coming from his study window as he wearily made his way from the meadow where Lioth and N'ton had just left him. He was very tired, but well satisfied with the results of his efforts over the last four days. Zair, balancing on his shoulder, cheeped an affirmative. Robinton smiled to himself and rubbed the little bronze's neck.

"And Sebell and Menolly are going to be satisfied, too. Unless, of course, there has been word from that scamp that they haven't been able to send me."

He saw the half of the great Hall door swing into darkness and wagered with himself who waited for him there in the dark.

"Master?"

He was right; it was Menolly.

"You were away so long, Master," she cried in a soft voice as she closed the door behind him and spun the wheel to lock the bolts tightly in floor and ceiling.

"Ah, but I've accomplished much. Any news from Piemur?"

"No," and her shoulders drooped noticeably. "We would've sent you word instantly."

He put his arm around her slender shoulders comfortingly. "Is Sebell awake as well?"

"Yes, indeed!" She gave a chuckle. "N'ton sent Tris to warn us. Or you'd've been locked out of your own Hall."

"Not for long, my dear girl, not for long!"

They were climbing the steps now, and he noticed that she slowed her pace to match his. He was tired, true, but, worse, he no longer commanded the resilience that made no bother of late hours.

"Lord Groghe was back two days ago, Master. Why did you have to stay so long at Nabol?" He felt her shoulders give a convulsive shudder under his arm. "I wouldn't have stayed at that place a moment longer than I had to."

"Not the most of congenial of Holds, to be sure. I can't think what can have happened to all the wine Lord Fax appropriated in his conquests. He had some good pressings, too. Meron can't have drunk it all in a bare thirteen or fourteen Turns."

"You'd no Benden wine, then?" Menolly teased him.

"None, you unfeeling wretch."

"Then I'm more amazed than ever that you stayed so long."

"I had to!" he replied, amazed at the irritation in his voice. But they had reached his rooms now, and he opened the door, grateful for the sight of the familiar disorder of his workroom and the welcoming smile on Sebell's face. The journeyman was on his feet, helping his master out of his flying gear and guiding him to a chair, while Menolly poured a goblet of a decent Benden wine.

"Now, sir, have you a tale to tell?" asked Sebell, lightly taunting with his Master's usual greeting. "Could we not have come to Nabol and helped speed matters?"

"I would have thought you'd seen enough of Nabol Hold to last a Turn or two," said Master Robinton, sipping at his wine.

"He's got news, Sebell," said Menolly, narrowing her eyes to glare at her master. "I can tell that look on his face.

160

Smug, that's what he is. Did you learn what happened to Piemur at Nabol?"

"No, I'm afraid I didn't find out about Piemur, but among other, equally important, things, I have arranged matters so that we don't have to worry about Nabol Hold supplying the Oldtimers with northern goods or receiving a further embarrassing riches of fire lizard eggs in that otherwise impoverished Hold."

"Then, none of the disappointed heirs caused trouble during the confirmation?" asked Sebell.

Master Robinton waggled his fingers, a sly smile on his face. "Not to speak of, though Hittet is a master of the snide remark. They could scarcely contend the nomination, since it had been made before such notable witnesses. Besides, I never bothered to disabuse them of the notion that Benden and the other Lord Holders would call the heir to account for the sins of his predecessor." Master Robinton beamed at the reactions of his journeyman to his strategy. "It afforded me considerable pleasure to help the new Lord Deckter send the worthless lot back to improve their beggared holds."

"And Lord Deckter?" asked Sebell.

"A good choice, however unwilling. I pointed out to him, adroitly, that if he merely regarded his Hold as a flagging business and applied the same ingenuity and industry with which he had built a flourishing carting trade, he would find that the Hold would respond and repair. I also pointed out that in his four sons he has able assistants and ministers, a fortune few Lords can enjoy. However, he did have one matter he was particularly anxious to resolve." The Harper paused. He looked at the expectant faces. "A matter that just happens to march kindly with a problem we face." He turned to Menolly. "You'd best ready that boat of yours. . . ." he had started referring to her skiff in that manner after he and Menolly had been storm-lost on his one voyage to the southern hold the previous Turn. Now Menolly's face brightened, and Sebell sat up straight, eyes wide with anticipation. "We won't locate Piemur by whistling for him from the north. You two go south. Make certain that Toric lets the Oldtimers know, if you can't carry the message discreetly to them yourselves, that Meron is dead and that his successor supports Benden Weyr. I believe that Master Oldive wants you to bring back some of those herbs and powders. He used up a large portion of his supplies on Meron.

"But don't you dare return until you've found Piemur."

Chapter 10

Stupid bleated, his rump, as he struggled to his feet, pushing sharply into Piemur's belly. Curled on Piemur's shoulder, Farli gave a sleepy complaint, which rapidly changed to a squeak of alarm. Piemur rolled over, away from both his friends for fear of injuring either and got stiffly to his feet. There wasn't anything alarming in the clearing about his small shelter but, as his eyes swung about, he caught the unexpected distant blur of bright red on the river. Startled, he brushed aside an obscuring bough and saw, just where the river began to narrow between the plains, three single-masted ships, carrying brilliant red sails. Even as he watched in surprise, the ships altered course, their red sails flapping as they were first turned into the wind and then were carried by momentum up onto the muddy beach.

Fascinated at the sight of ships on his river, Piemur moved further from his shelter, stroking to reassure Farli, who chittered questions at him. He was marginally conscious of Stupid brushing against his bare leg as he reached the outermost screen of trees. Not that anyone from the ships could possibly see him at this distance. He watched, as one will review a dream, while people jumped out of the ships: men, women and children. Sails were furled fully, not just thrown across the boom. A line was formed to convey bundles and packages from the ships across the muddy beach to the higher, dry banks. Holdless men from the north? wondered Piemur. But surely he'd heard that they were passed through Toric first, so that their inclusion in the Southern Hold was unobstrusive and the Oldtimers had no cause to complain. Whoever these people were, they looked as if they intended to stay awhile.

As Piemur continued to watch the disembarkation, he became aware of a growing sense of indignation that anyone would dare invade his privacy, would have the audacity to make a camp and set up cooking fires with great kettles balanced on spits across the flames, just as if they belonged here. This was his river, and Stupid's grazing grounds. His! Not theirs to litter with tent, kettle and fire!

What if the Oldtimers just happened to fly this way? There'd be trouble. Didn't those folk know any better? Setting up in the sight of everything?

Farli distracted him by protesting her hunger. Stupid had fallen to his customary sampling of every type of greenery in his immediate area. Absently, Piemur reached in the pouch at his belt for a handful of nutmeats he'd kept there to pacify Farli. Daintily she took the offerings, but informed him with a querulous cheep that this had better not be all she was given to eat that morning.

Piemur chewed on a nut himself, trying to figure out who these people were and what they were about. One group was now separating itself from those bustling about tents or filling the huge kettles with water drawn from the river. This group moved purposefully toward the far end of the field and then the individuals spread out. Long chopping blades flashed in the sun, and suddenly Piemur knew who they were and what they were doing.

Southerners had come to harvest the numbweed bushes, now full of sap and strong with the juice that eased pain. He wrinkled his nose in disgust: it'd take them days to harvest that field; and each kettleful would require three days of stewing to reduce the tough plant to pulp. Another day would be required to strain the pulp, and the juice had to be simmered down to the right consistency to make the numbweed salve. Piemur knew that Master Oldive took the purest of the resultant salve and did something else with it to make it a powder for internal use.

He sighed deeply, because the intruders would be here for days and days. The camp may have been set up a good hour's walk from him and undoubtedly he could keep from being noticed. He wouldn't escape however, even at this distance, from the stench of boiling numbweed, for that smell was pervasive, and the prevailing breeze right now was from the sea. It was infuriating to be forced out of *his* place just when he'd gotten everything arranged to his convenience so that he could feed himself, Farli and

Stupid, had shelter from the tropical storms at night and safety from Threadfall whenever it came.

Then it occurred to him that perhaps these weren't Southerners, but a work party from the north. He knew that Master Oldive preferred southern grown herbs; that was why Sebell had made that trip not long ago to bring back sacks and sacks of medicinal things. Surely he'd brought enough or maybe this was a new arrangement with the Oldtimers, who surely couldn't object to the Healer.

But northern ships had many-colored sails; Menolly had told him that seaholders prided themselves on the intricacy of their sail patterns. Plain red sail did suggest Southerners, whom everyone knew broke northern tradition whenever possible. Also those work groups were moving with the familiarity of much practice.

Piemur grinned to himself. One thing sure, he wasn't going to announce his presence right now. Sure as eggs hatched, he'd get himself included in harvesting numbweed. He'd just take what he needed and work around them, through the forest, until he got to the seashore, well east of them. And well away from the stink of boiling numbweed.

So he made a neat bundle of his woven mat and tied it with a vine thong, ignoring the chittering of Farli, who disapproved of his activity and of the fact that he was ignoring her gradually more insistent requests for food. He stared at the walls of his little shelter and decided that there was just the chance that someone might hunt in the forest and discover his rude hold. He dismantled the sheets of woven grass and hid them in the thick leaves of nearby bushes. He couldn't remove the clearing he'd made, but he scuffed up the tamped-down earth and scattered dead fronds here and there so that a casual glance would make it appear a natural clearing. He silenced Farli's now-urgent complaints by heading for the river. His fish trap, tied to his sunken Thread-tree, held more than enough to feed her amply. He gutted what remained after she was sated, and wrapping them in broad leaves, added that to his bundle. He hesitated a few moments before tossing the fish trap back into the water. Surely no one would notice it unless someone tripped over the silly thing, which seemed highly unlikely, and the fish it captured wouldn't suffer. He'd leave it, and then he'd have ample eating when he returned here.

He made his way through the forest, skirting the wide plain, pausing to drink when he crossed a small contributory stream and to let Stupid rest awhile. The little fellow's short legs tired quickly, and while the creature was no great weight, he did seem to get heavier on those occasions when Piemur took pity and carried him awhile. Farli flitted ahead of them and behind, venturing up through the trees into the sky occasionally, twittering a scold that Piemur didn't understand but assumed was directed at the invaders.

"At least, you're not afraid of them," said Piemur, when she returned to her perch on his shoulder, begging caresses. She leaned against his finger as he stroked her neck, murmuring sweetly for him to continue, and she twined her tail lightly about his neck. "If only they weren't making numbweed, I'd be willing to introduce us all."

Or would he? Piemur wondered.

It would have been so simple to go down and find out if they were Southerners. Imagine their surprise when he wandered in, as easy as you please. They'd be startled, they would! And amazed when he told them his adventures here in the south. Yes, but then they'd want to know how he'd got here, and he wasn't at all certain he ought to tell the exact truth. Surely it wasn't unusual for a bold holdless man to try to sneak south, particularly if he had merited his Holder's displeasure! Piemur didn't have to mention that he'd acquired Farli in the North and certainly not that he'd removed her from Meron's hearth in Nabol Hold. Southerners would naturally assume that he'd found the little queen fire lizard here in some beach clutch. Stupid's acquisition posed no problem at all. He could tell the truth there. Piemur could always pretend that he didn't know where the Southern Hold was, and had been endlessly searching. Yes, that was it, he could say he'd stolen a small boat and had had an absolutely ghastly trip south, which was only the truth. Yes, but where had he sailed from? Ista? That was too small a hold to steal a boat from. Igen? Maybe even Keroon? The Southerners were not likely to check with anyone . . .

"Hello! What are you doing sneaking around here?"

A tall girl stepped into his path, blocking his way. On one shoulder was a bronze fire lizard, on the other a brown, both eyeing Farli intently. She let out an apologetic *squak*, as startled as Piemur. As she also dug her talons into his shoulder and tightened her tail about his neck, all that came out of his mouth was a choked cry of astonishment. A quick chirp from the little bronze caused Farli to relax her tail. Piemur turned his head toward her, annoyed that she hadn't warned him.

"It's not her fault," said the girl with a wide smile, easing her weight to one leg as she enjoyed Piemur's discomfiture. She had a pack strapped to her shoulders; a belt with a variety of pouches, some empty; dark hair wrapped with a band tightly about her head so strands wouldn't tangle in branches; and thick-soled sandals on her feet as well as shin guards tied about her lower legs. "Meer," and she indicated the bronze, "and Talla know how to be silent when they wish. And when they realized that she was already Impressed, we all wanted to see who had got a gold. I'm Sharra from the Southern Hold." She held out her hand, palm up. "How'd you get down here? We didn't see any wreckage as we came along the coast."

"I've been here three Threadfalls already," said Piemur, crossing her palm quickly in case she was the sort of person who sensed when someone lied. "Landed up near the big lagoon." Which was also partially true.

"Near the big lagoon?" Sharra's face expressed concern. "Then you weren't alone? The others were killed? That lagoon is treacherous in high tide. You don't see the outside shelf of rocks until you're right on them."

"I guess being little, I sort of slid over okay." Piemur felt it was safe to seem sorrowful.

"That's all past history for you, lad," said Sharra, her deep, musical voice compassionate. "If you survived the southern seas, and three Threadfalls holdless, I'd say you belong in the south."

"I belong here?" Suddenly the prospect heartened Piemur. Sharra was as perceptive as the Harper. The thought of being permitted to stay on in this beautiful land, walking where no one else, maybe not even Sharra, had ever trod before, made Piemur's heart tip over.

"Yes, I'd say you belonged," said Sharra, wide mouth curled in a smile. "So, what name shall I call you by?"

If she hadn't given him the option to state a name, any name, not necessarily his own, Piemur might have prevaricated. Instead, he answered her with a grin. "I'm Piemur of Pern."

Sharra threw back her head and laughed at his audacity, but she also laid her arm about his shoulders and gave him a companionable squeeze.

"I like you, Piemur of Pern. What have you named your little queen? Farli? That's a pretty name, and is that little runner beast a friend of yours, too?"

"Stupid? Yes, but he's just joined us. His mother was threadscored last Fall, but he keeps up with us—"

"Keeps up with you? You mean, you saw the ships land?"

"Sure. Saw 'em going to harvest numbweed, too."

Sharra laughed again at the intense disgust in his tone, and Piemur found himself grinning at the infectiousness of her humor. "And that decided you to make tracks away from wherever you were? Can't blame you, Piemur of Pern." Her eyes glinted with humor and she added in a conspiratorial tone. "I make it my special job to gather other leaves and herbs that grow in this area. Generally takes me the entire time they're rendering the numbweed."

"I wouldn't mind helping you with that, you know," suggested Piemur, slyly giving her a look. He was only just aware of how much he had missed the interchange with someone of like mind.

"I'd be glad of the right sort of help. And you'll have to keep up with me. I've got a lot to do while they muck about with the numbweed. There's a northern Healer who's sent me a special request."

"I thought you Southerners kept away from the north?" Piemur decided it was time to be ignorantly discreet.

"Well, there are some things that need to be traded back and forth."

"But I thought Benden Weyr doesn't permit—"

"Dragonriders, yes," and there was curious tone in her voice when she said "dragonriders" that caught Piemur's quick ear. It was a mocking derision that surprised him, accustomed as he was to the respect with which all dragon-riders—except the Southern Oldtimers—were treated. But Sharra meant the Southern Oldtimers when she said "dragon-riders." "No, we trade with Northerners." Again that odd derision, as if Northerners weren't up to southern standards. "All manner of southern plants grow bigger and better than the same things in your old north. Numbweed, for one, feather herb and tuft grass for fever, red wort for infection, pink root for bellyache, oh all manner of things."

She had begun to walk now, gesturing Piemur to follow her deeper into the forest, her stride swinging as if she knew exactly where she was going in the tangled depths, had traveled this way many times before.

At some stages of the next few days, Piemur had occasion to regret not harvesting numbweed, a comparatively simple task compared to Sharra's search, which included digging, scrambling under thorny bushes that scratched his back raw, and climbing trees for parasitic growths. He felt he had found a taskmaster in her equal to old Besel at Nabol Hold. However, a taskmaster far more interesting, for Sharra talked about the properties and virtues of the roots for which they dug, the leaves for which they climbed only the healthiest of trees, well-sheltered from the worst ravages of Threadfall, or equally elusive herbs that lived obscurely where other bushes had thorns to scratch. Sharra had a wherhide jacket with her, but he had nothing to shield him from lacerations. She was quite ready and prepared to daub him with numbweed whenever necessary, but she did have to point out that his size made him the logical person to pursue the shyest herbs in their protective environment. Nothing would permit Piemur to lose honor in Sharra's eyes.

The first evening, she built a tiny, hot fire, knowing which of the southern woods burned best, and cooked him the finest eating he'd had since he'd left the Harper Hall; his contribution was fish and hers a combination of tubers and herbs. The three fire lizards devoured their portions of the stew with as much gusto as he did.

To Piemur's pleased surprise, Sharra did not question him again about his journey south nor his imaginary companions. When she commented on his knowledgeable handling of little Stupid, he did admit to having been a herds-man's boy in mountain holds. Otherwise Sharra seemed determined to introduce him to the south and gave him endless lectures on its beauties and advantages. She told him of explorations up the river—his river—which had ended in an unnavigable and dangerous marshland of tre-mendous breadth. The explorers had reluctantly decided that rather than get lost one by one up blind waterways they had better abandon the search until they could make an aerial survey of the area; a survey unlikely to be accom-plished until one of the Oldtimers boredly agreed to the outing.

Piemur hadn't been in Sharra's company for more than several hours before he learned how poor her opinion was of dragonriders. While he had to agree to her estimate of the Oldtimers, he found it very difficult not to call N'ton to her as comparison. He felt he was being disloyal to the Fort Weyrleader when he forced himself to keep silent. But a favorable mention of N'ton might bring a query as to how he, a lowly herdsman's boy, came to know so much about a Weyrleader.

Sharra had a light blanket, which she was quite willing to share with Piemur at night. She also acquainted him with the thick bush leaves, which made a more fragrant and comfortable bedding than the springier fronds he'd been using. The leaves also had no tendency to drive an-noying splinters into soft flesh.

Sharra knew a great deal, Piemur realized, for she also had him feeding Stupid on a particular plant that would make up for the lack of nourishment from his dead mother. Piemur would never have known that that was why Stupid had browsed so continuously; a dietary in-stinct rather than an insatiable appetite.

The second day, after a light meal of fruit and tubers, which Sharra had baked in the ashes of the fire, the two continued on a steady course south. The thick forest gave occasionally onto grassy meadows, dotted with herdbeasts and runners who would gallop wildly away when the first scent of the humans reached them. By the middle of the next day, they had reached higher ground, more frequently broken by meadows, until suddenly, they came to a low bluff, as if the land had suddenly fallen away from the level on which they stood. Below, stretching to the far hazy horizon, was a marshland, fingered with black strips of water, which wove and disappeared about the clumps of drier land on which grew giant bushes of stiff, tuft-topped grasses.

"We were well met, Piemur," said Sharra. "With you to help, we can get twice as much, manage a larger raft with two to steer it, and return down the river to the ships in very good time. But not," she grinned down at him, "until they've had time to barrel the numbweed. Here's what we do now."

She showed him, by a map she scratched in the dirt at their feet with her knife belt, and by pointing in the appropriate directions. The third large channel to their right was actually the river that led to the sea. That much the earlier exploration had determined. There was plenty of the valuable tuft grasses between the bluff and that safe, third channel. They would be able to half-swim, half-wade across the intervening channels, using the fire lizards to scare away the water snakes, which could wring the blood out of a person's arm or leg. Piemur didn't believe that water snakes could grow that big, but he had to credit her warning when she showed him the fine band of puncture marks on her left arm where a water snake had wound its coils and left the myriad points of its toe-teeth. Not a denizen of these parts, Sharra assured him blithely, and brushed aside his pity by saying that the marks would fade gradually. Then she suggested that, being taller, she'd better carry Stupid across the waters on her shoulders.

As they reached each grassy island, they cut the tufts from the grass for the therapeutic seeds that grew along each stem. The larger branches were laid aside and tied in bundles to be bound together for the raft. Sharra said that the branches absorbed water gradually, but the raft would float long enough to get them safely to the river's mouth. The heart of the grass plant, just above the root ball, was its most important part. This was dried and pounded into a powder that was the best medicine known for reducing fever, especially firehead fever, about which Piemur had never heard. Sharra told him that it seemed to occur only in the south, and generally only during the first month of the spring season, now well past. Something, they thought, rolled up on the spring tides so that beaches were avoided during that month by everyone.

Piemur might have avoided both numbweed stench and water snake puncture, but he certainly worked as hard beside Sharra, as he had that one day in Nabol Hold, a day that seemed to belong to another boy entirely, not this one that was alternately soaked and dried to parchment as they harvested the precious fruits of the swamp grass.

The fourth day they made the raft, binding layer after layer of the grass stalks and then forcing them into a vaguely boatlike shape by tying the ends into stubby prows, leaving a central hollow for their precious cargo and Stupid.

Sharra had taught her fire lizards to hunt when they were in the wild, but she had also managed to train them to bring their catch to her. They returned that fourth evening with the strangest-looking creature Piemur had ever seen. Sharra identified it as a whersport. It was far too small to be like the watchwhers that Piemur knew as nocturnal hold guardians in the north, but it was bigger than fire lizards, which it also somewhat resembled. Fortunately it was almost dead when the delighted Meer and Talla deposited it on the ground by Sharra's feet. She dispatched it with a deft prick of her knife and, grinning at Piemur for his horrified expression, proceeded to disembowel it, throwing the offal far out into the black waters, which ruffled briefly as the snakes took the offering.

"May look a sight, but roasted in its skin, a whersport is very good eating. So, we'll stuff it with a bit of white tuber and some grass shoots, and we'll have a meal fit for a Lord Holder."

When she saw Piemur's dubious expression as she completed her arrangements, she laughed.

"There're a lot of strange beasties in this part of the south. As if all the animals you have up north got mixed up somehow. A whersport isn't a fire lizard, and it isn't a wher. For one thing it's a daytime beast, and whers are nocturnal; sun blinds them. Then there's far more varieties of snake here than in the north. Or so I'm told. Sometimes I'd like to go north, just to see all the differences, but then again," and Sharra shrugged, her eyes wandering over the lush, deserted and strangely beautiful marshlands, "this is where I hold. I haven't seen half enough of it yet to begin to appreciate all its complexity." She pointed due south with her bloody knife blade. "There're mountains down there that never lose their snow. Not that I've seen snow, on them or on the ground, though my brother has told me about it. I wouldn't like to be as cold as he says it gets in the north when there is snow on the ground."

"Oh, it's not bad," replied Piemur reassuringly and a trifle pleased to be able to talk on a subject he did know, "rather invigorating, in fact, cold is. Snows are fun, too. Then you don't have to—" He caught himself. He'd been about to say "you didn't have to report to all work sections at the Harper Hall." "—do as much work."

Sharra didn't seem to notice his brief hesitation or that he had substituted another phrase. She gave him a grin.

"We don't always work this hard in Southern, either, Piemur; but now it's time to harvest numbweed and get the tuft seeds and bush hearts. If we didn't have them. . . ." and she shrugged to indicate a very unpleasant alternative. Then she made a trench in the red ashes of their fire, lined it with thick water plant leaves, which began to hiss and exude a steamy fragrance, deftly inserted the stuffed whersport, folded over the leaves, then carefully knifed the hot ashes in place, and sat back. "There. Dinner won't be long, and there's enough for all."

Chapter 11

Once out of the grip of the Great Current, Sebell wrestled with the gaudy striped mainsail, untying it from the runners on the boom and folding it away neatly in its bag. Then he and Menolly bent the bright red southern sail to the boom and mast. Practice had made it a smooth operation, though the first time Menolly and he had changed the sail halfway to the Southern Continent, it had taken them hours, with him cursing at his ineptness and she patiently explaining the trick.

No sooner had they hauled the red sail up the mast than the wind, which had so favored their journey, dropped to a mere whisper.

With a sigh, Menolly surveyed the bright blue and cloudless sky and then laughed as she sank to the deck by the all but motionless tiller handle.

"Wouldn't you just know?"

"All right, weather eye, breeze at sunset?"

"Possibly, usually does come up again, then," she replied, squinting up to see what made Sebell so irritable.

"Sorry, Menolly," he said, running his hand through wind-disheveled hair. He dropped to the deck beside her.

"You're not worried about Piemur, are you? Something you've kept from me?"

"No, girl, I've kept nothing from you." Her anxious query seemed at this moment more of an accusation to him than a plea for reassurance, and he had answered with more asperity than was customary for him. She was quiet, though he could sense her confusion at his manner; he was unable to explain it to himself. "I didn't mean to snap, Menolly," he said, realizing that she wouldn't speak until he had. "I just don't know what's gotten into me. I honestly believe we'll find Piemur in the south."

"Maybe we ought to have taken someone else to help with the sailing—"

"No, no, it's not that!" Again his tone was churlish. He bit his lips together, took a deep breath and carefully added, "You know I like sailing. Better, I like sailing with you alone!" That came out sounding more like himself, and he gave her a smile.

Menolly started to respond to his oblique apology, but then stared at his face, her eyes widening. Suddenly, she glanced skyward, where the fire lizards were aerially following the skiff in swoops and glides. She watched them for a long moment, frowning slightly as she saw one dive into the waves. Sebell, puzzled by her abrupt curiosity, identified the fisher as his own Kimi and smiled indulgently as she brought the neatly captured yellowtail back to the prow of the ship. Oddly, the others stayed aloft while Kimi tore savagely into the flesh of her still-struggling prey.

Sebell wondered why the other three fire lizards didn't come to share the feast, but the thought didn't absorb him long. The ferocity with which Kimi ate fascinated him; he felt as if he were somehow involved in tearing the strips, as if he could savor the warm salty flesh in his mouth, as if—

"I'm sending Beauty to Toric at Southern Hold. She can't stay here now, Sebell."

Sebell heard Menolly's voice but made no sense of the words, his entire attention was concentrated on the unusual actions of his fire lizard queen. He wanted to go to her, but he couldn't move. He found that he was alternately clenching his hands and then rubbing his sweating palms against his legs. He was unbearably hot and tore at his shirt to open the throat.

"Oh!" he heard Menolly exclaim. "Oh, what else can I do? I can't send Rocky and Diver away. That's not fair to Kimi. We're too far from land to raise more fire lizards, and there's not a breath of wind to attract them here!"

Sebell pulled off his shirt and tossed it aside. The coolness of the day seemed to have no effect on the heat that consumed him. Then he noticed the two bronze fire lizards, crouching on the roof of the small cabin. They made no attempt to join Kimi in her feast. She was growling,

175

too, her eyes glowing orangely at the two impertinent bronzes, and she seemed to be glowing in the sunlight.

Glowing? Unwilling to share food? What had Menolly mumbled about sending Beauty away? And to Toric? Why would she send Toric another message? What *was* the matter with Kimi?

He wanted to reprimand her but could frame no message in his mind. And why were those bronzes waiting? Why didn't they go away and leave Kimi? Why . . . ?

The "why" suddenly penetrated Sebell's fire-lizard-linked confusion. Kimi eating alone, savagely; Menolly sending Beauty, another queen, away; Kimi, glowing golden and taunting the bronzes, her good friends, with her staring, whirling orage-red eyes! Kimi was about to fly. And it was Menolly's bronzes who would fly her. A surge of elation swept Sebell, who could scarcely believe his good fortune. And yet . . .

"Menolly?" He turned to her, hands outstretched, palms up, pleading with her and apologizing for what he knew was about to happen since there were only the two of them on this becalmed boat in the middle of the windstill sea. He hadn't wanted Menolly coerced, as she now must be; he'd wanted to be in full command of himself, not overriden by the mating instinct of Kimi.

"It's all right, Sebell. It's all right."

Smiling, Menolly put her hands in his and let herself be drawn into his arms where he had so yearned to have her.

As if their contact had been a signal, Kimi uttered a shriek and flung herself skyward from the prow, the two bronze fire lizards a length behind her. Sebell wasn't standing on the deck with Menolly in his arms; he was with Kimi, exulting in her strength, in her flight, determined to outsmart those who pursued her. Just let them try to catch her!

Never had her wings responded so fully to her demands. Never had she flown so high, soaring, veering, gliding. The sun flowed across her body, its rays burning into her eyes as she flew on and ever upward. The heat was unendurable. She glided obliquely to the right, caught movement below her and, sweeping her wings back, dropped down, screaming with delight as she fell between the two startled bronzes.

176

One of them tried to entangle her with his lashing tail and fell, his flight rhythm disrupted. She beat upward again, calling defiance and deliberately cutting across the path of the second bronze. But, in her desire to flaunt her flight superiority, she brushed just too close to him, and he veered, jamming his wing tip against hers. Her forward speed was momentarily checked. Before she could get away from him, he had caught her, neck twining hers in that instant. Locked together, they fell toward the shimmering sea so far below.

On the tiny bright oblong that was but a mote on the glistening water, Sebell and Menolly, too, were together, lips, bodies, hearts and minds as they, linked by and in the love of their fire lizards, experienced and repeated the joy that enveloped Kimi and Diver.

The flapping of the untended sail roused Sebell first, the rising sea breeze cooling his cheek. He moved aside, shaking his head, trying to orient himself. Menolly stirred against him, awakened by the same sea sounds. Startled, she opened her eyes and saw him, propped on his elbow above her. Surprise, and then memory, changed the color of her sea green eyes. Holding his breath, Sebell watched, fearful of her reaction. Her smile was tender as she lifted her hand and brushed his hair back from his eyes.

"What chance did you have, dear Sebell, with Rocky and Diver so determined?"

"It wasn't just Kimi's need," he said in a hurried voice, "you know that, don't you?"

"Of course, I know, dear Sebell." Her fingers lingered on his cheek, his lips. "But you always stand back and defer to our Master." She did not hide from Sebell then how much she loved Master Robinton, nor would that ever come between them since they each loved the man in their separate ways. ". . . but I have so wished—"

The ominous creak of the boom swinging across the cockpit warned her just in time to pull him back against her, out of its way.

"I wish," said Sebell in a growl, "that the bloody wind didn't choose to rise right now."

"We need the wind, Sebell," she replied, laughing with a spontaneous gaiety that drew a laugh from him because they had finally spoken of what had kept them apart too long.

He put up his hand to grab the boom before it could swing back. She half rose and reached the lines to secure the boom, then pulled herself onto the seat to unlash the tiller. As Sebell rose to join her, he caught sight of a curled ball of bronze and gold on the forward deck, but Kimi and Diver were too soundly asleep to be roused by considerations of sea and wind. He envied them.

"Where did Rocky go?" he asked Menolly, who frowned slightly in thought.

"He either joined Beauty . . . or found himself a wild green. I suspect the latter."

"Wouldn't you know?" asked Sebell, surprised.

Menolly shook her head from side to side, with a half-smile, and Sebell realized that she'd been unaware of anything except their rapport with their two fire lizards. He relaxed, thoroughly content with their new understanding.

"If this breeze continues to follow, we'll make Southern by tomorrow high sun," she said and deftly played out the line, making the most of the wind that filled the red sail. Then she indicated that Sebell should bridge the distance between them in the cockpit.

Neither left each other for very long all through that brilliant, lovely night.

Menolly's sea-sense was acute, for the sun had just reached its zenith when they eased the little skiff into the pleasant cove that served the Southern Hold as harbor. Sebell counted the ships bobbing at anchor and wondered where the largest three vessels were. They'd seen none fishing as the Great Eastern Current had raced them toward their destination. Not that Sebell expected anyone in the Southern Hold to be moving about in the heavy heat of high sun.

Suddenly Beauty appeared, chittering a wild welcome. Rocky arrived more sedately, settling on the tied boom. Menolly scooped him from his perch and caressed him, murmuring loving reassurances until Sebell heard her laugh.

"What's so amusing?"

"He must have found a green. He looks far too smug, but he's trying to make *me* feel guilty!"

"Not your fault Diver lived up to his name!"

"*Hello down there!*" The loud hail attracted their attention up to the small precipice that bulged out above the harbor. The tall, tanned figure of the Southern Holder, Toric, waved an imperious arm at them. "No use sweltering! Come where it's cool!"

With Beauty and Rocky as escort, they waded ashore, leaving Kimi and Diver still asleep. Sebell firmly captured Menolly's hand as they raced across the hot sand to the steps that would lead to the top of the white stone cliff, which rose above the sea to make a safehold for its inhabitants.

Toric was gone from the halfway lookout when they reached it, but they were both accustomed to the southerner's habits, and indeed, it was only sensible to get out of the burdening heat.

Toric had been able to keep the lush vegetation of the south only so far from the entrance to the cool white caves by strewing the area deeply with seashells. The crunch and break of shell also served to warn the hold of visitors. Toric awaited them just inside the hold's entrance, gripping each by the arm with fingers that threatened to leave bruise marks.

"You were mighty short on words with that message Beauty bore me," he said as he escorted them to his private quarters.

The Southern Hold differed from northern ones in many respects, and, at this time of day, was uninhabited. The large low cavern was used for mealtimes, bad storms or Threadfall. The Southerners preferred to live apart, in shelters set in the shade of the thick forest of the bluff. When the wind was from the wrong quarter, this cavern could be breathlessly hot. Today, however, as Toric handed them each long tubes of cooled fruit juices, the temperature was a distinct drop from the heat without.

"To expand on Beauty's terse message," said Sebell, without the usual harper preambles, for Toric was a bluntspoken man and appreciated the same in return. "Meron is dead and his successor, Lord Deckter, wishes it clearly understood that he is in no way to be bound by previous commitments."

"Fair enough. I'd expected it. Mardra and T'kul won't *like* it, and they may try Deckter's resolve—"

"He'll remain firm—"

"So he has no problem." Then Toric laughed to himself, shaking his head from side to side in his amusement. "No, Mardra won't like it, but it'll do the old one good to be thwarted. She was going to give Meron every dead fire lizard egg she could find for sending her a half-empty sack."

"Half-empty?" Sebell caught Menolly's eye.

"Yes, the sack arrived with the top loosened and she's certain some of the shipment, some materials she's been plaguing the Masterweaver for, dropped out *between*. Why?" Toric caught the significant glances between the harpers. "Oh, that missing lad you queried me about several sevendays back? You think *he* came south in it?"

"It's a possibility."

"Never occurred to me to connect the two before now." Toric stroked his cheek thoughtfully. "A small lad? Yes, he'd doubtless have fit in that sack. Anything else about him I should know perhaps?"

Sebell thought how like Toric to want answers before he gave his own.

"A queen fire lizard egg was involved. . . ."

"Oh ho," and Toric's eyes crinkled with satisfaction. "Then it's not a possibility anymore, but a probability that your lad got here." He stressed the word "got," strangely, but went on before Sebell could question his emphasis. "Four, no three Threadfalls ago, weyrmen went after a wherry circle. Most of the time that means fire lizard hatchings so they do stir themselves to investigate." Toric gave a sour laugh. "Not that that energy will profit them now if this Deckter fellow won't follow Meron's ways. The strange thing was that when they reached the area, the wherries flitted away through the forest, and they found only a queen's shell on the beach. They spent a good deal of time going up and down that strand, but there wasn't any trace of a full clutch."

"Piemur does have his friend after all," cried Menolly, grabbing Sebell and dancing about with him in her relief.

"Piemur? That's your missing boy? Hey, stop that, you'll set every fire lizard in the place a-wing."

Kimi and Diver swooped into the cavern at that point, and with Beauty and Rocky bugling their delight, some of the southern fire lizards were also reacting. Sebell and Menolly called their four to order, and Toric sent his away.

"Yes, it's Piemur who's been missing, our apprentice," said Menolly, so jubilant that for a moment Sebell thought she'd swing Toric into their joyful antics.

"He and I were at Meron's Gather," said Sebell. "Somehow he got into the Hold itself and purloined the queen fire lizard egg. Meron was livid. . . ."

"I can well imagine," said Toric with a snort.

"Only none of his men could find Piemur or the egg. Kimi said she couldn't reach him," Sebell went on.

"That was when he'd hidden in the sack,'" Menolly said. "Oh, that wretched, that clever rascal."

"More clever than he knew, or could guess," Sebell continued, for Toric's expression told him that he didn't think so highly of Piemur's escapade. The harper explained to Toric all that had occurred after Piemur's daring theft: the fear of the main contenders for the Holding that Benden Weyr would discover Meron's dealings with the Southern Oldtimers. The heirs apparent now wanted no part of the succession, nor did they want the Hold in contention, so they pressured Meron to name a successor, who would then try to placate the Benden Weyrleaders. But Meron had collapsed, and both the Master Healer and the Masterharper were summoned, for the Harper could act as mediator. He convoked other Lord Holders and the High Reaches Weyrleader to force Lord Meron to name his successor. About the methods, Sebell remained discreet. Nor did Toric inquire, since Sebell's recitation was limited to facts rather than story-telling embellishments.

"So we think," Sebell finished, "that since Kimi specifically said it was too dark, as in a sack, and she couldn't 'find' Piemur, or room enough to get to him, he did secrete himself in a sack, which the Oldtimers collected that night—I saw the dragons—and brought here. That would also explain why none of our fire lizards could find a trace of him anywhere in Nabol."

Toric had listened with keen attention to Sebell's summary, but now he cocked his head to one side and made a rueful noise with his tongue against his teeth.

"It's true a boy could have fit in that sack, and it's true that a queen fire lizard egg was found. But . . ." and he held up his hand warningly, ". . . Thread fell that day . . ."

"Piemur knew you could live holdless through Thread-fall!" said Menolly with the firmness of one trying to convince self.

"Wherries were circling that shell. They could have got the little queen at hatching—"

"Not if Piemur was alive! And I *know* he was," said Menolly more stoutly now and utterly convinced. "Is that place far from here? Could your queen take our fire lizards? If Piemur's anywhere about, *they'll* find him."

Toric was dubious, but he called up his queen. To the surprise of both harpers, the queen didn't, as Kimi or Beauty would have done, land on Toric's shoulder, but hovered awaiting his pleasure. Toric issued the sort of order one would give a stupid drudge. She chirped at Kimi and Beauty, disdaining the two bronzes, and flitted out of the cavern, the other four fire lizards right behind her.

"Lord Meron's death won't bother *them*," and Toric jerked his head in the direction of the Southern Weyr, "for a while. They just brought in all they'll need for some time. I would prefer that we somehow keep them supplied. *I* . . ." and he jerked his thumb at his chest in emphasis, ". . . do not wish to jeopardize my arrangements with Lessa and F'lar. *They*" and again he meant the Oldtimers, "don't care how they get what they think they need. Meron was just convenient." He took the harpers' solemn assurance of assistance as his due, but then grinned, not pleasantly. "Has any one of Meron's people figured out just how many green fire lizard eggs got foisted off on 'em?" Toric plainly thought little of people who would be taken in by such a deception.

"You forget that the small holders don't know much about fire lizards," said Sebell. "In fact, the enormous fire lizard population at Nabol is one of the reasons why Piemur and I were there: to make certain Meron was the source of so many green fire lizards."

Toric half-rose, his usually controlled expression showing anger. "No one suspected *me* of cheating traders?"

"No," Sebell said, though that had been one of his problems. "Don't forget that I collected the clutches you've sent north in barter, but it was necessary for the Harper to find the real culprit. Green clutches could have been brought in by sailors who have been so conveniently losing themselves in southern waters."

"Oh, all right then." Toric subsided, his honor unchallenged.

"The Oldtimers have not questioned those lost sailors?"

"No," said Toric, shrugging negligently. "So long as the sails are red. They never have bothered to count the number of ships we really own."

Toric then noticed that they had drained their juices so he replenished the cool drinks.

"Have you some ships out now?" asked Sebell, because he had thought it odd to see so few at anchor when the sun was high.

Toric smiled again, his good humor completely restored by Sebell's observation. "You are well come, Harper, since the ships have sailed on your account. Or, I should say, Master Oldive's. It's harvest time for the numbweed, and for certain other herbs, grasses and such like that Sharra says the good man requires. If you stay until they return, then you can sail home full laden."

"Good news, Toric, but we'd best sail home laden with Piemur as well."

The southerner clicked his tongue pessimistically. "As I said, there've been three, maybe four Threadfalls since that queen egg shell was found."

"You don't know our Piemur," said Menolly, so insistent that Toric raised his eyebrows in surprise at her fervor.

"Maybe, but I know how other Northerners act in Threadfall!" Toric was plainly contemptuous.

"You're having trouble with their adaptation here?" asked Sebell, worrying that the Harper's masterful solution of sending holdless men south to Toric in unobtrusive numbers was in jeopardy.

"No trouble," said Toric, dismissing that consideration with a wave of his hand. "They learn to cope holdless, or stay holdbound without the additional privileges of being ranked as holders here. Some have adapted rather well," he admitted grudgingly. Then he noticed Menolly's anxious glances toward the entrance. "Oh, I told her to give the forests a good raking, too. The fire lizards'll take a while if my queen has followed her orders. Now that drink is not enough to soothe a sea thirst; there's sure to be ripe fruit cooling in the tanks." He rose and went to the kitchen area of the cavern where he scooped a huge green-rinded fruit from a tank set in the wall. "Generally we save heavier eating for the evening, when the heat has eased." He sectioned the fruit and carried a platter of the pink-fleshed slices to the table. "Best fruit in the world for quenching thirst. It's mainly water."

Sebell and Menolly were licking their fingers for the last of the succulent juices when a twittering fair of fire lizards swooped in. Beauty and Kimi made immediately for their friends' shoulders, Rocky and Diver settled near Menolly on the table, but Toric's queen hovered, chirping out a message, her eyes whirling with the orange-red of distress.

"I told you he might not survive," said Toric. "My queen really looked for any trace of a human, too."

Menolly hid her face on the pretext of reassuring her fire lizards, who were imaging to her endless distances of forest and deserted stretches of beach and sandy wastes.

"You sent them west," said Sebell, grasping at any theory that would give them hope, "to the place where the egg shells were discovered. If I know Piemur, he wouldn't have stayed anywhere that he had left clues. Could he have worked his way east? And be further down this side of the Southern Weyr?"

Toric gave a snort of laughter. "He could be any bloody where in the whole great southlands, but I doubt it. You Northerners don't like to be holdless in Threadfall."

"I managed quite well, thank you," said Menolly, her face bleak despite the sharpness of her reminder.

"There are undeniably exceptions," said Toric smoothly, inclining his head to indicate he meant her no insult.

"Piemur avoided discovery by fire lizards at Nabol, he told me, by thinking of *between*," said Sebell. "He could have tried that trick again today. He'd have no way of knowing they were our friends. But there's one call he won't ignore or hide from."

"And what would that be?" asked the skeptical holder.

Sebell caught Menolly's suddenly hopeful expression. "Drums! Piemur will answer a call on drums!"

"Drums?" Toric threw back his head in an honest guffaw of surprise.

"Yes, drums," said Sebell, beginning to find Toric's attitude offensive. "Where's your drumheights?"

"Why would we need drumheights in Southern?"

It took the astounded harpers a little while to understand that drumheights, traditional in every hold in the north, had never been installed in the Southern's single hold. Granted, there were now small holdings established as far to the east as the Island River, but messages came back and forth either by fire lizard or by ship.

To Sebell's impatient query for any sort of drums in the hold, Toric said that they had a few to aid rhythm in dances. These were found in the quarters of Saneter, the hold's harper, who roused from his midday rest to show them to Sebell and Menolly. They were, as Sebell sadly found, no better than dance drums, with no resonance to speak of.

"Still and all, message drums would be handy to have nowadays, Toric," Saneter said. "Easier than sailing down the coast to discuss something. Just drum 'em up here. Safer, too. Those Oldtimers never learned drum measures. Come to think of it, I'm not sure how much I remember myself." Saneter regarded the journeymen harpers with an abashed surprise. "Haven't had to use drum talk since I came here with F'nor."

"It wouldn't be hard to refresh your memory, Saneter, but we must have proper drums. And that would take time with all the Master Smith has on his plate right now," said Sebell, shaking his head with the disappointment he felt. He'd been so sure. . . .

"Must drums be made of metal?" asked Toric. "These have wooden frames." He tapped the stretched hide across the larger drum, and it rattled in response.

"The metal message drums are large, to resound—" Sebell began.

"But not necessarily metal; just something big enough, hollow enough over which to stretch your hide, and resonate?" asked Toric, ignoring the interruption. "What about a tree trunk . . . say . . ." and he began to hold out his arms, widening the circle while Sebell started in disbelief at the area he encompassed. ". . . about this big? That ought to make a bloody loud drum. Tree I'm thinking of came down in the last big storm."

"I know things grow bigger here in the south, Toric," said Sebell, skeptical in his own turn, "but a tree trunk as big as you suggest? Well, now, they don't *grow* that big."

Toric threw back his head, laughing at Sebell's incredulity. He clapped Saneter on the shoulder. "We'll show this disbelieving northerner, won't we, Harper?"

Saneter grinned apologetically at his crafters, spreading his hands out to indicate that Toric was indeed telling the truth.

"Further, it's not all that far from the hold. We could make it there and back before dinner," said Toric, well pleased with himself, and strode out of the harper's quarters ahead of the other three to rouse assistants.

While Sebell didn't doubt that the fallen tree was "not far" from the Southern Hold, it was also not an easy trek through steamy hot forests where the trail had to be hacked out afresh. But, when they finally reached the tree, it was every bit as large in girth as Toric had promised. Sebell felt much like Menolly, awed, as they reached out to caress the smooth wood of the fallen giant. The insects that had burrowed out the monster's core had also made meals of its bark until only a thin shell remained, the last skin of the once-living tree. Even that shell had begun to rot away in the steam and rain of its environment.

"Will this make you enough drums, harperman?" asked Toric, delighted to confound them.

"Enough for every holding you've got, with more left over," said Sebell, running his eyes down the fallen trunk. Surely it must be several dragon lengths: queen dragons! It must be the biggest, oldest tree ever grown on Pern. How many Threadfalls had it survived?

"Well, how many shall we cut you today?" asked Toric, gesturing for the doubled-handed saw that had been carried by his holders.

"I'll settle for one just now," said Sebell, "from here . . ." and he marked the distance with an arm and his body, pointing to the limit with his right forefinger by his ribs,

". . . to here. That would make a good, deep, long-carrying sound when the hide is stretched."

Saneter, who had come with them, stooped to pick up a thick, knobby-ended branch and pounded the tree trunk experimentally. Everyone was surprised at the hollow boom that resulted. The fire lizards, who'd been perched on the surface, lifted with shrieks of protest.

Grinning, Sebell held out his hand to Saneter for the stick. He beat out the phrase "apprentice, report!" He grinned more broadly as the majestic tones echoed through the forest and started a veritable shower of tree-dwelling insects and snakes, shaken from their perches by the unexpected loud reverberations.

"Why move it?" asked Toric. "You could hear this at the back of the mountains."

"Ah, but site this on that landing over your harbor, and a message would carry to that Island River of yours," said Sebell.

"Then we'll cut your drum, Harper," said Toric, gesturing for another man to take the opposite handle of the big saw. He held the blade for the initial cut. "Then we shall . . . take the rest . . . out in sections . . . as big as we . . . can carry them," he said, thrusting mightily at his end of the saw.

With a man of Toric's brawn and the willing help of the other holders, the first drum section was quickly detached from the trunk. A long pole was cut, vines quickly laced to secure the section to the carrier, and the party was soon making its way back to the Southern Hold.

By the time they had arrived, Sebell and Menolly were dripping with sweat, tortured by scratches and insect bites, which did not seem to bother the tougher, tanned hides of the Southerners. Sebell wondered if he could find the energy to cover the drum that day. Toric had firmly assured him that there were hides large enough—since herdbeasts also grew larger here in the south—to fit this mammoth drum. But the journeyman was determined to work as long and hard as the Southern Holder if he had to. And he had to, to find Piemur.

They had positioned the drum in front of the cavern "for the sun to dry up the insects," so Toric announced, when the big holder frowned at his guests.

"Man, you will die an early death if you work this hard all the time." Toric waved toward the westering sun. "The day is nearly over. This drummaking can wait till morning. Now we all need a wash," and his gesture went seaward. "That is, if you harpers swim . . ."

Menolly gave a sigh, partly composed of relief that Sebell was not going to insist on finishing the drum tonight and partly of disgust since Toric would never remember that she had not only lived holdless but had been a seaholder's daughter and could outswim him. Sebell hesitated briefly before he surrendered to Toric's suggestion.

The seawater, not as warm as Sebell had anticipated, was indeed refreshing as well as relaxing. The four fire lizards zipped in and out of the gentle evening waves, chittering with delight to frolic with their friends, though if Menolly disappeared for long beneath the waves, her three fire lizards dove after her, pulling her surfacewards by her hair.

Suddenly Toric's queen, who had held herself aloof from the antics of the visitors, hovered above Toric's head, twittering urgently. Toric glanced around. Following his gaze, Menolly and Sebell saw three red-sailed sloops, their sides lined with people, rounding the arm of land that protected the southern harbor.

"The harvesters have returned," said Toric to the harpers. "I'll just see if all is well. Stay on and enjoy yourselves."

With strong strokes of his powerful arms, he made a diagonal line to the shore that would intercept the landing of the lead ship.

"Sometimes that man is too much," she said, shaking her head at this latest exhibition of the southerner's strength.

"Which is as well for me," said Sebell, laughing, and pulled her under just to let the fire lizards rescue her.

They played that game bit, reveling in the freedom of the water and its coolness until Menolly suddenly wondered if she had enough energy left to swim back to shore. But they got there safely, fire lizards escorting, and paused to lean against the seawall to catch their breaths before continuing back up to the hold.

Toric was now directing the unloading, his tall figure moving here and there. Abruptly, they saw a tall, dark-haired girl, only a head shorter than the big Holder, approach him and hold him in a long conversation.

"That must be Sharra," Menolly said, noticing several fire lizards converge over the girl's head. One of them landed on her shoulder, and Menolly gave a snort. "Toric certainly has his queen well-trained, hasn't he?"

Suddenly a sound paralyzed them: the sharp thudding of a practiced hand against what could only be the newly acquired drum round. A practiced hand that beat a measure, "Harper here, anyone else?" and the staccato that was a question.

"It has to be Piemur!" Menolly's cry was half-gasp half-scream, but the words weren't quite out of her mouth before both harpers were on their feet and running toward the ramp up from the harbor.

"What's the matter?" they heard Toric yelling after them.

"That was Piemur!" Sebell managed to gasp out as he charged a bare stride ahead of Menolly. But when they skidded to a halt on the shell-strewn area before the cavern, there was no one about.

Sebell cupped his hands about his mouth. "PIEMUR! REPORT!"

"Beauty! Rocky! Where is he?" gasped Menolly, half-angry with Piemur for that heart-stopping shock.

"SEBELL?"

The harper's name echoed and re-echoed coming from the cavern. Sebell and Menolly were halfway there when a tanned, bare-legged, shock-haired figure ran straight into them.

Menolly, Sebell and Piemur were entangled in mutual cries and thumpings of rediscovery when a tiny fire lizard queen began attacking Sebell, and a small runner beast tried to butt Menolly's knees from under her. Beauty, Rocky and Diver immediately drove off the little queen, but it wasn't until Piemur, dashing tears of relief and joy from his eyes, called Farli to order and reassured Stupid, that any sort of coherent conversation was possible. By that time, Sharra, Toric, and half the Southern Hold were aware that the lost had been found.

A celebration for the successful return of the harvesters would have been held in any case, but the evening was certainly crowned by Piemur's appearance, especially after he was reassured that his absence would be forgiven by the Masterharper in view of the extraordinary outcome of the initial folly of stealing the queen egg from Meron's hearth.

Sebell and Menolly listened intently when Piemur accounted for his continued absence once Farli had been Impressed.

"He was wiser not to come back right then, anyhow," said Sharra before Toric could speak. "If you remember, Mardra was in a taking over that unclosed sack and ready to flay the hide off the back of the culprit. Though what she wants with more to wear here, I don't know!"

"The wilderness has its own thrall," said Toric, eyeing Piemur so closely that the boy wondered what he'd done wrong now. "Tell me, young apprentice harper, how did you survive Threadfall the day your queen hatched?"

"In the water, under a ledge in the lagoon," said Piemur as if that ought to have been obvious. "Farli didn't hatch until after Threadfall."

Toric nodded approval. "And the other Threadfalls?"

"Under water. Only by that time I'd sort of found a camp by the river, above the numbweed meadows. . . ." He glanced at Sharra, whose eyes twinkled at the truth he now chose to speak, "where I found a submerged log to hold onto and a long reed to breath through."

"Why didn't you come back after the second Fall?"

"I found Stupid, and I couldn't travel far or fast until he was grown up."

Sharra bubbled with laughter then, for the ingenuous expression of Piemur's face was just short of impudence.

"You were certainly making tracks eastward to the sea when our paths crossed," she said.

"You expected me to stay anywhere near people making numbweed?" asked Piemur with such disgust that everyone laughed.

"I'll bet there were times in the marsh when you wished you were back just harvesting numbweed," said Sharra, grinning at Piemur, who rolled his eyes upward.

"You went alone to the marshes?" Toric was not pleased.

"I know the marshes, Toric," said Sharra firmly, as if this were a continuation of previous arguments. "I had my fire lizards and, in fact, I had Piemur, Farli and little Stupid. And I'll add one thing"—now she turned to the harpers—"your young friend is a born Southerner!"

"He's apprentice to Master Robinton," said Sebell, with a warning to Piemur that brought a sudden silence to the main table.

"He's wasted as just a harper," said Sharra after a moment. "Why, I—"

"And I'm not really a harper right now, either, am I, Sebell?" asked Piemur, suddenly collecting his wits. "I was only good as a singer, and I have no voice. Is there *really* a place for me at the Harper Hall? I mean," and he rattled on, his eyes going from Sebell to Menolly, "I know you and Menolly thought you could get me to help you two, but a fine help I turned out to be, getting sacked up and sent south without even knowing it. It's not as if I was good at anything except getting into trouble—"

"Useful trouble, as it turned out," said Sebell, "but I just had an idea . . . to keep you out of trouble for a while." The journeyman turned to the Southerner. "You rather like the idea of message drums, Toric? And, Saneter, you say you've forgotten most of the measures you learned. Well now, Piemur hasn't."

"I could be drum messenger here?" Piemur was suddenly open-mouthed with shock.

Sebell held his hand up to get a word in, and the radiance in Piemur's face faded. "I can't be certain until I've asked Master Robinton, but frankly, Toric, I think Piemur could serve his Hall very well right now as drum . . . no, drum apprentice-master . . . if Saneter wouldn't mind being taught by one of lower rank." Sebell then turned to the startled hold harper to explain. "Rokayas who is Master Olodkey's senior journeyman said that Piemur was one of the quickest, cleverest apprentices he's ever had to beat measures into. If you wouldn't mind him refreshing your memory. . . ."

Saneter laughed and beamed encouragingly at Piemur, whose face once again shone. "If he can put up with a fumble-fingered old harper . . ."

"Toric, as Southern Holder?" Sebell paused delicately, for he had caught the narrowing of the big man's eyes and wondered if he had presumed too much.

"Troublemaker in the Hall?" Toric frowned, giving

each one a long, expressionless look, pausing to stare hard at Piemur. The boy held his breath so long his face began to turn bright red under his tan.

"Actually, not a troublemaker, Toric," said Menolly. "He just has a lot of energy."

"We could certainly use drums for messages to the coastal holds," said Toric in a slow drawl, his face closed on his thoughts. "Can Piemur make the drums?" he asked Sebell.

"I'd prefer to stay and supervise," Sebell murmured.

"Well, in the ordinary way I wouldn't accept another Northerner, but as Piemur has already proved he can survive on southern lands, I will make an exception in his case."

At the shouts of joy, he held up his hand once more, commanding instant silence. "Contingent, of course, on the approval of the Masterharper."

"He'll be so glad to hear that Piemur's alive and well," cried Menolly, fumbling in her pouch for the message tube.

"Aw, Menolly, it's not as if I hadn't listened to everything you told me about fire lizards and your life in the Dragonstone cave and all—"

"You'll find this lad has ears in every pore of him," said Sebell, giving Piemur's right one an affectionate twist.

"And tell Master Robinton I've got a queen and a tame runner beast," Piemur told Menolly who was busily writing. "I wouldn't have to leave Stupid behind if I have to go back to the Harper Hall, would I, Sebell?"

Sebell said something soothing and watched as Menolly made the message tube fast to Beauty's leg, told her to go back to Master Robinton and return as soon as possible.

"D'you think he'll let me stay?" Piemur asked Menolly then, his eyes round with hope and anxiety.

"You did put your time in the drumheights to good advantage," Menolly said, hoping that this solution to the problem of Piemur's immediate future did indeed meet with Master Robinton's favor. The boy so clearly had thrived in his few sevendays' here. She could swear he was taller and had broadened through chest and neck. And there was no question but what his unexpected trip to Southern had altered him in many subtle ways. She caught Sebell's glance and knew that he had observed those changes, too. That the journeyman must see that this broad and unexplored southern land could absorb the energies and intelligence of their young friend far better than the more traditional Harper Hall. "Bet you didn't think it would result in an opportunity like this?"

Solemnly Piemur shook his head from side to side. Then the laughter that always lurked in his eyes shown through. "Bet you didn't, either."

Most of the Southerners then prevailed on the two visiting harpers for the latest northern songs, always a happy importation. So the time passed quickly for most while Beauty delivered her message.

The moment the little golden queen swooped into the cavern, every sound died, for by now the prospect of Piemur as drum messenger had filtered to every Southerner present and the suspense was universal.

But Beauty was so attuned to the message she carried that her carolling answered Piemur's question before the confirming words were read aloud.

"Well done, Piemur. Safely stay. Drum-journeyman!"

Congratulations were loud and cheerful, with Piemur's back being thumped and hand shaken until he was nearly dizzy with such sudden acclaim after so much solitude. When Sebell saw him take an opportunity to leave the cavern and the continuing festivity, he started to follow, but Menolly shook her head, already halfway to the door.

So it was only Menolly who heard Piemur say to the tired little golden queen that clung to his neck: "I wish I had a drum big enough to tell the whole world how happy I am!"

ABOUT THE AUTHOR

ANNE McCAFFREY had this to say about herself.
"Born on April first, I did nothing else of particular significance until I wrote my first novel during Latin class. I think things would have worked out better if I'd written it in Latin, but I didn't. Then, I wrote *Flame, Chief of Herd and Track*, an impossible Western. I gave up writing in favor of the theater and, among other things, was involved in the first musical tent circuses in summer stock, directed operas and operettas and studied voice for nine years. I also got married and had three children, two boys and a girl. All of us write, and so do my older brother and three of my nieces.

"Now I live and work in Ireland with my two younger children, who are still in school. I can sew for anyone except myself, embroider, knit an Arran sweater in ten days, cook well (I've edited a cookbook) and play some bridge. I particularly enjoy taking care of my heavy-weight, dapple grey gelding, Mr. Ed. He answers as readily to 'Horseface,' because he knows he's beautiful, and he bullies all of us, including the cat, Mr. Magoofey.

"My hair is silver, my eyes are green and I freckle; the rest is subject to change without notice."

Anne McCaffrey has also written *Dragonsong* and *Dragonsinger* for Bantam.

The Harper Hall Trilogy

BY ANNE McCAFFREY

One of the most popular and widely read science fiction/ fantasy writers today, Anne McCaffrey is the winner of the coveted Hugo and Nebula Awards. Her growing success is based upon her two dragon trilogies—"Dragonriders of Pern" and "Harper Hall." The three books of "Harper Hall" are DRAGONSONG, DRAGONSINGER and DRAGON-DRUMS.

DRAGONSONG

In the land of Pern, Menolly is unhappy because her father has thwarted her love of music, and betrayed her ambition to be a Harper. Menolly has no choice but to run away. In flight she chances upon a group of fire lizards and finds happiness among them.

DRAGONSINGER

Menolly returns in triumph to Harper Hall aboard a bronze dragon. But her future becomes uncertain because she's always late, her fire lizards are forever underfoot and the other girls don't like her.

DRAGONDRUMS

This last book continues the adventures of Menolly and the people of Pern. A young man comes of age as he takes a journey beyond his wildest imaginings and the inhabitants of Pern finally discover the secret of their heritage.

All three novels by Anne McCaffrey are now available from Bantam Books, wherever paperbacks are sold.

"LITTLE, BIG is indescribable:
a splendid madness, or a delightful sanity,
or both. Persons who enter this book
are advised that they will leave it a different
size than when they came in."

"LITTLE, BIG is a book that all by itself
calls for a redefinition of fantasy."
—Ursula K. LeGuin

Little, Big

An enchanting new novel by

John Crowley

It's about Smoky Barnable, who falls
in love with Daily Alice of the Drinkwater
family—and all the things that keep
happening... or seem to.

On sale August 15, 1981.
#01266-5 • $8.95 • A large format paperback

OUT OF THIS WORLD!

That's the only way to describe Bantam's great series of science fiction classics. These space-age thrillers are filled with terror, fancy and adventure and written by America's most renowned writers of science fiction. Welcome to outer space and have a good trip!